Knight Predator

Jordan Falconer

Mindancer Press

Bedazzled Ink Publishing Company * Fairfield, California

978-1-934452-38-7 paperback

Library of Congress Control Number: 2009940689

Cover art
by
C.A. Casey

Mindancer Press
a division of
Bedazzled Ink Publishing Company
Fairfield, California
http://www.bedazzledink.com/mindancer

For Carolyn . . . This would never have come out without you. Rest in peace, my friend.

For Tammy . . . Who just won't ever let me give up . . .

ACKNOWLEDGMENTS

Thanks to Carrie for making me sound good and trimming all the excess baggage I'm so good at.

PROLOGUE

"MynameisBronwynHunterandI'mfiveyearsoldIliveat7Georges Road."

I looked down at the puddle of little girl by the side of the road. It was early evening, and I was starving, just out cruising for a bite to eat. I dismissed her; she was a bit young for my liking.

Her luminous jade eyes were shadowed and tear-stained as she looked anxiously up at me, silky blonde hair disheveled, dirty pink dress pooled around her upper thighs, feet scratched and filthy in her once clean white sandals. There was a bubble of snot under one nostril, a testament to her distress. She sniffed mightily and her shoulders hitched as she sobbed again, clearly afraid.

What was a child that young doing out in the night by herself? Did I want to bother with a human child? Was it really my problem? Nope, I didn't think so. So I made an effort to keep walking and set aside the small stab of sympathy and guilt that needled into me. I squared my shoulders and tried to ignore her.

From behind me, the little forlorn voice continued on. "Please? Missus? MynameisBronwynHunterandI'mfiveyearsoldIliveat7Georg esRoad."

My legs betrayed me and stopped moving. I tried to stop myself from doing it, but I had to turn around, go back to her, and squat down in front of her.

I sighed in disgust at myself. So much for being a cold-blooded killer.

I smiled carefully at the little girl. Her wide eyes were bloodshot and swollen from her tears.

"Well, BronwynHunter," I said, my voice soft and low. "Why are you sitting by the side of the road?" It was something to say, more to make her trust me than anything else. She was obviously quite rattled and any misstep was bound to result in me chasing her all over the world, trying to get her home. I would end up missing my dinner, and that would not a good thing.

She yawned mightily. "Because I'm tired."

Kids. Glad I never had any. What brilliant question could I ask next?

I sat in the gutter next to her, arms encircling my long legs. "Why are you tired?"

"Because I've been walking."

"Where are you walking to?" It was a bit like playing Master-mind. Eventually I would hit on the right question, and all would be revealed.

"I'm trying to go home. I'm—I'm—I'm lost." This was punctuated with a fresh bout of tears from her swollen and red eyes.

I knelt in front of her. "Hey." I dug into the pocket of my black jeans, searching for a clean handkerchief. Personally, I didn't need the things, but Mum always told me never to leave the house without one.

I leant forward with a comforting smile. I gently took her small head in my large hand and wiped her eyes a bit. I then held the handkerchief against her nose.

"Blow," I instructed.

Like the obedient child she obviously was, she blew her nose into my handkerchief. When she was done, she threw herself into my arms, sighing, and gave me her hardest hug. Surprised, I hugged her back, trying not to notice her torrid, animal scent and the hot, throbbing veins in her neck.

After a few moments, I pulled back and looked closely at her. "There." I smiled, putting the gentlest expression I had in my eyes.

She answered with a hesitant smile and much drier radiant green eyes.

"Okay." I blew out some air from my lungs. I no longer needed to breathe, but just the simple actions of pretending I was alive, some-times let me think more clearly. It also stopped me from standing out in a crowd like a neon sign. "Your address is 7 Georges Road, right?"

She gazed at me solemnly and nodded.

"You want to go back home to Mummy, right?"

Again, she nodded, this time with more confidence.

"I think I can help you with that. Take my hand." I stood up and held out my hand. She hesitantly slid her small hand in to my large one. I gently squeezed her hand, struck by the creamy warmth and soft smoothness of her child's skin.

I started off down the old and pitted road, careful to shorten my long-legged stride so she could walk beside me. We had no sidewalk, so we made our bumpy way over darkened front lawns, careful to avoid mud, spider webs, and suspicious dark spots in the sometimes overgrown grass.

She glanced up at me, wide-eyed. "Your hands are cold. And they're pretty hard." She stroked the back of my hand and traced the outlines of my long fingers.

I chuckled softly, helpless at the barrage of comments and questions I had known would come from her as her confidence in me grew. "I know." I hoped she wouldn't ask me why my skin was alabaster and my burning blue eyes almost shone in the darkness.

She pulled me to a halt and peered up at me. "You're pretty."

I raised an eyebrow and looked down at the small face, which was now considerably happier than it had been not five minutes ago. I gave her a gentle smile. "Yeah? Thanks."

I pulled her back into motion. The last thing I needed was for her to give her mum a vivid story about the friend who had brought her home. It would lead to questions about me, and I would no doubt be forced to run again. I'd only just settled in here, and I really liked the neighborhood. Nice and quiet during the day, just the way a vampire likes it.

She stopped and pulled a startled me to a halt again. I hoped each question she threw my way would not require a pause. Could she think and walk at the same time?

"MynameisBronwynHunter, what's yours?"

Oh dear. What should I tell her? If I told her my real name, perhaps her mother would come looking for me to thank me, and I couldn't have that. It would not do at all.

"Carlisle Crowley. My friends call me Crowley."

"Can I call you Crowley?"

"Are you my friend?"

She looked at me with furrowed brows. Inwardly sighing, I realized my joke had gone way over her head. Well, she was maybe five after all, what was I expecting? Quantum mechanics?

"You're *my* friend," she said with an intensity that surprised me. Her serious eyes were wide and trusting, completely without guile.

I didn't know how to respond. I returned her solemn expression, while smiling inside. "Okay, then, call me Crowley."

I led her through the quiet suburban streets, relishing in the power of the night and the beauty of the blackness, with her constant child's chatter in the background. I found out all about her brother Tim and her best friend Amy, her boyfriend Robert, her Mummy, Daddy, and I think almost all of clan Hunter, including crazy uncle Edward who smelt "really bad" of baby powder. Somehow I ended up with her in my arms, keeping her warm. She yawned mightily as we approached her house, her soft breath teasing the sensitive skin of my throat. I struggled to remember to breathe so I looked like a living human being.

We finally reached the front gate of her house, and I leant down to undo the latch, with her soft snoring in my ear. It undid with a quiet snick that spoke of regular maintenance. The entire house and yard appeared to be in the same good repair. The house was newly painted, the garden beds weeded and freshly watered. I could see small plants in the rich earth all around the yard, markers indicating what grew there. I grinned and made my way up the neatly swept, cracked concrete path to the newly varnished front door.

I adjusted her weight in my arms, gently so as not to disturb her, freed a hand, and opened the screen door. I held it back with my foot while I knocked on the front door. I had to get in and out of the house as quickly as possible because my stomach was giving me hell. I needed to feed.

The porch light sprang on, making me wince and stagger back slightly in the unwelcome blaze of light. I blinked, trying to get rid of the spots that disturbed my vision, and Bronwyn awoke and looked all around without recognition.

The door was pulled wide open with a creak, and a young, pretty, well-dressed woman flew out, yelling for her daughter. Followed close on her heels was an equally young man, dressed in a clean polo shirt and blue jeans. He was pale and strained, pausing a moment to eye me with nothing less than full gratitude.

"Bronwyn! Bronwyn! Where have you been?" Mrs. Hunter pried the reluctant young girl from my arms. Bronwyn's arms finally encircled her mother's neck, squeezing tight, and she brayed sobs once more.

I stroked her back with a hesitant hand, feeling awkward, as Mr. Hunter's long arms encircled his family.

I smiled. It was nice to know my status as a vampire had not condemned me to a life of evil and torment, much to the potential disgust of the more religiously inclined in the general population.

There were tears of relief all around, and I turned to leave, feeling as though my presence was an intrusion. I needed to leave to resume my hunt for my evening meal. A large hand descended to my shoulder, and I turned, smiling pleasantly at Mr. Hunter.

He looked considerably more relaxed, but he still seemed to be shaking. He drew an unsteady breath. "I . . . I . . . I . . ."

"It's okay," I said softly. "I was out for a walk and I found her sitting by the side of the road."

Mrs. Hunter appeared to notice me for the first time. She freed a hand and grabbed my arm. I allowed her to do it. It took a couple of attempts before her words came out. "I can't thank you enough for this. We were out of our minds with worry."

I smiled at her, wondering where the hell the police were. Surely they would have been called?

"We only noticed she was gone a little while ago," Mr. Hunter said, as if reading my mind. "She was meant to be playing with her friend Robert and staying the night with him. His parents called to tell us she was gone and they were going to look for her." He was babbling a little, but seemed to be calming down. He exchanged a relieved glance with Mrs. Hunter. "I was just about to go out and look for her as well."

I nodded. "You have her back now."

"Where did you find her?"

"I found her about an hour's walk from here."

Their eyes widened in shock.

"How on earth did she get that far?" Mrs. Hunter asked.

They eyed me, as though I could supply an answer. They'd have to ask Bronwyn.

I shrugged. She walked? "I have no idea."

"I got lost. I tried to find my way home, but I got loster." Bronwyn gazed at me with watery and trusting eyes.

I smiled at her. "Well, you're not lost any more, are you?"

"No you're not, thanks to your angel," Mrs. Hunter cut in. She gave me a serious look that was eerily like Bronwyn's. "I have no way to thank you enough for what you've done for us."

I held up a hand, concerned about tea and scones or crumpets.

My stomach rolled uneasily, and I focused on her neck to try and settle it. It was a bad mistake. My stomach did a flip flop, and I felt my fangs with the tip of my tongue as I began drooling. I knew I had to get out of there before my bloodthirsty nature overran my manners.

"It's fine. No worries. It's my pleasure." I followed that up with a broad smile.

Mr. Hunter stepped forward again. "Can we at least offer you a cup of tea?" He peered at me, and I had no doubt that my pale skin was causing no small measure of alarm. I longed for my natural element of darkness again.

"No, thank you. I was out for a walk because I haven't been feeling well, and I thought I could use the fresh air. I'm afraid eating is a little too much for me at the moment." I patted my stomach, hoping they would just drop it and allow me to go on my merry way. I was only half lying. If I ate their food I'd be retching before it even hit my stomach. Welcome to the world of vampires.

They both gave me another concerned look. Bronwyn stared at me. "You want to go, don't you?"

When I had died, I had lost the ability to blush, something that I was eternally grateful for, never more so than now. I nodded. "I really should be going home. I really should go back to bed."

It was the wrong thing to say. Her parents leapt forward, ready to battle every imaginary germ in my body. They were hell bent on doing something nice for me, and I could hardly refuse them. Finally, I graciously gave in and allowed them to lead me into the house, which was as immaculate as the land it rested on. I hoped against hope that chicken soup would not be thrust at me.

It took what seemed an age, but I was finally allowed to leave, and in my wake were requests to drop by again, more gratitude and general well-wishing. By the time I left, I was ravenous, and it had taken all of my willpower not to drain every last drop of sweet blood from their animal bodies.

Just as I reached the front door, I heard the pounding footsteps of Bronwyn crashing up the hallway behind me. I turned and knelt in front of her so we were eye to eye.

She smiled at me and threw her arms around my neck for a hard parting hug. I returned it as gently as I was able. I desperately ignored her neck as I almost shook with my need for blood.

"Good bye, Crowley. Mummy says you're *my* angel, and I think so too."

I smiled and gently touched her cheek in a farewell gesture. I left the house, shaking hands with Mr. Hunter on the way, and took in a huge breath of fresh, almost perfumed night air.

I could feel her staring at my retreating back. Mustering every scrap of self-control, I strolled down their front path on shaky legs and turned to wave at her parents one last time. Bronwyn hid behind her father, peering around his jeans clad thigh and staring at me intently, then lifted a small hand and almost wistfully waved at me. The front door closed and the light was extinguished.

I ran down the street, a blur, faster than the human eye could see. I ran all the way home. I had planned on hunting the streets close to my house, but my encounter with Bronwyn had changed that. Pure laziness had spurred that decision, and now I listened to the small voice in the back of my mind that told me feeding close to home would be a horrible mistake. It was always a bad idea to attract attention close to one's daylight hideaway.

When I got back to my house, shaking like a leaf, stomach grumbling loudly, I barely paused to grab my black helmet. I ran out to my garage on rubbery legs. I mounted my trusty motorcycle and roared into the city through the heavy traffic at breakneck speed, keeping an eye out for a snack. When I got to Kings Cross, the festering, black heart of Sydney, I made sure I parked in the space that was reserved for motorcycles. It was bare of anything other than my mount, and I smiled grimly. I knew what would happen when I parked there, but I was too hungry to care. My vampiric nature had full rein as I hunted for a meal.

It didn't take long before I finally found her, and as I plunged my sharp teeth into her sweaty, aroused neck, I could almost swear that she came as she died.

Nice to know I hadn't lost my touch.

As I strolled back through the masses of humanity to my trusty steed, I saw about thirty or so hairy, sweaty human men leaning on my gleaming Japanese bike. I had parked it at the end of the Harley riders' parking spots on Darlinghurst Road. The spots did not really belong to them, but they bullied anyone who ran in the face of their tradition. Well, to hell with them and their attitudes. It was a public place, wasn't it?

I sauntered toward them, restless as always, ignoring the wolf whistles. Rough, obscene gestures came from the ones at the back of the pack who thought I couldn't see them. The ones at the front stood up straight, eyeing me curiously, whispering uncouth comments about my physical attributes to each other. They obviously thought I couldn't hear them. Well, they were wrong.

I turned to the largest of them, who was leaning against my bike, his arms crossed. He was of middle age, clothed in leather pants, leather vest, and large, scuffed, motorcycle boots. His eyes were small, brown, and mean. His long, oily brown hair was tied at the base of his dirty neck with a leather thong. Tattoos scudded up and down his tanned, wiry arms. Every one of his muscles stood out in sharp relief.

Ugly, smug, smelly bastard.

He eyed me from top to bottom, his gaze lingering on my breasts.

I smiled.

"Hey, love," he said. "You shouldn't park this thing here."

"What did you say your name was?" I asked. The fresh blood that I'd consumed flowed through my system, temporarily warming my cool skin, working its magic on my muscles and my senses.

He frowned at me. "I didn't. It's Allenby. Why?"

"Well, Allenby," I said, making a show of inspecting the asphalt under my bike. "I don't see your name here. So why shouldn't I park here again?"

He snorted, exchanging a glance with his annoying, somewhat childish friends. "Fuck you, love. Get this piece of shit out of here. Go get yourself a real bike or a real man that has one." He got off the seat and turned around, preparing to kick my motorcycle over. I glared at him.

He gave a hissing intake of breath and then howled as my hand squeezed his testicles. He had not seen me move.

"Now, now," I said. "I *do* own a real bike, and if I ever need a real man I'll know who *not* to ask."

I threw him into his shocked compatriots. He collapsed in a heap, wheezing and clutching his battered manhood. The gawkers at the back stared at me then lunged forward to beat the living shit out of me, or worse.

I decided to play with them a bit and threw some of the closer ones back and flicked out a heavily-booted foot and knocked over all the nice, shiny Harleys parked next to my humble steed.

In the middle of the carnage and chaos, I leapt on the back of my bike and roared off, flipping off the ones who were still standing and staring at me in disbelief. I cut through traffic, almost causing several minor accidents.

My hair streamed in the wind out from under my helmet as I laughed all the way home. I never had a lot of time for human men, and thanks to my status as a vampire, I now had the power to do something about it.

Perhaps I should tell you a little more about myself, or at least the way I was back then. I looked—and still do—not a day over twenty-one although I was born seventy-one years earlier. I am a vampire. I allowed myself to be made into one when I was twenty-one by a creature I knew as Sembur, so by the night I had taken a little girl home I had been a vampire for almost fifty years. Sembur had given me a choice: eternal life, youth, and beauty far exceeding the span of normal humans or slow aging and death. Once upon a time these things concerned me, so I said yes to eternal life.

The problem was, I didn't know what effects it would have on my life. At that time I really started to realize what it was all about, and I wasn't sure I wanted to be immortal anymore. I was always a survivor, though, and all I really needed was some time to work it all out.

Where am I headed with this? Patience! I'm telling you about how it all began, all those years ago . . .

CHAPTER ONE
TWELVE YEARS LATER

"Hey, watch it, ya dumb bitch! Women!"

The gangly drunken boy, still staggering, turned to glare at me as I made my way down the narrow sidewalk of Darlinghurst Road through Kings Cross. His friends stood behind him, grinning, equally underage, and smirking as their brave comrade put a woman in her place. They were all wary and dressed the same in garish Hawaiian shirts and dark jeans about three sizes too large, and therefore quite fashionable in their eyes. They watched me curiously, clearly thinking that I would sense their importance and manliness, fearfully apologize and scurry off into the thick crowds of humanity that buffeted us.

I gave my best smile, burning my eyes into him, and flashed my sharp, hungry fangs. The expectant and overbearing expression on his pimply face did not change, so I decided to give him a quick demonstration on stranger danger.

With contemptuous ease, I lunged forward to grab his carefully ironed shirt. To me it was a leisurely movement, but to him it was faster than the blinking of an eye. Combine that with a six foot, muscular body, and I knew it scared the pants off him.

"Now, now," I said. "Is that any way to treat a lady?"

I lifted him so we could see eye to eye. I noted with disgust his dirty, sparsely bearded skin, and almost unbearable blast of cheap aftershave. His bleary gray eyes widened with anger laced with a surprised glimmer of fear.

He didn't say anything, just sort of gaped at me like a landed fish, and I laughed to myself. He was all bluster and attitude and no guts to back it up. His friends, the big strong men that they were, backed away, trying not to look embarrassed. He was on his own. It didn't matter; it would have been no challenge at all if I had wanted to wipe the street with all of them.

"Are you going to apologize?" I asked, smiling.

I was starved; it took all of my self control to be even this patient with him. His friends straightened and shifted as though ready to leave at a second's notice. I was not about to let him go without an apology. If I did not get it, I would make them run and I would throw him into the bushes and let him tell them whatever lies he wanted to when he met up with them next.

He nodded frantically, and his shaggy, greasy hair flopped against his forehead. It had finally sunk in that he was the one in trouble and he was appropriately terrified.

"Good. Don't do it again." I followed that up with an intense stare, daring him to argue with me. I just wanted to be done with him so I could go back to the more serious pursuit of hunting for a bite to eat.

Again, he nodded so hard I thought his filthy neck was in danger of dropping off.

With no particular gentleness, I put him back on his feet and watched him scurry away like the dung beetle he was. His friends leaned toward him, closing ranks, trying not to make eye contact with him because it would imply that he had not taken the upper hand in our disagreement. His stride was already cocky again, ready for the next engagement. Alcohol had taken precious amounts of the minimal intelligence he probably enjoyed. I shook my head in disgust. One thing I hated about young men was they were so arrogant and self-absorbed. I enjoyed putting them in their place as much as I could.

It was time for me to hunt, and I took in my surroundings with a fond gaze. Humanity teamed all around me, looking for the next flesh show, a whore, a loose wallet, more drink. For the most part they were a happy bunch, more interested in getting laid than getting into fights. Alongside the more heavily scented, well-dressed people were the usual filthy one or two that yelled obscenities at people and things both real and imagined. Some tried to avoid the beggars in the street while mingling with the police walking up and down the dirty pavement, keeping alert for any signs of trouble. Cars crawled along the congested two lane road, bathed in a sea of flashing electric light that turned night into day.

I wanted to scent the cool night air, so I pulled a deep breath into my lungs. I could smell the masses of humanity all around me, the soft scent of young girls' perfume, the stench of the exhaust of all the cars, the vomit, the beer, and the brine from Sydney Harbour that lay close to us.

It was my favorite time. I had always loved this, even when I was alive.

I always took deep pleasure in scouting the world, looking for someone to nibble on. I toyed with the idea of finding that stupid boy and draining him to the last drop, but quickly discarded it. The amount of alcohol in his bloodstream would make him taste rather odd, plus probably make me a little drunk, and quite frankly I didn't feel like it. There was also the small problem of the group he was with. I did not relish having to kill all of them. I only really needed to feast on one human victim.

I checked the fringe dwellers of the busy crowd, looking for the lone, unaccompanied person that would be my next snack.

Then I spotted her.

She was young and beautiful and leaning behind one of the buildings, puking her guts out.

With a soft smile of satisfaction, I made my way to her. The sea of humanity parted and allowed me through, without even knowing why they did it. That small gift was courtesy of my vampire blood.

The darkness was no barrier to my keen eyesight. I saw the puddle in front of her, the tears staining her smooth, pale skin—her long, blonde hair in real danger of falling into her waste. Her mini skirt had ridden up her creamy thighs, and I could smell the stale, sugary odor of the spirits she'd consumed and so recently parted with.

I knelt down behind her, and with one hand gently pulled her hair out her face, and with the other hand, massaged her back as she heaved again. I leaned forward and kissed the back of her neck, breathing in the delicate, feminine scent of her humanity. I smiled.

She realized she was not alone and shifted to stare at me with dazed, bloodshot green eyes. They would have been quite beautiful if they had been clear. Struck, I gazed closer at her. Those eyes were familiar, but I could not place them.

She collapsed back so that she was sitting on the ground, unmindful of the view of skimpy underwear that she afforded me.

"Thanks." Her voice was soft and gentle, with no trace of slurring.

I captured her gaze, willing her to want to come with me. I smiled, radiating good humor. I'd always had a strong personality when I was alive, and now with the brighter eyes I had inherited on my death, I was able to make humans do what I wanted them to do.

It worked on her, and as I stood, I took her with me and pulled her in close. *Bingo*, I thought with satisfaction as her arms slipped around me, and she buried her face in my chest. She gave me a quick, soft kiss on my neck. She sighed and shivered.

"You're so beautiful." The words were so quiet I almost missed them.

I was glad she couldn't see my face as I slipped my arm around her and led her down a dark side alley. Obviously she thought she was going to get laid. She was quite right—but it was going to be her coffin and not my bed.

We stood in the shadows of the side street, and I pulled her around so she was in my arms. I extended my fangs, knowing she could not see them in the darkness, although I could make out every valley and curve of her face and body. Stroking her cheek, I leaned in close, kissed an ear—careful to avoid her pukey mouth, and then whispered, "What's your name?"

I brushed her rib cage with my fingertips. I normally did not ask the name of my victims, but she had me intrigued. I hadn't seen her before, I knew that for certain, but I recognized something in her eyes.

She leaned into me, running her hands over my body, causing the skin to prickle, my hair to stand on end, the most delicious sensation on my cold body. She gazed at me hungrily, shameless face flushed, her eyes dark with desire. Her intent study struck a chord in me, and I focused my attention on the song of memory inside of me that sounded its melody just out of my hearing. Her yearning stare was for me alone.

I was hungry, oh so hungry.

"My name?" Her voice was a whisper as she sank into my eyes, and she began to breathe heavily, skin flushed. "My name. My name is Bronwyn Hunter."

Good Lord.

Oh my God.

Hell's bells.

Bloody hell.

The floodgates to memory opened. Once again a young girl sat despondently by the side of the road, waiting for an adult to bring her home.

I remembered her, all right.

I remembered her like it was yesterday.

Goddammit!

"Bronwyn Hunter," I said quietly. "My name is Crowley."

Her eyes widened. The spark of recognition that flared in them as I'd pulled her to her feet burst into a bright flame as she gazed at me.

"Crowley." The word was soft and drawn out, filled with a million emotions. Longing, trust, and an aching desire for something. Her arms tightened around me, and she leant into me, sighing. "I missed you."

I allowed the familiarity and rested my cheek on the top of her head, tightening my arms around her. "You remember me?"

"I remember," she said in a soft, trembling breath.

Of course she'd remember me. My white skin, black hair, and blue eyes, combined with my six feet of height would be difficult to forget.

"An angel. *My* angel."

I almost missed the words, and smiled ruefully to myself. I was no angel—I was a cold-blooded killer who enjoyed doing what she did far too much for moral comfort.

That reminded me. I was starved and had to eat. Well, I most certainly couldn't snack on her, could I? What was she doing out at this hour and at this place? She was too young and she had no business here. I would have to bring her home, just like I had twelve years previously. I also had to take a human life, but I could not take hers. I was a killer, that was certain, but I wasn't *that* brutal. I enjoyed doing what I did, but I didn't kill people for the sheer hell of it.

"Please excuse me for one moment," I said, and slipped out of her grasp.

Faster than the eye could follow, I ran out of the alleyway, careful not to look behind at her, searching for the evening's nourishment. In the distance I heard her soft cry of loss as she watched my retreating back.

I found him almost straight away, puking his guts up in a private stretch of bushes. I tapped him on the shoulders, and when he looked up at me, bleary eyed, runner of saliva hanging out of one corner of his mouth, I noted with satisfaction that it was the boy who had tried to push me around. How fitting.

"You bitch!" He snarled, trying to prove his courage, and staggered to his feet to take a swing at me. I sighed—I really didn't have time for this.

I caught him and pulled him in close. He struggled, and looked more and more frightened as he realized his strength had no effect on my iron grip. I gazed into his bleary gray eyes, revolted by the genuine hostility I saw in them. I contained my temper with minimal effort. I was to have the last word in our disagreement, and there was no need to be annoying about it.

"You're a bitter little thing, aren't you?" I whispered and held his arms by his sides as I leaned in and pushed my drooling fangs through his pulsing jugular vein. I did it with no particular gentleness; even at his weakest he still had wanted to hurt me. I had no time for people like him. Revenge and retribution had always bored me, and I had other things on my mind. I had to get back to Bronwyn.

I felt the heady heat of the salty blood as it filled my mouth and jetted down my throat, a raw flood of vampiric power that satisfied me like nothing else. He moaned and made one last attempt to throw me off, but it was no use.

The liquid hit my stomach, and fire spread through my veins. I relaxed my grip on his slackening arms as his struggles became weaker.

His body almost drained, I dropped him to the ground and nipped a wrist with my sharp fangs. I knelt over him before the wound closed and dribbled my blood on his neck, closing the wounds. He lay there like a rag doll in the expelled contents of his stomach, his cheap, loud shirt half pulled out of his equally cheap, soiled jeans, with the waistband of his boxers sticking up. He seemed so young and defenseless, but I felt no pity for him. He was just another stupid kid who had too much to drink.

He was still alive, and at first glance people would suspect he collapsed from alcohol poisoning. He would be in hospital for a few days as his body, in a coma, replenished some of its blood supply, and then he would either live or die. It made no difference to me. I would remain undiscovered by humans in either case.

The alcohol he'd consumed leeched into my system.

Oh my God. That was really the last thing I needed. I had to be alert and aware, on guard for any signs of trouble.

My first priority was to get back to Bronwyn and take her home, like I had done twelve years ago.

For a normally graceful vampire, I was staggering back to the young, blonde woman I had left down a darkened street in the worst part of town. The lights seemed dazzlingly bright, and now the sight of all the humans annoyed me. I had fed and I wanted to go home and sleep off whatever was in that blood.

I was lucky I had not gone far from Bronwyn, and that I had encountered no people on either trip between her and my victim. I entered the alley and looked around anxiously, unable to see her. I was alarmed. What had become of her?

I forced patience into myself and used my piercing gaze to cut through the darkness. The ultra keen eyesight of a drunk was with me now, and I saw the collapsed body by the side of the pathway. I did my best with my lack of usual coordination to rush over to her. She had been alone for no more than two minutes. Yet even that minute amount of time was often enough for this morally destitute place to claim another victim.

Humans murdered each other on these backstreets, as did vampires. I wasn't afraid of humans—I was more cautious of other vampires. They could be territorial, aggressive, invariably moody, and sometimes irrational. It was particularly bad when they traveled as a pack. I looked around. I couldn't see any, but that didn't mean they weren't there.

As I unsteadily leant over her fallen body, I touched her soft, smooth neck. I found a pulse with my fingertips and heaved a deep sigh of relief as I turned her over.

Her beautiful green eyes fluttered open, and her red lips curved into a smile as she saw me.

"Crowley." The word was a sigh. "Are we going home?"

I nodded, cursing my inability to co-ordinate my movements. I would soon be drunk as a skunk. "Yes, I'm taking you home."

Amazingly, she got to her feet with a little help from me and boldly slipped her arms around my waist as I supported her. I took a deep breath, preparing myself for the almost overwhelming task of going to my car.

"You're beautiful." The words were louder this time, and I looked down at her. She was staring at me adoringly, with a healthy dose of lust thrown in for good measure. I smiled to myself.

"Uh huh."

"And you're strong."

"Really?"

"I love you."

I stopped and smiled at her in genuine amusement. "No, I don't think so. You just want to fuck me stupid."

Her face darkened in a flush of embarrassment, and her earnest eyes skittered away from mine. I realized that she'd been trying to do her schoolgirl's interpretation of the seduction of an older woman. I cupped her face in my hands, forcing her to meet my eyes. I had not intended to humiliate her.

"Forget it." I willed her to not remember what she'd just said.

She blinked, bleary eyed, and her face returned to its normal coloring.

I peered at her bloodshot eyes. "Let's go."

We supported each other as I led the uncertain way back to my car. I had parked down one of the side streets that ringed Kings Cross, a horrible morass of narrow, one way streets that were heavily patrolled by police who should have more productive things to do. Humanity teemed all around us, most people gazing at us in disgust, making a wide berth around us. Since we were forced to carry each other, it looked as though we were trying to make out while walking down the street. I tried to remember where I'd parked my car, glad that I had not brought my bike with me. I still had it, but I knew what the Harley riders were like in this area, so I only rode it into the city when I wanted to tease them.

After a fair bit of fumbling around the streets, trying to avoid drug dealers, whores, and murderers, I finally stumbled onto my car, heaving a sigh of relief as I took in its sleek, silver lines.

I couldn't shake the feeling that we weren't alone, and it wasn't the humans in the streets around us. It was something else, a presence . . . most likely another vampire. It didn't come close to us, but it also wasn't far. It made me feel almost uneasy. I forced myself to move faster.

I led the limp Bronwyn to the car, leaned her against it, and then unlocked the door—something that took more than one attempt, much to my vague embarrassment. I scanned the darkness near us for the presence, but it was gone.

Although Bronwyn had forgotten what she had said to me, she did not forget that she wanted to get in a good grope before I took her home. I finally managed to get her hands off my body and both of us into the car.

I maneuvered myself behind the wheel and leant back in the seat, closed my eyes, and sighed. I sat like that for a few moments, trying to prepare myself for the arduous task of getting us home. When I finally felt a little more energetic, I glanced at Bronwyn. She lay slumped in the passenger seat, clearly struggling to stay awake. As though they contained magnets, her eyelids slid down to cover her eyes, then snapped open again as she reminded herself to remain conscious.

"Where do you live?" I remembered the answer, but I wanted to hear her say it.

"7 Georges Road." Her voice was exhausted and followed by a bone-cracking yawn. "Where do you live?"

I could not refuse her puppy-like emerald eyes. Besides, she was almost unconscious and would never remember the answer I gave, so I told her.

"Wow," was her only comment.

I'd been dead for quite some time, and with the tricks of robbery I'd picked up from Sembur, I'd managed to amass quite a large amount of money. I had bought a nice, big, private house, complete with healthy security system, so I could sleep the days away with some peace of mind. It was in the deep south of the city, in one of the better suburbs, not far from where Bronwyn herself lived.

I smiled and nosed the car out into the crawling traffic. I hoped that the gods were with us and we arrive home unmolested by police wanting to do random breath tests. I wasn't very keen on finding myself behind bars, and I didn't relish the idea of being barbecued by sunlight in a jail cell.

Thank God for a vampire's reflexes, I thought as I at last steered my car down her street thirty minutes later. I was glad she'd passed out not long after I'd headed out from the city. The ride had been an unending nightmare of honking horns, unfriendly finger flipping, and squealing brakes. I wasn't sure how many accidents I caused, or how many I'd almost participated in, and I vowed that I would never take another drunk person again.

I saw the Hunters' house in the distance and it was almost the same as I remembered it. It was freshly painted and the luxurious lawn green and well kept. The garden had more than ten years of growth behind it and had transformed into a flourishing meadow of wildflowers, a fountain, and several obligatory, happy gnomes.

I pulled up to the front of the dark house and gazed at Bronwyn, sprawled out in the passenger seat. Time slipped away as I took in her dirty dress, pooled about her upper thighs; her tear-stained face and the fact that one of her shoes was missing—something I'd failed to notice in the city. The relaxation of sleep washed years away from her face, an almost jarring contrast to her gorgeous, grown woman's body. I almost expected her to wake and give vent to some heart-rending sobs and a need to use my handkerchief to blow her nose. The only thing that spoiled the illusion was the unlovely, open-mouthed drooling.

"Bronwyn." I leaned over and nudged her.

"Fuck off!" She tried to roll over and ignore me.

Well, that wasn't what had happened the first time, was it? I grinned and nudged her harder. The alcohol in my system had given me a major headache, and my stomach was uneasy with its meal of blood.

"C'mon now." My voice was soft as I gripped her shoulder harder. "You're home."

"Home." The muffled voice was apprehensive. "Home. With you?"

I frowned, unsure of what she meant. Did she mean that she'd come home to her parents' house with me, or that we'd gone home to my place? I decided just to answer the literal meaning of her question. "Yes, with me. Home."

"Okay."

She struggled to sit upright from her position against the door and shook her head. She swallowed with a grimace and rubbed her eyes with the heels of her hands.

"Mum's going to kill me." The mumble made me smile. I had often had that thought as a teenager, but it'd never been caused by a bender like this. I had never been a saint by anyone's definition, but this was not something we did so openly in my day. I had never had a taste for alcohol anyway, and I'm sure that pleased my poor, sighing mother no end.

"Face the music, Bronwyn Hunter." I stared into her apprehensive green eyes. "Take responsibility for your actions."

That was the one piece of advice my father had tried to give me, and it fit here. The fact that I'd never been able to follow it myself had nothing to do with anything.

She glared at me and climbed out of the car without a word of thanks for my generosity, but that didn't bother me. She would undoubtedly remember her manners after she had spoken to her mother. Like a good and concerned date, I watched as she walked up the neatly swept path to the front door, just in case an axe-wielding madman leapt out of her father's flourishing rose bushes to turn her into sushi. As she fumbled in her handbag for her house keys, the porch light came on, and the front door opened. Her mother, dressed in a dressing gown, gray hair standing on end, arms crossed, glared angrily at her hung-over daughter.

"Well?" Mrs. Hunter demanded.

I couldn't see Bronwyn's face, but I could feel her struggling to find something to say.

"Hi, Mum," she began lamely. I smacked my forehead and rolled my eyes. That was a far too open-ended thing to say to your mother. It practically begged for a vicious tongue-lashing.

"What did I say to you?" Mrs. Hunter's voice was cold and hard, a wonderful match to her hazel eyes. She had certainly changed from the younger woman I had met twelve years ago. Through my alcohol-induced haze, I wondered what had happened to them.

Bronwyn, I could see by her expressive back, was still struggling to say something. Hopefully, whatever she dug up next would be smarter than her last words.

"You told me if I walked out the door I wasn't coming back." Bronwyn's shoulders sank and her head drooped in dejection. I winced at the tension that must have been flying around in the house before she left. I felt an instant of sympathy for her and tried to push it aside. This was not my problem.

My guard began to rise, as I sensed what was coming next. I hoped Bronwyn could talk herself through the front door.

"Slut! Nice to see you remembered something I said. Now go and stay with your whore or pimp, whichever you rolled up with this time. They can look after you. You're no daughter of mine. Get out and don't come back, you ungrateful, selfish bitch!"

The door slammed shut, and I winced as Bronwyn's back stiffened, and then her shoulders sagged and began to hitch.

Oh my God, I thought, knowing what I had to do next. Well, I couldn't just leave her there, could I? She was a striking young thing, and while clearly not the best daughter ever to walk the face of the earth, not the worst either. Perhaps all her mother needed was to calm down before they talked this through like rational people. In the meantime she needed a place to stay.

I sucked a deep lungful of air and blew it out as I growled and slapped the steering wheel. "Fuck!" I cursed the conscience that wouldn't let me walk away from her.

I climbed out of the car, leapt over the front gate, and jogged up behind Bronwyn. As my hand touched her shoulder, she whirled and threw herself into my arms. Her tears rained down on my chest.

I sighed as I held her close and stroked her long, silky, blonde hair. Her tears eased up a bit. Slowly, she calmed herself.

"C'mon." My voice was soft, and she looked up at me as we went back to my car. We were half-way down the path to the front gate when the light came on, the front door flew open, and a large, heavy object sailed out the door, followed close behind by its friend.

I turned to see her father slam the front door shut. They were more serious than I thought. More serious than needing to spend the night apart and then reconcile.

Stumbling, Bronwyn went back up the path to the bags her parents had packed and thoughtfully deposited out into the front yard.

She sobbed as she collapsed on the ground, trying to find the handles of the suitcases. I drew her back to her feet and into my arms for a brief, comforting hug. "C'mon."

I slung both suitcases under one arm, then slipped my free arm around her shoulders and guided her back to my car. We left the front gate open. Mr. Hunter could close it himself. His hands were free now, thanks to his recent demonstration of Olympic Suitcase Throwing.

"You can stay with me for a couple of days until you find somewhere else to live." A couple of days? Where had that come from? I didn't want her to stay with me at all. She added a complication to my life that I simply did not need.

She encircled her arms around my neck for a quick hug. "Thanks, Crowley." The relief in her voice was almost palpable. Her green eyes were stressed and miserable, but held a thin thread of relief.

Wonderful, I thought as I helped her into the passenger side. I opened the trunk and threw in her bags, amazed I had the room for them in the sports car.

I could guarantee that I wouldn't be thanking myself before dawn.

It only took a couple of minutes at the speed I was driving to get to my place. Dawn was sneaking up on us, and I had to get her into bed before the sun forced me into mine. I wasn't keen on trying to explain my lifestyle to her if it wasn't necessary. I didn't doubt for one second she'd be gone fairly quickly to stay with a friend, and I could go back to my comfortable solitary existence.

I punched the button on the remote for the electric gates, willing them to hurry and open. They did so with slow obedience, barely open enough as I drove through with something less than my normal deliberation. They slid shut behind me with a firm rattling of metal as I tore up the driveway quicker than normal, but that didn't really concern me. I could feel dawn approaching and I didn't have much time to get to my bed.

I drove the car into the three car garage next to my motorcycle, pleased with my returning co-ordination. The doors rattled down behind us, and I hopped out of the car, barely remembering to undo my seatbelt. My head thumped away, but that seemed to be less as the alcohol in my stomach was slowly banished by my vampire's body. Bronwyn was fast asleep again, tears trickling from under her closed eyelids. I'm sure she thought she was having a nightmare, but the reality would come home all too soon, and I thought it best to play along with her subconscious and get her settled.

I opened the car door, and she fell out into my waiting arms. It was enough to wake her up, and she blinked uneasily, and then stared up at me with anguished, red rimmed eyes.

"Where are we?" she asked.

"We're back at my place, just like I said. Can you stand?"

"Uh." She got out of the car, tripped over her own feet, and landed on me again. "I guess not. You'll have to carry me." She giggled, and I raised an eyebrow.

"Okay." I scooped her up, and she giggled again. She slipped her arms around my neck.

"You're the beautiful princess come to carry me away from my evil stepmother."

"She's your real mother, and I don't think so." A soft snore greeted my words. She had passed out again, hopefully for the last time. I opened the side door of the garage and stepped onto my stone path with Bronwyn cradled in my arms.

I never locked the door to the kitchen, and I opened it now with a little difficulty. I went out of the kitchen up my hallway, lighter now than it normally was during full night. I ran when I hit the living room. I raced with her up broad, thickly carpeted stairs that were almost painfully bright in the predawn hours. The doors at the top of the stairs were to the master bedroom, and I always left them open. I was glad of that now as I put her on the satin sheets in my king-sized bed. It was comfortable enough, undoubtedly a hell of a lot better than she was used to.

I pulled the remaining shoe off her foot and covered her with a light, summer doona, and cursed under my breath that I couldn't do more. I abandoned her and raced downstairs, hands covering my eyes. I stumbled through the kitchen and tore open the door to my basement hideaway. I slammed it shut behind me, barely pausing to lock it. I sagged in relief against the door, thankful I'd made it in time and that I could sleep safely for another day. I straightened and then barreled down the steep, creaky wooden stairs to the door of my bedroom.

I only just made it through the door. There was just enough time for me to slide the lock home, before the sleep of the vampire came over me and I collapsed where I stood.

CHAPTER TWO

"Oh my aching head." I came to my senses, cramped and compressed by my crumpled position by the door. I winced. Even those words were too darned loud for me. I cursed my rotten luck at having run smack into Bronwyn overnight and being forced to consume a drunken boy. Then it hit me.

I'd invited Bronwyn home.

Invited her *home* to my place.

Just what the bloody hell had I been thinking? Had I taken leave of my senses? For crying out loud, I knew I should never have feasted on that drunken boy. I knew what was going to happen to me and I still did it. If only I had walked an extra couple of steps I may have run into one of his friends, and most of them were decidedly less inebriated than he was.

I threw up my hands. Moron.

Fine.

What to do now?

I looked down at my dirty, wrinkled shirt. Well, the first order of business was to clean up. I only ever needed to shower if I got covered in dirt or blood. Most of the time I didn't need to bother because my body wasn't alive like a human body was. I didn't sweat or excrete, I didn't breathe and I didn't eat in any conventional sense. I liked showering because it gave me a good chance to think, particularly when I had to get my life in order.

After that, of course, I needed to find out what happened to my houseguest.

At my best guess she had been awake for several hours already. Without a doubt she'd gone through my kitchen cupboards and noticed they were somewhat empty. Would she have run screaming from my house? I didn't think so, because that scenario would have been the easiest to deal with, and my luck was not running that way. The worst thing was that she'd probably collected all her friends and was engaged in wrecking my house with an out of control slumber party. I didn't know the first thing about Bronwyn and the almost woman she'd become, but if her parents' reaction was anything to go by, she was a typical teenage shit or worse.

I shrugged as I continued on down the hallway into my bedroom with its king-sized, four poster bed and dark carpet, and then into my bathroom. I left the lights off as I shucked my clothes. The extra light added nothing to visibility for me, anyway. I flicked on the hot and cold water taps and put a hand under the water to test the temperature. When I was satisfied, I strolled into my shower. Fine—let Bronwyn find out the hard way that pissing me off wasn't a particularly good idea.

As I stood there, luxuriating under the warmth of the hot water, it occurred to me that I was pretty hungry. Wonderful. I would have to go out hunting, and I couldn't take her with me. Should I drain her to the last drop?

It seemed somehow quite rude to take her life after inviting her into my home. The idea made me uncomfortable. I was no serial killer, luring young women to their deaths, after all. I simply fed on humans because I needed to eat, no more, no less. If I were ever to take her life it would be from sheer self preservation. I would not kill her because it struck my fancy to do so.

What had she done to make her parents think she was such an unredeemable arsehole? Why had they kicked her out of house and home? Was it because she really was an animal masquerading as an attractive young woman?

Would it be a good idea to kill her? If she went missing, would her parents care? Struck, I walked around this thought for a moment or so. My obedient memory from twelve years ago brought up the unremarkable features of Mrs. Hunter. She had had a twinkle in her hazel eyes, such kindness. The love she held for her daughter shone bright and true in her heart and eyes.

I shut off the water and got out of the shower, humming, and dried myself off with one of my favorite towels. I ran a brush through my thick hair.

What would Mrs. Hunter be thinking now? Would she be regretting her actions, questioning where Bronwyn was, wondering how to find her, how to bring her home again? Or would she be thinking that it was about time her rebellious daughter found out that living at home wasn't the worst thing that could happen to her? There were, after all, a lot of questionable humans out there that took great delight in tormenting young people.

Bronwyn, quite frankly, intrigued me, I mused as I pulled on my long, black, baggy shorts and long sleeved white shirt. She had been a pretty young girl and had grown up into an equally lovely young lady. Her long, blonde hair and stunning emerald green eyes combined with her lithe, muscular body made her quite an appealing package, a promise of spectacular beauty to come. Yet she was such a rebel—she had habits that were quite unseemly for a child of her tender years. She had seemed an obedient child when we had first met, so what had happened to her?

All right. My simple curiosity would decide her fate over the course of the evening.

I pushed my long, damp, hair out of my face and back over my shoulders. I grabbed my discarded shorts and dug in the pockets for my keys. I threw my dirty laundry in the hamper I had in the bathroom. My first order of business was to find my guest, if she was still here.

I walked up the hallway and climbed the rickety wooden stairs to the door that led to the kitchen. With a steady hand—my headache had already disappeared—I put the key in the lock and opened it with a firm snick.

My stomach growled mightily. Needless to say I was bloody well starving.

"Quiet!" I slapped it to get it to stop yelling at me.

I looked around the kitchen, half hoping a victim was there for me to snack on. It was empty—a slightly water-stained glass sat on the damp sink from where Bronwyn had obviously helped herself to something to drink. The doors to all the cupboards lay shut, my bare fridge hummed away quite happily in electric contentment.

I first tried the master bedroom. It was jarringly different to its normal sterile state, with crumpled sheets and her discarded clothing. I checked the master bathroom. The shower was wet. At least she had some concept of hygiene. Not like a typical human slut, so that part of her mother's assessment was wrong.

I checked the dummy wardrobe I kept upstairs and noticed one of my white shirts and another pair of green cargo shorts was missing. That made sense. Her luggage was still in my car. She needed something clean to wear. Where was she?

Sighing, I ran a hand through my now dry hair and wandered back downstairs. I already knew what I was going to do—step out for a quick bite to eat and go cruising the city on my bike—the kind of therapy I needed this evening. I could worry about Bronwyn's whereabouts later on after I'd eaten.

Downstairs in the living room, I looked out the bay windows to the roadside, struck as always by the pull the night had on me. I didn't know what it was. Was it the streetlights, casting a small pool of light on the gray and oily road? Was it the clean smell of the air? Was it the stillness and the nightlife that came out to bask in all its glory? The night had something I'd always loved, and nothing had ever been able to stop me from sitting alone for hours watching the sleeping world drift all around me, often until the cold light of dawn came up over the river behind my parents' house.

It was so beautiful.

I let my eyes wander, darkness entering me, soothing me, whispering its secrets to me. The full moon shone brilliantly down onto the road that ran by the front of my house, bright and silvery.

I saw her silhouette in all its glory, as she bent down to pick at the twigs in the gutter. Each one she examined and replaced, clearly deep in thought, shoulders slumped in dejection.

I had to talk to her. I had to get her out of my life.

The irritation of being forced to live with another person crashed down on me—the knowledge of how she could not stay with me leaping foremost into my mind. My life as a vampire was radically different to a human life, and quite frankly I did not have room for a human to share it.

I steeled myself for the coming confrontation. Bronwyn would no doubt be upset by my news.

I let myself out the double front doors and padded down the path. I slipped through the open driveway gates and straight up behind her, relishing the feel of the freshly mown grass beneath my bare feet.

I dropped a smooth, cold white hand on her shoulder, and she gasped.

She whirled around and blinked, trying to make me out in the darkness. I smiled to myself. My eyesight was now so acute that darkness for me was the same as bright daylight for mortals.

I said nothing, my face unreadable.

"Hi." Her voice was soft and dejected as she looked into my mask-like features. "Crowley?"

"Bronwyn Hunter." I dropped down to sit by her on the curb and eyed her without mercy, then softened my gaze. I wanted to know what was going on in her mind as her eyes skittered away from me as though burned. I could see her steeling herself to talk to me. Was I really that threatening?

"What happened last night? Where am I? Did my parents really throw me out?" Her voice dropped to a whisper, and her breath hitched as the tears formed in her lovely eyes.

"You got drunk and passed out. You're at my place. Yes."

Bronwyn leaned forward, face in hands, and cried in earnest. Inwardly I sighed, ever mindful of my raging hunger as I relented and pulled her into my arms. The events of last night had obviously registered deep inside of her, and she knew she was in major amounts of trouble.

After she cried for a bit, she pulled back and wiped her nose almost apologetically with the borrowed sleeve of my nice, clean shirt. Inside I grimaced. As part of my protective coloring, I'd developed an over fondness for neatness. I pulled out my ever present, clean, striped handkerchief from my pocket.

She gave a watery sniff. "I have nowhere to go." She bowed her head in dejection.

"Nice to see you know where you're at." My voice was calm and unemotional. "You can stay with me for a few days until you sort out something else." I did not trust myself to say any more. I didn't want to engage in a conversation that would give her an opening to worm her way into my life.

"I have nowhere to go." The words were muffled. She covered her wet face with her hands as she tried to wipe away her tears.

I felt like the shit that I was for being so blunt with her. I was an adult and used to taking care of myself, and she wasn't. She was nothing more than a child who had been thrown out into the real world far too soon. She had just learnt that it was fine to run amuck, but another thing to realize she was on her own to fix the resulting mess. I gripped her wrists and pulled her hands from her face, forcing her to look up into my eyes.

I kept my voice gentle and quiet. "You can stay with me for a few days until you sort out something else." Once she realized she had friends, and that her parents loved her no matter what, she would be able to go home and resume her life. She was in shock, and it was stopping her from thinking clearly.

The gratitude was almost tangible in her expressive green eyes. "Thank you, Crowley."

Just then, my stomach picked the most ridiculous time to rumble. As I stared at my midsection, she snorted with laughter.

"I'm starved," I said, slightly embarrassed.

"So am I," she said in almost a whisper as she captured me with her emerald eyes.

Although they were gentle, I was wary. Her parents had thrown her out of their house, and it wouldn't have been for an over fondness for stuffed toys and sleeping in. I was a good hostess and I knew that I had to see to the needs of my guest. The problem was, it had been so long since I had eaten human food I did not have the faintest inkling of what appealed to a mortal stomach.

"Okay." I got to my feet and took her hand so she came up with me. Her gentle study of me never wavered as I led the way across the grass to the garage and sleek, low slung sports car. My hand was there to steady her when she tripped on the deceptively smooth lawn. I unlocked the car door for her, opened it, and helped her into the passenger side. I hoped that my coordination was fully recovered from the alcohol.

"So. What would you like to eat?" The car purred as I backed out of the garage.

"Something quick."

"Okay, I know just the place." I smiled at her for the first time and planted my foot down as we took off for the favorite bastion of young adulthood—McDonalds.

Lucky for me, the traffic wasn't heavy and all the lights turned green in my favor, so about ten minutes later we pulled up at the drive-through. It was busy, and it looked like each of the four cars ahead of us had placed big orders, forcing everyone to wait for them.

We hadn't spoken one word to each other, comfortable in the silence, though I could feel her sneaking a glance at me every now and again. Her expression was unreadable.

I knew what was causing that. I looked so different to mortals, and after the initial shock of actually seeing me, the differences became more pronounced. The fact that this child had a pretty large and healthy crush on me certainly didn't help things at all. I silently cursed as we moved forward in the queue.

"Why don't you have any food in your fridge?" She was hesitant— clearly she still didn't know how to approach me yet.

"I eat out a lot." My words were clipped, and I was careful to avoid her eyes.

"Oh." That came after a moment or two more of silence, as she realized I wasn't going to add to my response.

Something caught my eye. The McDonalds was at the corner of a multi-story parking lot. At any hour of night, there would either be couples making out—too young to drive, let alone be in the back seat of their mum's car, or humans stuffing their faces on fast food as they tried to ward off the aftereffects of a heavy night out. A young girl was being forcibly pulled off into the darkness by two young men, as they furtively looked around to see if they'd been discovered. They had—by me.

"Here." I kept my keen eyes on the two men as I climbed out of the car. "Drive. I'll see you in about two minutes. There's change in the center console."

"What?" Bronwyn's voice was more than confused as I fled the vehicle. I broke into a fast run, eager to track my quarry. The car door opened behind me, and Bronwyn slipped around to my recently vacated seat.

I slowed to a jog, silent as I stopped pretending to breathe for Bronwyn's sake. Ahead of me, I could see the two men, one of them holding down the woman, as the other rifled through her purse. Her black slacks were unzipped and half torn down over her large hips, flashing pink, floral underwear.

As fast as I could go, I slipped up behind the man pinning the struggling woman to the ground. With no particular gentleness, I grabbed him and ran for my life across the car park, bare feet making almost no sound on the smooth concrete. He struggled mightily in my grip, but it was almost no challenge to hold his hands by his side. His frightened eyes stared into mine, and I gave him a quick, savage smile, to let him know that his opponent outclassed him and would never fear him. He squeaked in a most girlish way as he realized I held his life in my hands, and I intended to squeeze them shut.

In the darkest recess I could find I wasted no time, extending my fangs and plunging them into his carotid artery. Air hissed out of his lungs, and his body became dead weight as the life fled from him.

I was greedy and so hungry. I drained him in almost one mighty draft, the heady power of the blood causing a huge, silly grin. As I dropped the corpse and tidied up the fang marks, I wondered if I was in the mood for another.

I thought about his hot, throbbing neck. I thought about her floral underwear.

Yes.

Oh my goodness yes.

Was I a greedy pig or what?

Smirking to myself, I went back to the place where they had held the woman captive. As usual, I'd been quick and there hadn't been enough time for the remaining thug to continue with the woman. I zeroed in on her and lunged. Before she had time to scream, she was draped over my shoulder and the cold wind of my passing encircled the other man as I pulled the purse out of his hands. I grabbed him by the shoulder, pinned his wrists, and tugged him right along with us. She kicked my back and stomach, while he bit at my hands, but to no avail for either of them.

In the blinking of an eye we were in my dark recess, and I just missed stumbling over the corpse of the first man. The woman fell onto his corpse in an untidy heap, while pawing and struggling with her torn underwear and tattered slacks. She breathed in with a hiss and prepared to give vent to an almighty scream. At the same time, she frantically backpedaled when she realized what cushioned her from the concrete.

I couldn't let her go unscathed for fear of discovery, but I also didn't want to kill her. Instead, with a move that used to amaze my fellow vampires, I plunged the struggling man's knife into his gut and lunged over to sink my ravenous fangs into the woman. She moaned softly and went limp and I held her and nicked the smooth skin of my wrist with a fang. I dribbled my blood on the wound in her neck, and it closed over slowly.

In about a minute it was all over, and I was left with the heady feeling of the fresh blood coursing through my system, and two fresh corpses lying at my feet. Great gusts of air flowed in and out of the woman's lungs, and I knew that she would be terribly weak when she woke up, but would still be alive.

I cocked my head and decided what to do next. I grinned. They had tried to rob a woman of more than her possessions while she was alive, and I would do the same for them after death.

Five minutes later, I finished dusting myself off, and whistled to myself as I strolled across the busy parking lot to my car and the wide-eyed Bronwyn. She had parked, badly, not far from the drive-through. She picked away at fries, obviously unwilling to plough into her hamburger until I had rejoined her. I noted with interest that she seemed to have some concept of good manners.

As I approached the car, I smiled broadly and climbed into the passenger seat.

"Uh, I bought you a burger." Her voice was apprehensive as though she was waiting for me to explode.

Okay, so she was wondering if I was a bomb, just as I wondered the same thing about her. On the other hand, she was also probably wondering about my sanity. Who else would suddenly leap out of a car in the middle of the parking lot at a fast food restaurant?

"Thanks. I'm fine though." I patted my stomach. The volume of the blood was making me feel lightheaded, the vampire equivalent of drunk. It was a wonderful feeling of fullness and raw, heady power.

Bronwyn raced through her food and tried not to peer at me, concerned. "Are you okay? You look a little flushed."

"I'm fine." All I wanted was to move and roam the night, looking for trouble. "Wanna go out for a while?"

Bronwyn looked at me in surprise. "Love to." She pushed her shaggy blonde hair out of her face. "Where are we going?" She balled up her feed bag and threw it through the open window toward the overflowing plastic garbage bin not far from us. Much to my surprise, she made it first hit.

I smiled. "Ahh. We're going for a ride on my bike."

She grinned in return. "I love those."

"So do I. Home, Jeeves."

Her eyebrows drew together in an uncertain frown. "You want me to drive?"

"Of course. Who else was I talking to? I just wanna sit and cruise. I trust you." I could afford to say that. Okay, so she wrapped the car around a tree. So what? I would get up and walk away unscathed. She wouldn't come off so lightly, but at least she wouldn't be my problem anymore.

Bronwyn smirked and adjusted the mirror. While she wasn't looking at me, I threw the burger out the window, reclined the seat, and crossed my hands across my pleasantly full stomach.

With a feral grin I'm sure Bronwyn thought I couldn't see, she slammed the car into reverse, and we skidded out of our parking spot. Without even casting a look at the light traffic she floored it, and we screamed down the road. I was amazed we escaped in one piece, considering the extent of Bronwyn's driving skills consisted of looking straight ahead and pushing the accelerator as hard as it would go. She raced the traffic lights, speeding up when they went orange, rather than slowing down to avoid attracting attention.

I stayed in my seat with nary a flicker of emotion, completely relaxed, and closed my eyes. "Take it easy there, Bronnie. If the coppers book us you're paying for it."

I could feel her smirk as her fantasy of being a race car driver took over. "They won't catch us."

"They better not." I aimed a severe blue eye at her. "If they arrest me, I'll kill you."

She must have realized I meant it literally. I didn't think for one second she had a real driver's license, so if the cops bailed us up on the road we'd both be arrested. I would not last long during daylight in a cell. I let her know by the glittering in my eyes that her death would precede mine.

She gulped and slowed down considerably.

"That's better." I shut an eye and let her go about her business in the heavier traffic on the road.

"Ah, Crowley? Where do you live?" Bronwyn asked after a few moments.

I chuckled and gave her directions without opening my eyes. The amount of blood I'd consumed left my senses more acute than usual. I could tell where we were by the smell on the wind.

That, of course, was when I remembered to breathe.

By the time she pulled up into my garage, she was pale and looked a little nervous. I stared at her, confused.

"Are you okay?"

"I'm fine." Her forced words said one thing, her mannerisms another. I could see her sitting as close to the car door as she could, looking at me as though I'd grown horns.

"Still want to go for that ride?" I reached out my hand, curious to see if she would take it, wondering what I had done that had scared the bejesus out of her. I hadn't done anything other than sit and call out directions.

"Love to." Again, her words said one thing, her tone another. She hesitated and then took my hand.

I loved the feel of the smooth, warm, mortal skin in my hands. She was fine boned and though quite muscular, still a delicate creature. I ran my hand over her knuckles, struck by the life held within its warm confines, and smiled.

"Okay, let me just grab a helmet, and we'll be off."

She looked down at herself, sweaty hand firming around my grip as she relaxed slightly. "Like this?"

"You were thinking of taking your clothes off? Novel but rather cold. Yes, like this. Trust me?"

She froze and gaped, obviously fishing for a witty reply.

Okay, so she didn't trust me. I didn't mind. I wouldn't have trusted me either. I knew why I didn't trust myself; the real question was why *she* didn't trust me. Curious, I leant forward.

"Boo."

Bronwyn squeaked and jumped out of the car. I admit it—I'm an arsehole, so I'm afraid I laughed.

"C'mon, you're perfectly safe around me." I got out of the car and held out my hand again. I could see her fighting with herself over whether to take it or not.

Finally, curiosity won out and she took it. "C'mon." My voice was soft and gentle. "The bike can wait."

I kept a firm grip on her hand and led her into the house, shivering as the light of the moon touched me, washed over me. I left her standing in the living room, knowing she would not move, as I went to the CD player and put on some soft music. I turned to her.

She stood in place, arms moving as she fidgeted and fought with the idea of running away as fast as she could. The moonlight, softened by the slightly tinted windows, lit up her face, which was pale and expressionless, green eyes with their now familiar wariness, watching me closely.

I held out my hand. "Dance with me."

She shook her head, trying to keep firm and to keep me at arms length, as though that would protect her. Nothing could protect her if I put my mind to hurting her.

"Dance with me." I held out my hand, my eyes locked onto hers, as I willed her to relax a little. She hesitantly reached out and took my hand.

I pulled her in close to me and slipped an arm around her waist. I took her around the room, whirling and moving in time with the music, careful to keep her ensnared in my calm gaze. Her muscles remained tense as her body molded to mine.

A tiny smile teased the corners of her mouth. "MynameisBronwyn-Hunter. What's yours?"

Once again I found myself by the side of the road with a five-year-old girl.

"Carlisle Crowley. My friends call me Crowley."

"Can I call you Crowley?" Her smile came out of hiding.

"Are you my friend?" My gentle smile matched hers.

She frowned, and her eyes glistened with unshed tears. "You're my friend." Her voice was so soft even I had to strain to hear it.

I knew what was going to happen next and wanted to let her down as gently as I could. "You can't stay with me. I'm a complete waste of time." Our lives were so different I could not see how the two could ever meld, even if I were of a mind to do it. I was also rare for a vampire—I did not take humans in thrall and use them as servants, as Sembur once showed me how to do.

"Please? No, you aren't." The question in the liquid green eyes was painful to see. She was young enough to think that there was such a thing as living happily ever after and that there would never be any problems. How wrong she was.

"I will bring you nothing but trouble. My lifestyle does not have room for you." Though the words were harsh, I made certain my tone stayed gentle. I had never been blessed by tact.

"I'm eighteen, and have only two months of school left. After that I'm out of your hair." She sounded so desperate.

I remained expressionless, studying her. She really was begging me. Could this work? No, I didn't think so. If she stayed with me it was only a matter of time before she found out what I really was. For now, she appeared to have some glorious childhood image of me as her savior firmly planted in her head, and the truth was so far removed from this concept it was embarrassing.

What would happen if she found out? Would she try something exceptionally stupid like hammering a stake through my heart as I slept? More importantly, could she keep her mouth shut about what she saw when she was with me? I didn't know the first thing about her, and quite frankly her reputation had preceded her. I didn't trust her any further than I could throw her. I could not afford to trust her with my secrets.

"Do you trust me?" My voice caressed her.

We continued to dance, and not once did she lose her firm grip on my body. In fact, her fingers gained confidence and traced the outlines of my hard muscles moving under my cool skin as we danced around the living room.

"I think you're an animal."

I laughed. "The feeling's mutual."

Her face became expressionless as she absorbed the implications.

I took pity on her. "So, BronwynHunter. Still want to stay with me, given that you're terrified of me and you don't trust me?"

She smiled. "Given that I have no real choice, I'd still like to stay with you. Besides, I can't help thinking you're not the fucking bitch you sound so much like. It's in your eyes, Crowley." She sucked in a breath. "Are you still going to kill me?"

That was it. I laughed outright, spun her around, and dipped her. I leaned forward so our lips were almost touching and planted a quick kiss on the end of her nose.

I moved so suddenly she gasped, and equally suddenly she was upright in my arms as I whispered into her ear, "No, I'm not going to kill you." I looked deep inside myself and knew this for the truth. I had two firm rules. One, if the gut hesitated about killing someone, then it was usually quite wise to listen to the objection, and second, don't kill anyone you know. "As for my being a bitch, well, there's a lot you don't know about me. But don't say I didn't warn you."

Much to my intense surprise, she slipped her arms around my neck and gave me a deep kiss on the lips, pushing her whole body into mine. Shock prevented me from stilling the hungry hands that roamed all over my body. "I could be dead tomorrow, and if I die then at least I want to be able to say I kissed one of the hottest chicks alive. Does this mean yes?"

That was it. I was gone, laughing like a complete loon. I fell over backwards onto my sofa. "It means yes."

"Thank you." She stared at me in amusement, then more seriously as I recovered some of my self-control and raised an eyebrow. In one swift movement, I stood facing her.

"Don't thank me too soon. My house does have some rules. I get up in the evening and go to bed at dawn. End of story. Not negotiable. Stay out of my room at all times. Do as I say when I say, and do *not* tell anyone about me. And above all, clean up after yourself. I'll leave it to your imagination to find out what happens if you break any of these rules."

As I enunciated each rule, I took one step closer to her until we were so close our bodies were only a hairsbreadth apart. I gave her a cold, feral grin.

She gulped, and went pale. "I can do that."

"Was that 'yes I agree to these rules' or 'yes I can imagine what you'll do to me if I break them'?"

"It means 'yes I agree to these rules.'" She forced herself to meet my fiery eyes, so I would see the truth. "I don't intend to break them."

"All right, then, let's see how it goes."

"My princess."

"Trust me, sweetie, I am *no* princess." I grinned and swept her into my arms, and we continued to dance late into the night.

In the predawn hour, I picked up her sleeping body and took her to the master bedroom. I placed her in what was now her bed and covered her over with the colorful doona.

As I walked downstairs and into my own bedroom, locking myself inside, it occurred to me that I actually liked the girl. I could feel fire in her, her youthful energy. She wasn't stagnating as I was. She was intelligent and challenging and had a spirit that matched mine. She reminded me of what it was to live, and not be alone and lonely. She was not afraid to stand up to me, although I clearly scared her badly at times.

Could this work?

Not in a million years. Something would happen, and I would have to leave.

Did I want it to work?

Yes. Yes, I think I did.

CHAPTER THREE

I woke up the next evening, hungry as always. I dressed and made my way upstairs to see what my young charge was doing with herself.

I opened the door to the basement, and found her amusing herself in the kitchen. I sniffed. It was quite an event to actually see my kitchen being used. She had not heard me, and leant over a chopping board, cutting up something I barely recognized.

"Good evening, sunshine!" I said.

She started and hissed as she nicked her finger. I winced. I smelled the blood, and I was hungry.

"Hey, Crowley," she said, turning and sticking her forefinger into her mouth. I was by her side, gazing at her finger before she could blink.

She stared at me.

"Let me see," I said, gently extracting her damaged finger from her mouth.

The droplets of sweet blood from the cut made my stomach grumble. The hot, metallic scent of the blood was almost more than I could bear.

I tried a smile. "Careful."

"I know," she said, extracting her hand and taking a step back from me. She gave me a wary stare.

"I won't hurt you," I said softly. "I thought we got that sorted out last night."

She was silent for a moment. "We did. You're just so . . . so . . ."

"Sexy? Attractive?" I asked, a grin tugging at my lips.

"You have no idea," she said, shaking her head and tearing her eyes away from me.

"All right." I shook from the hot, animal blood that still teased my starving senses. My stomach grumbled. "I'm going to go out for about half an hour. I'll see you when I get back."

"Wait!" Bronwyn said as I strode out of the house on shaking legs. "Don't you want something to eat?"

"No! I'm fine."

I dug in my pocket for the keys to my car. I saw Bronwyn's silhouette in the doorway as I pulled away and tried to erase it from my mind.

I didn't have time for my usual leisurely hunt in the city, so I went to the local train station and waited for one of the young men I knew would go into the city for a night out on the town.

I didn't have long to wait. I grinned when I saw him, a young man in his early twenties, handsome and well-dressed. I stepped out of the bushes and smiled at him.

"Are you all right? Can I help you with something?" he asked, walking toward me.

"Yes."

I pounced on him, pinned his arms, and sank my fangs into his neck. I willed him to relax and to forget all about me. Once I was pleasantly full, I nicked my wrist and carefully dribbled the blood over the marks I had made.

He would live. I had not taken all his blood. He would be weak when he awoke, but that was all.

I made my way home again, seeing by the clock in my car that my timing was perfect.

By the time I arrived home, Bronwyn was settled at the dining room table, happily demolishing a steak.

"Hey," she said as I walked in. "Where did you go?"

"Out." I sat down at the chair close to her and watched her eat.

"Okay," she said. "Um . . . I hope you don't mind, but you have an awful lot of change lying around. I kind of helped myself. Did you know you have nothing to eat in the cupboards?"

I laughed. "Yes, I know. I eat out a lot."

"Why?"

"Because I can. You said you noticed all the change around the house. I don't have to eat here if I don't want to."

"So when are you going to take me out on a date?"

"A date?"

"Yes. You know, one of those things where you pay for dinner and kiss me good night?"

I leaned forward and kissed the edge of her jaw. "You just don't give up, do you?"

Her arm brushed against my breast. "No," she whispered in my ear. "I love you." I felt the heat from her skin as she blushed. "And I don't care how much you scare me sometimes."

I tilted my head. "I promised you a ride on my bike last night, didn't I?"

She cut another piece of steak and put it into her mouth. "Yes, you did."

"Then finish up and I'll take you out."

She smiled, and it transformed her beautiful face into something that was elegant and stunning.

"I'll just go and find you a helmet."

I got up from the table, feeling her eyes on me, and went to the hall closet and dug around.

"I got it," I said triumphantly as she put the last of her dishes in the dishwasher.

She grinned. "Okay, then, let's go."

I led her out to the garage, and backed the bike out. I got on and turned to her. "Usual rules. Stay with me. Lean with me. It's easier if you hold on to me and not the bike. I'd say nothing personal if you happen to slide into my back, but I know with you it would be."

She snickered and got on the bike. I shot down the driveway, feeling her weight shift in the pillion seat as I headed into the city.

Bronwyn was a natural pillion. She did hold onto me—not groping me as I half-suspected she would, but simply enjoying the cool, night air.

We headed down Park Road and turned left onto Darlinghurst Road.

"You want to go to the Kings Cross Hotel?" she asked. "I love that place. That and the Test Tube Factory."

I shrugged as I took us down a side street. "Sure. Let's do the Test Tube Factory."

I was going slowly, and I felt Bronwyn shift forward.

"Crowley," she said. "There's something I've always wanted to try. Can you keep going this slowly?"

I glanced back at her. "Sure."

I felt her warmth leave my back and her knees tightened around my ribs. She was standing up on the rear footpegs. I glanced back, and her hands were thrown wide. She had a grin plastered from ear to ear.

"You want me to go a bit faster?" I asked.

She gave her best war cry and looked down at me. "Yeah!"

I laughed and pulled the throttle back a little.

"Yes!" she screamed. "This is fun!"

"I know," I said. "But I think you better sit down again. I just saw a spot."

She sighed and sat down as I pulled up. She got off, and I backed into the spot. She took off her helmet and shook out her shining, blonde hair. My gut clenched. God, she was so beautiful.

I hid my churning emotions with a rakish grin and held out my hand. "C'mon, let's go."

She threaded her arm through mine and took my hand. We walked toward the main road.

"Why are you always so cold?"

"I'm not always cold. We've been on the back of the bike, remember? It's pretty windy."

She frowned, and her face darkened.

"What does it matter, anyway?" I asked.

"You're so strange," she said. Her eyes were shadowed as she peered at me.

I was just thinking about how to respond when we found ourselves in front of the bouncer. I was relieved I didn't have to think up a witty reply.

We walked in, and heads turned.

The club was not packed—it was too early. She led us to a corner table as a luscious redhead dressed in a nurse's uniform came to us and leaned over the table to take our order. My gaze wandered over her delectable, full breasts and up to her eyes. The waitress's brown eyes were dark and turbulent as she took me in. She leaned over a little further, on the pretext of hearing over the noise in the dark club. I was surprised her assets did not tumble out of her uniform. I sighed and leaned forward, lips twitching.

"Is there something I can help you with?" she asked.

"I'm not sure," I said. "Is there?"

"We'll have a rack," Bronwyn said, beautiful face carefully expressionless.

"That'll be—" the waitress began.

"Thirty bucks. Here." Bronwyn handed her the money, and I stared at her in amazement.

She and the waitress exchanged unfriendly stares before the waitress stalked off to get our drinks.

I stared at Bronwyn. "What was that about?"

"Nothing," she said.

"Bronwyn—"

"I'm fine."

"You're not—"

"Yes, I am. Let it go, angel."

The waitress returned and put the rack on the table. Bronwyn grabbed the first test tube—a shot of Midori—and downed it without a thought.

I watched as she poured another six out of the twelve in the rack down her throat in quick succession.

"Well," I said, "since nothing's wrong, why don't we get out there and dance?"

The alcohol was beginning to have an effect on her, and her eyes spat less fire as she smiled. "Sure."

I led her to the dance floor, and within seconds found her in my arms, our bodies touching along their entire lengths. I grinned.

She slipped her arms around my neck, and her green eyes flashed as she gazed deep into my eyes. I wrapped my arms around her waist and cupped her behind. She trembled in my arms. She kissed the hollow of my throat.

I glanced at the waitress, whose eyes were now flashing fire.

We moved around the dance floor, and Bronwyn slowly relaxed.

We spent a few hours alternating between the dance floor and our table as the club filled.

Every trip to our table was a duel between our waitress and Bronwyn, each shooting daggers at the other.

I finally got sick of it, and we left the club at around three in the morning. I put my arm around Bronwyn and helped her back to the bike. When we reached it, I found myself in her arms and the recipient of a firm, deep kiss.

I gently extracted myself. "You're going to have to stop doing that, Bronnie."

"Why? I love you."

"No you don't," I said as I mounted the bike. "You barely know me and you're afraid of me."

"What is there to know?" she asked as she wobbled behind me. "You're as hot as they come."

"So you're saying you just want to fuck me but you don't want to know anything about me."

"No, I'm saying you won't tell me anything about yourself."

I smiled as we headed out of the city. "If you want to talk, this isn't the time to do it."

I pulled the throttle back, and she held onto me for dear life. We arrived home about half an hour later, and by that time Bronwyn was unconscious.

I gently nudged her as I hit the kill switch. "Wake up, sleeping beauty. I think it's bedtime for little girls."

"I'm *not* a little girl," she said, and I caught her as she fell off and put her on her feet. I held her elbow, but she pulled out of my grasp.

"I can do it," she said with drunken dignity. She took a step forward and tripped over her own feet. I caught her and scooped her up into my arms.

"You're so strong," she said as her arms crept around my neck. She kissed my chest.

"Really?" I said, pushing the back door open with my foot.

"You're so beautiful." She sighed.

"Uh, huh."

"I love you."

"No, you don't. We've been through this before," I said as I put her onto the bed. Her grip never loosened, and I found myself lying on the bed beside her. She snuggled into my arms, her head on my shoulder.

"I want to know everything about you," she whispered.

"Like what?"

"Where did you come from?"

"Right here, actually," I said, slipping my arm around her.

"How long have you lived here?"

"I think you already know the answer to that one," I replied. I traced a soothing, circular pattern on her back.

"For an old chick . . . you're . . . you're . . ." Her breathing deepened and became regular.

I laughed softly.

I made sure she was asleep before I extracted myself from her gentle embrace and covered her. I gazed down at her.

She looked so much younger when sleep robbed her of her maturity. It was almost as though the child she had been lay in my bed. The only thing that belied it was her sensual, woman's body.

She called *me* beautiful? I thought as I descended the stairs toward my basement hideaway. God, she was so beautiful she made my teeth ache.

ⅎ

The next evening when I ascended the stairs, I found her sitting in the living room waiting for me.

"Good evening, sunshine," I said cheerfully.

She gave me a sour look. "If you say so."

"Really?" I asked as I settled onto the sofa beside her. "Why is it not a good evening?"

"It's the tail end of a bad day." She sighed and gazed at me.

"Don't make me drag it out of you," I said. "What happened?"

She sighed again. "Well, for starters I got to school late. How come you don't have any clocks in here?"

"I tend not to need them. We'll get one."

Her smile lit up her eyes. "Thanks." She looked away. "I had a splitting headache and not enough sleep."

I shook my head. "That's my fault. I'll wear that one. I shouldn't have taken you out on a school night."

"I'm just tired."

"You want a quiet night in?" I asked.

She nibbled her lip and nodded.

I smiled. "You want a burger to eat or something?"

"I guess so."

"All right, then," I said. I stood and pulled her to her feet. She sank into my arms.

"Thanks," she said.

"For what?"

"For not being mad at me."

"Why would I be mad at you for something stupid *I* did?" I asked, gazing at her in confusion.

"There's something else I have to tell you about that," she said.

"All right," I replied as I led her out to the car. "What else do you have to tell me?"

She got in and fastened her seatbelt. She was blushing. "I'm not eighteen yet."

"By how much?" I asked, raising an eyebrow.

"By about four days," she whispered.

I sighed. "Look at me."

She stared straight ahead, nibbling her lip, with unshed tears in her eyes.

"C'mon, Bronnie, look at me," I said softly, willing her to look in my direction.

Her eyes stuttered to my face.

I cupped her chin. "Stop nibbling, will you? Better. Look, don't worry about it. We went out; we didn't get caught; we came back; we were stupid enough to do all three on a school night. We won't be doing that again in a hurry, now will we?"

She nodded, her eyes showing relief, but there was still something lurking in their green depths.

"What else?"

"I asked a couple of my friends today about moving in. No go."

I sighed again, and closed my eyes. I ignored the swift feeling of relief that shot through me. "I know what you're going to ask."

"Please, Crowley? Please?"

I flinched at her begging. She sounded so raw.

I opened my eyes and met her pained gaze. She opened her mouth to speak, but I silenced her with a gentle finger to her lips.

"No more begging," I said. "Please. All right. You can stay with me for a while."

She threw her arms around me and sobbed against my chest. I put my chin on her head and stroked her hair.

"I'm so sorry," she said after a while. "It just hurts, that's all."

"Your parents?" I asked, tightening my arms.

Her breath hitched. "Yeah."

"If your parents love you half as much as mine loved me, you can fix it."

"Not while I'm with you," she said, pulling back and gazing into my eyes. "They can't handle the fact that you're a woman for starters. They also can't handle . . . look, never mind."

I sighed. "It's all right. I'll take you back to them whenever you want me to."

Her arms tightened around me. "I don't want to. I want you. The choice just hurts, that's all."

"Shh . . . easy. It's not a choice you need to make now, if ever. Just relax and try to get your bearings back for a few days and then decide how you feel about it all."

She nodded and then pulled back. "Thanks."

"You're welcome." I smiled. "Still hungry?"

"Yeah." She sighed.

"Let's go get something to eat."

I pulled out and thirty minutes later both of us had eaten in the parking lot of McDonalds.

Bronwyn, giving me a puzzled stare, slid into the passenger seat while I slipped behind the steering wheel. I tapped the wheel and then turned and gave her a dazzling grin.

"I know just the place," I said.

"For what?" Bronwyn asked, still glancing at me with a surprising wariness.

"You said you wanted a clock, didn't you?" I said. "Well, I know just the place."

"Will it still be open?"

"I think so," I said, glancing at the light traffic on the highway.

Half an hour later we were in St. Peters, standing before an old clock shop. Bronwyn looked around in interest at the turn-of-the-century townhouses along the road.

"Gotta love the inner city, don't you?" I said.

She shrank next to me, watching the group of five young men walking toward us. They were exchanging glances and whispering to each other. I barely paid attention to what they were saying. I knew we were both good looking and felt no need to listen to comments about our sexual attributes.

I glanced at Bronwyn. "You're perfectly safe with me. They can't hurt you."

"Are you sure about that?" she asked, gazing at the one at the front who seemed to be a body builder.

I laughed. "Hell, yes. Look, if it makes you more comfortable, we'll go inside."

I pushed open the door, and the bells tinkled. We found ourselves in an ancient, shadowed shop, resonant with the sound of ticking clocks. Cuckoo clocks hanging on the walls, grandfather clocks scattered along the walls, mantelpiece clocks, kitchen clocks, traveling alarm clocks, and display cases filled with pocket watches and wrist watches.

"Wow," Bronwyn said, turning in a circle as she took in all the timepieces.

"Cool, huh?" I said. "Check this out." I pointed to a glass mantel-piece clock close to us. Its internals were bronzed springs, gears, and cogs, each wheel turned by a small man. It looked as though an entire factory of tiny people worked to keep the clock ticking.

"Oh, that *is* cool," she said.

"You like it?"

She nodded.

"Can I help you?" a voice asked behind me. I turned and saw an old man. I smiled at him. I had last seen him when he was much younger.

"Yes. We're after a—" I glanced around and saw Bronwyn staring at a grandfather clock, as tall as I was. "—grandfather clock."

He smiled fondly when he saw Bronwyn's round-eyed expression. I found myself mirroring it. Her expression was nothing short of endearing.

"You like that one?" I asked her.

"Check this out," she said.

I followed the direction of her extended finger and was equally awkstruck. Every millimeter of the clock's silver face was intricately carved, and the roman numerals understated and classic rather than ornate. The weights looked aged and sturdy, the wood well-kept and loved. It ticked with a quiet authority that was soothing.

"Wow," I said.

"I like this one." She blushed and nibbled her lip.

I caught her chin in my hand. "No nibbling. I like it too." I turned back to the clockmaker. "How much do you want for this one?"

He mentioned a price, and Bronwyn sagged and clutched me for support.

I smiled. "I'll take it. When can you deliver it, and can you do it in the evening? I'll be out until then."

"We can do that for you tomorrow. But it would have to be night," he said. "How do you want to pay for that?"

"Sounds perfect. Will you take a check?"

He nodded. "Certainly."

Five minutes later, Bronwyn and I were on our way back to my car. She held a small alarm clock, almost an afterthought, in her hand. She slipped her hand into mine and pulled in close to me. "That is the most beautiful clock I've ever seen, beloved angel."

I nodded. "I know. It's superb."

"Where are you going to put it?"

"Where do you think it needs to be put?"

"How about at the bottom of the stairs near the front door?" She blushed. "I really like looking at it."

I laughed. "I have no problem with that at all. I think it would be stunning."

As I opened the car door for her, she turned and slipped into my embrace. "Thanks, Crowley."

My arms tightened around her. "You're welcome, Bronnie." I finally pulled back and gazed into her eyes. "I promised you an early night and that's one promise I intend to keep."

She nodded. "All right. Sounds good. I really don't feel like partying tonight."

When we were safely back in my house, I beckoned to Bronwyn. "I *do* have a fun idea if you're interested."

"If it involves slow dancing with you I'm more than interested," she said. I opened my mouth to protest, but she cut me off. "It's not because you're hot or because I love you. I want to do it because it feels good."

I nodded as I went to my stereo. "I get it." I grinned as I put in one of my favorite compact discs. Slow music filtered through the speakers.

Before either one of us really knew what was happening, we were tangled together and moving in time to the music.

"So, beloved angel," Bronwyn murmured against my chest. "What was this fun thing that you wanted to do?"

"You like terrible movies?" I asked with a grin.

"Depends on how bad."

"Absolutely rotten. Scum of the earth. So bad you can't even be bothered to puke."

She giggled and nodded. "Yep. I also like lotsa blood and guts."

I laughed. "Oh, yeah, I'm right there for that one." I pulled her to a halt. "Come with me."

I took her by the hand, and she stayed close to me as I led her to her room. I pushed her onto the bed, pulled out a remote from a dresser drawer, and flicked on the television. I tuned it to my favorite horror movie channel. We just hit the start of the evening horror show.

"Oh, geez," she said with a groan. "This isn't *The Thing With Two Heads*?"

"You betcha," I replied. "Or would that be—if you listen to Elvira—The Head With Two Things."

"Who?"

"Watch."

Elvira appeared on the screen, and Bronwyn's eyes goggled.

"Good lord," she said.

"Stacked, isn't she?"

"Yes," she said in a strangled voice.

"I know," I said, patting her arm. "Lovely. I really like this show."

Bronwyn mock glared at me and playfully slapped my arm. "I'll just bet you do."

I laughed and pulled her into my arms. She rested her head on my shoulder and put her arms around me with a happy sigh.

We watched for a little while, and I heard Bronwyn whisper, "I love you," before her breathing deepened as she sank into a deep sleep.

I stayed with her until the wee hours of the morning, holding her close. Every time I tried to leave, her grip tightened, but as the night lightened she let me go. I leaned over her and smoothed her golden hair away from her forehead. I brushed my lips across her temple.

"Relax, Bronwyn," I whispered. "I'll take care of you for as long as you need me to."

I wanted to kick myself for that statement as I spoke it, but I really couldn't. I meant it.

I really liked my fierce, mortal friend.

CHAPTER FOUR

The next night our new clock was delivered by two large, burly men. One of them looked remarkably like the clock maker, and I was amazed at the delicacy he displayed in placing the clock and hanging the weights inside it. When they were done, Bronwyn and I sat side by side on the stairs, hearing it tick, gazing at its beautiful face.

"Looks great, doesn't it?" I asked, nudging Bronwyn.

She put her head on my shoulder. "Oh, yeah, sure does." She glanced at me. "Thanks, Crowley."

"What for?"

"Everything."

I put my arm around her and pulled her in close. "You're welcome."

We were quiet for a moment or so, simply enjoying the feel of one another.

"What do you want to do this evening, angel?" Bronwyn finally asked.

"You want to go for a ride on the bike?" I had slipped out of the house and fed before she knew I was awake, so I was really only offering a ride.

"I don't know," she said.

"Yes?" I asked, nudging her again, very gently. "You wanted to do something else this evening?"

"I'd like to go out, all right," she said. "But not as far as the city. How about to the Civic Center?"

"What's in the Civic Center?"

"There's an art display by all the seniors from the local schools. It's a parents and friends thing, and I promised one of my friends ages ago that I'd go." She braced herself. "I was kinda wondering if you were interested in going?"

"Sure."

"Look, it's okay if you . . . what did you say?"

"I said yes."

"Really?"

"Really."

"You'd go with me to a school function?"

I chuckled. "Why wouldn't I?"

She blushed and fidgeted. "I don't know."

I looked at her curiously. "That's not the only one, is it?"

She shook her head.

"Ah," I said. "Which other one is there that's so important?"

"I have my graduation ball in a couple of months."

"And you want me to be your partner? Sure. Why not?"

Her beautiful face lit up. She had a broad smile as she finally met my eyes. "Could I ask for a special favor, just for me?"

"Okay . . ."

"Would you consider wearing a top hat and tails for my grad ball?"

I laughed. "Sure. Any particular reason why?"

"Is there any reason you keep agreeing to what I'm asking you to do?"

"We're friends, aren't we?"

She hesitated, studying me closely. Her eyes misted. "Yeah, I guess we are," she murmured and chewed her lip.

"Hey," I said, cupping her chin. "Why are you chewing your lip? And you haven't answered my question yet."

"I just think you'd be hot in a tuxedo . . ."

"Yes, but I'm sure I'm hotter in an evening gown."

Her face darkened as I expected it would. "Stop teasing me with that beautiful body of yours."

I smiled. "I'm a grown woman and a free spirit."

A thin sheen of tears glistened in her eyes. "Oh, god, I know. Stop baiting me."

I flinched. "Look, you're the only person I've ever agreed to wear a tux for."

She slipped her arms around me and buried her face in my chest. Hot tears stung my cool skin, and I stroked her back.

"C'mon," I said, pulling back and smiling into her slightly blood-shot eyes. "Let's go to this exhibit of yours. Sounds like a lot of fun."

She nodded. "Some of the work is pretty good."

"Okay, what are we waiting for?" I asked, standing and pulling her with me.

Half an hour later, I was parking the car, and we were looking at the thick crowd of parents and teenagers milling around the front of the Civic Center.

As we approached them, Bronwyn scanned the crowd for her friends, while adults glanced at us, some dismissing us, some looking at us curiously. One or two older brothers eyed us from top to bottom, and I returned each stare, taking in the blushes and dropped eyes with an internal smile.

One of the onlookers kept his eyes on us. He was about my height, and seemed to be all of nineteen years old. He had a handsome face, one that would be rugged in later life, and stylishly unruly hair. There were a cluster of girls Bronwyn's age surrounding him, but he ignored them and focused on me.

"That's Chris Carlton," Bronwyn said, following the direction of my gaze and moving in closer to me.

"Okay."

"He's the big brother of one of the most popular girls in school. All the girls are after him." She rolled her eyes.

I gazed into his eyes and saw something flickering in them that I didn't like. Perhaps it was a species of young arrogance, or the reflection of the cruelty lurking around his mouth.

"I don't know why," I said.

"Don't you think he's cute?"

I glanced at Bronwyn. "No."

Her brow furrowed. "Okay." She looked back at the doors. "You want to go inside and stare at the art work?"

I nodded, and she took my hand. She led me through the throng of hot, throbbing humans and into the cool interior of the Civic Center.

An older man approached Bronwyn. He was balding and had a thin mustache. He glanced at me. "Bronwyn, it's good to see you."

"Hi, Mr. Rowland," she said cheerfully, as we brushed past him.

He gave her an odd look.

"Thanks," I said.

She squeezed my hand. "Like I'm going to forget your rules any time in a hurry. 'Do *not* tell anyone about me.'"

I laughed. "Like I said, thanks." We continued through a field of bizarre and sometimes wobbly and self-conscious sculpture.

"Where do you want to start?" I asked as she pulled me into the main hall. There were less humans in there, and I was glad for the break from my prey.

"How about down the back corner?" She blushed. "I think I want to start where it's quieter."

She pulled me forward again, and I found myself in front of a painting that would have done Michelangelo proud. It seemed a cross between Whistler's Mother and the ceiling of the Sistine Chapel. It was a picture of a man on his death bed, surrounded by family, eyes closed and features limp. All the onlookers—and it was a mix of young and old—were in varying stages of mourning. Naturally enough, it was entitled "Last Moments."

I winced. The technique was brilliant but the subject matter was too close to home. I had seen my father die like that, and it brought back the sting of memory. I closed my eyes and sighed.

"Are you all right?" Bronwyn asked, concerned.

I opened my eyes and gazed at her. Her green eyes were gentle and kind, and I smiled at her. "I'm all right. This picture just brought back some memories, that's all."

"Oh. You want to talk about it?"

"No, I really *am* all right." I felt a little embarrassed. "It just reminds me of my father, that's all."

"Is he still alive?"

I snorted. "Oh, no, he died a long time ago."

"You were there when he passed?"

"Yes, right by his bedside. He was a good and kind man."

She slipped her arms around me and gave me a gentle squeeze. "How long ago was it?"

"A long time ago." I couldn't tell her it was going on fifty years.

Her eyebrows shot up at the sharpness in my tone. "You must have loved him very much."

"I did."

She was quiet for a moment. "You really don't like to talk about yourself much, do you?"

I looked at her and sighed. "There really isn't much to tell even if I wanted to."

"I really wish you would tell me more." She must have seen the traces of exasperation in my eyes. "It's not because I have a crush on you, and officially I don't. I love you. There's a difference."

"God, Bronnie," I said, rolling my eyes.

"Let me finish, will you? As I was saying, it's because despite your prickly, unapproachable exterior, your eyes are so gentle. You're not a bitch, and I don't understand why you keep yourself so isolated. You're so beautiful, why don't you take advantage of your youth and loosen up a bit? I don't get it."

I sighed and moved closer to her, cupped her beautiful face, and stroked her soft cheeks. "My life is very complicated, and I don't really feel young anymore. I'm also not as young as I look. I'm old and tired." I think it was the distress in her shining green eyes that forced the words from me.

"You look young enough to me," Bronwyn replied, sinking into my caress. "You're so beautiful and you're alive. What more could you want?"

"Peace," I said. "One day I think you'll understand."

"I want to understand now," she said.

"In time, I'll tell you more, if you're still around. But until then, leave a girl some secrets, will you?"

"In time? God, I want to be around you forever," she whispered and stood on her tiptoes to kiss my cheek.

I smiled at her. "Let it go and enjoy the moment, my young charge."

I pulled her toward the next painting, a surrealist piece involving a peach, a bicycle, and something else I couldn't quite identify. It looked almost geometrical.

I tilted my head. "What the fuck, people? Seriously, what the fuck?"

Bronwyn burst out laughing and blushed. "Shit, I thought it was just me. I had no idea what the hell it was, but people have been ooh-ing and aah-ing over it all week. I figured I was just an idiot."

I laughed with her. "Then we're both idiots."

"What about this one?" she asked, moving to the next painting.

"Cool," I said. "If I ever get the urge to paint a bowl of fruit, shoot me, will you?"

"If you ever put one on our kitchen table I'll shoot you. How's that?"

I laughed, letting the reference to "our" kitchen table slide by. We continued along the paintings, chuckling or exclaiming as the mood proclaimed. I became aware of eyes on us and extended my senses to see who it was. Bronwyn shifted beside me and glanced at me.

The stare was coming from our left, behind us, so I looked in that direction to find Chris Carlton's eyes on us. He was surrounded by a gaggle of schoolgirls, but he paid more attention to us.

I met his eyes.

He did not drop his.

He was the predator, we his prey.

I would have to watch for him, now that he had seen us.

"Crowley," Bronwyn said.

"Hmm?"

"What's wrong?"

I gave her an easy smile. "Nothing."

"You want to get out of here? I do. I think I've seen enough art to last me a lifetime."

"You don't like art?"

"I like the stuff I can understand."

"You ever feel inclined to go to the Art Gallery?"

"Only if it's with you. Otherwise it would be y'know . . . daggy . . . to go with any of my friends."

I laughed. "Does that mean that if you go with me I'm stodgy and staid enough for you to get away with pretending it was a forced excursion?"

"You're not stodgy or staid and you fucking know it."

"Language, Bronwyn. Language. You've quite a foul fucking mouth on you there."

She slapped my arm. "God, you're such a brat."

I inclined my head and smiled. "Thanks. What would you like to do with me now?"

"*With* you or *to* you?"

"And you're a forward little thing, aren't you?"

"I'm not little. I'm a grown woman and, on top of that, I'm almost as tall as you."

I folded my arms. "Grown, are we?"

"Oh, hell yes," she said, grinning, and pulled her tee shirt out a little, giving me a delectable view of her beautiful, full breasts, barely encased in a lacy bra. It took me a minute or so to reclaim my self control.

"Yes, Sweetpea, we certainly are grown, aren't we?" I reached out, amazed my hand wasn't shaking, and pulled out her tee shirt so I could ogle her a little more. I gently brushed her lips with mine.

Bronwyn fell against me, flushing. "God, Crowley."

I gave her a smug grin. "Gotcha."

"Let's go home," she said breathlessly. "I want your body against mine, even if it's only to dance."

I sighed. "Bronwyn, love, we aren't going to be together that way." I captured her green eyes. "You're only going to get hurt if you keep doing that."

She flinched. "Stop doing that. I can hope, can't I?"

"It's a bad idea to hope for something that can never be," I said. I took her cold hands into mine, and she tried to pull away from me, a glimmer of tears in her eyes.

"Look," I said. "Let's try being friends, all right? Like I said, I really like you."

"You won't hurt me?"

I flinched and cupped her face, soothing her tears. "No. I'd never intentionally hurt you."

"Okay." She nodded. "I still want to go home. I still want to dance. I like you too. Forget love, I really like you."

"Okay. Let's go home. We can keep dancing." I gazed into her eyes, and her smile returned, lighting up her beautiful, green eyes.

"I'm sorry," she said.

"It's all right. I really do think we're friends. I'm sorry I can't give you more."

"I know. One day you will, Crowley."

I gave her a sad and slightly frustrated smile, and saw the answering flinch in her eyes.

We held hands and walked through the sea of humans, which unconsciously parted to let us through. I scanned the crowd for Chris Carlton, but he was gone.

80

Bronwyn avoided me for the next two nights. She was not home when I got up. I went out to feed and when I got back she was normally home. She stayed in her room, door shut, television on in the background.

I didn't want to disturb her because I knew she was hurting. She needed a little time away from me, and I wanted to respect that.

It didn't last long. I broke.

I grinned as I went to bed at dawn. On the kitchen table was a crystal bowl of chocolates, held by a stuffed effigy of the Count from Sesame Street, along with a card. *Forgive me*, it said.

The next evening when I got up, I bounded up the stairs, expecting to see Bronwyn in the kitchen. When I burst through the door, my heart sank when I saw it was empty.

My shoulders sagged until I saw the crystal vase of red roses in the center of the table. I went to it and pulled out the card nestled in between two of the roses. I scented them, smiling at their fragrance.

My beloved angel, the card said.

"I was wondering when you'd get up."

I turned and saw Bronwyn leaning in the doorway, hands stuffed into the pocket of her jeans, crooked grin on her face.

We tangled together. I could feel her soft breath on the skin of my chest, and buried my face in her hair, taking in her warmth and gentle, feminine fragrance.

"Crowley," she began, "I . . . I . . . "

"Shh," I said. "It's all right."

She pulled back. "No, it's not all right. I don't understand. Your words say no but your actions say yes. You say you don't love me but everything else about you says you do."

I shook my head and sighed. "You keep teasing me, and I'm doing it back. I'll try to stop because I know you're not taking it the right way."

"It means I'd have to stop as well and I just can't."

I couldn't say anything to that. She was right. I liked touching her as much as she did me.

We stared at each other, then I tore my gaze from her eyes.

"It's Saturday night, isn't it?" I said.

She nodded, and I smiled. "Want to go out with me?"

"Sure," she said. "I love going out with you."

"I like taking you out with me," I replied and made the mistake of gazing into her intense, green eyes. This time she broke it, and I cleared my throat. "You want me to tell you where we're going, or you want it to be a surprise?"

"I think I like your surprises," she said, blushing.

I could not help myself. I took her hand. "Come with me."

Twenty minutes later we were in a dusty parking lot at the local recreational park. There was a carnival in town, and I had felt the urge to smell popcorn, teeming humanity, and animals. They also had a circus traveling with them, but we would only go to that if Bronwyn wanted to. I could do everything that the circus performers did and better at that, so they had lost some of their appeal for me.

We got out of the car and took each other's hands as we hit the first sets of tents. There were shooting galleries, a Ferris wheel, pony rides, cotton candy, parents, and children.

I was hungry. I had not fed. I looked around for my first victim and thought about how I could slip away from Bronwyn long enough to take them.

"Hey, Bronwyn," a young girl said, surrounded by her friends. They were all whispering and staring at us. Bronwyn and I both pretended not to notice.

"Hi, Lauren," Bronwyn said cheerfully, and they began to chat.

"Bronnie," I whispered into her ear. "I'll be right back."

"Sure," Bronwyn said. "Are you all right?"

I smiled. "I'm fine."

I really was. I scanned the crowd, looking for the eyes I could feel on us.

I found them.

Chris Carlton, aloof and alone, stood at the edge of the trees that bordered the carnival, staring at us. He had dropped all pretence of good humor, his expression and eyes feral as he took me in. I openly stared at him, and he returned it with malice.

I ran faster than an eye could blink and stood before him.

"What's going on in that nasty little head of yours?" I whispered.

We stood not two inches apart, meeting each other's eyes.

"I want her," he said. "You're unnatural."

"We feel exactly the same way on both scores," I replied.

I felt something sharp dimpling the skin of my stomach and looked down at the knife he had touching me.

"Put it away or I'll make it painful for you," I said.

He laughed.

I pounced.

He did not have time to scream before I had his arms pinned to his sides and my fangs in his neck. I pulled out great drafts of his blood, draining him almost as much as I normally drained my victims. I didn't want to kill him; I wanted to teach him a lesson.

I dropped him where he stood and cleaned up the fang marks on his body. As the flesh of my wrist closed, I thought about what I'd said to him, that I wanted Bronwyn.

Oh fuck, I realized. I liked Bronwyn, all right, and there was nothing platonic in it.

My heart sank as I ran back to her. Her friends had left, and she was waiting for me close to a shooting gallery.

"You want to win a girl a stuffed bear?" she asked.

I laughed. "Anything you want, my succulent young charge." I caught her expression and her half open mouth. "Ah, ah, ah—*almost* anything you want."

"Bugger," she muttered playfully.

I stared at the prizes at the shooting gallery. If she wanted a bear, I would give her one. The largest one I could find. The one I had spotted as we walked past the Test Your Strength challenge.

Two minutes later, Bronwyn was choosing her bear, and I was collecting applause. She hugged me and her bear—almost as big as she was.

"My beloved angel," she whispered.

"You're welcome, BronwynHunter," I said.

She gestured toward an empty shooting gallery close to where we were standing. The spruiker stood outside, staring at the passersby with glassy, disinterested eyes, calling for all he was worth.

"Step right up! Come and relive the wild west! You, young lady!" He zeroed in on Bronwyn. "You look like you'd be a great shot!"

She pulled me over to him and handed me her bear.

He gave her a smile and a rifle.

She gave him a pearly, polite grin. "Sure, I'll give it a go."

We both watched in amazement, the spruiker shocked into silence, as she shot the shit out of every target in the shooting gallery.

I laughed as she put the rifle down, giving the now morose, heavily painted man a dazzling smile.

"I'll have that one, please," she said, pointing to a bright purple dinosaur.

My laughter increased as he opened and closed his mouth several times, and fished out a toy. He glared and thrust it at her. Her smile did not falter as we walked away and stopped to exchange toys.

"It's been a long time since I've seen a real dinosaur," I said, capturing her gaze. "I like it."

Her eyes sparkled with mirth. "So did I," she said, taking my hand.

We walked aimlessly. Bronwyn saw the freak show nestled off to one side, down a roughly formed alleyway. We looked at each other and grinned like a pair of children.

We went toward the booth, and I bought us tickets. I gestured for her to lead the way, and she did so.

We went into the first darkened tent to see a genuine mermaid.

"Okay," I said, eyeing the exhibit. "No worries."

Bronwyn giggled. "C'mon. Where's your sense of fun?"

"Not in a tent looking at a wet, stuffed monkey wearing badly painted neoprene flippers."

"Where's your sense of adventure?"

"I think I lost it a long time ago."

"You're so strange," she said, pulling me to a halt as we left the tent to go on to the half man, half woman.

"How so?"

"You keep talking about how old you are, but you're young. You're alive. You're vital. It sounds corny, but you *shine*. You're amazing."

"Flattery will get you nowhere."

She put her hand on my shoulder and gazed deep into my eyes. "I'm trying to help you. I don't know why you've given up on life. You won't tell me. I'll live with that. But I have trouble with the fact that you're so much fun to be around, such a worthwhile person, and all you seem to want to do is lie in a rowboat, moan 'woe is me' and die."

I raised an eyebrow. "'Woe is me'? Good grief, Bronwyn."

"What's the matter? Don't you like being around me? Don't you think I'm fun to be around?"

I nodded, emotions churning. "I do, young Bronwyn, very much so. I like being around you, too."

"Then could you please enjoy every day you have with me? One by one? I know you want to get rid of me, fine. But while you're stuck with me, can't you just live for the moment?" She flinched, as if afraid of my response.

"I don't intentionally want to get rid of you. Don't think that. It's just that you're so young. I'm sure you're going to change your mind about me in a year or so." I stroked her face. "I thought I *was* living for the moment with you."

She braced herself. "I'm so afraid of you, of being hurt by you. I always get the feeling that you don't want me to get close to you at all, that you really want to get rid of me. I feel like all the kindness you're showing to me is lies."

"Hey! It's not lies." I cupped her face. "And stop nibbling." I held her pained gaze. "Look, let's go home. I don't know about you but I think I'm finished with the carnival for one evening."

She returned my gaze for a moment or so. She nodded. "All right, angel."

I took her hand, and we walked back to the car. She clutched her bear.

When we got home, she was the one who turned on the music and began dancing with me.

"I don't know where to begin," I said, breaking the gentle silence between us. "I don't hate you and I would never intentionally hurt you. None of the kindness I'm showing you is lies. I mean all of it. I don't just invite anyone into my life."

"But you didn't invite me into your life, I put myself here."

"What on earth makes you think I don't want you around? Where's this coming from?"

"You told me right from the start."

"Oh, Bronnie." I sighed, tightening my arms around her. I felt her tears against my chest. "Would it make it better if I spelt it out for you? Okay, I'll do it. I don't mind at all that you're living with me. I like you. You're fun to be around. You're not an inconvenience." I was surprised to realize that I actually meant all of those things.

She peered up at me uncertainly. "You mean it?"

I smiled and nodded. "I mean it."

"You won't throw me out?"

I flinched. "No, I'm not throwing you out any time soon. If you want to leave, that's your decision."

She nodded and snuggled into me again. I let the silence play itself out for a few minutes as we moved in time to the music. My emotions were tearing me apart. I meant every word I said to her. I really *didn't* want her to leave.

"Why are you so insecure?" I asked. "What have I done?"

She began to cry in earnest. "I went to see my mum and dad after school today."

We stilled, and I rested my cheek on her head. I rubbed her back as the tears came. "What happened? What did they say?"

"It was bad. I'm not welcome in their house any time soon."

I waited for a minute, but she remained silent.

"How about I go with you the next time you go and see them," I whispered. "Maybe it won't be so bad for you then."

She pulled back and gazed into my eyes. "No, and stay away from them. This is my problem."

"I'm part of it. They don't know me. I'm sure they're blaming me for all your problems. If I went with you, it would give them something to focus on aside from you. If they think I've done something to you, it'll all go away if they actually get to meet me."

"You can't do that and you know it," she said. "You don't look a day older than when you brought me home. They're not stupid, they're going to notice."

I nodded. "I have good genes. I aged well."

"Really? You don't look like you've aged at all."

"Like you once said to me—not bad for an old chick."

Bronwyn studied me closely for a moment or so, and then she smiled, and her face transformed from beautiful to stunning.

"The night is still young," Bronwyn continued, just as the grandfather clock struck ten. "You want to go out for a while?"

"Sure. Where do you want to go?"

She grinned.

I snorted and laughed. "You want to go to the Test Tube Factory, don't you?"

Her grin broadened, and I laughed. "Just for you, Bronnie, just for you."

Forty-five minutes later we were sitting at our table, with our waitress engaged in a tug of war with Bronwyn over my affections.

I took a good look at the waitress's luscious breasts, unfettered by a bra, while Bronwyn scowled at us both. I don't think it occurred to her that the waitress got her drinks more quickly when I did that.

"You want to get out there and dance?" I asked.

She gave me a curt nod. "Sounds good."

"Bronwyn, I know it makes you angry when—"

"No, it doesn't."

"But—"

"Are you coming?"

"Aren't you going to let me—?"

"Let's just go and dance, okay?"

I sighed. "Sure."

She grabbed my hand, squeezing my fingers to the point of pain, and pulled me onto the dance floor. She began to relax, and finally lost herself in the music. I loosened my grip, and we underwent an unexpected partner change. I frowned at Bronwyn, now in the arms of a muscular young man. He steered her away from me, and she stared at me, half-irritated, half-alarmed. She started to push herself out of his grasp, but his arms tightened around her. I was just about to rescue her when I realized I wasn't alone.

I gazed at the girl who was now clinging to me. She had luminous blue eyes, and a willowy, full-breasted figure. She was almost too thin, and she held me with what seemed like desperation.

I gazed deep into her eyes and scented the air.

She was very sick.

I saw the desire in her eyes as she held my gaze.

"I'm sor—" she began, but I gently held my finger to her lips, silencing her.

"No you're not," I whispered. I nuzzled her neck, scenting her soft, young skin.

Disease was not just in her, it was galloping through her system.

Her arms tightened around me, and she took in a shuddery breath. She radiated warmth as her body responded to my hands stroking her smooth back.

We slowed down, and the world slipped away.

"You're beautiful," she whispered, gently pecking my lips.

"So are you," I said, capturing her eyes before I pulled her in close.

"Do you want to get out of here?" she asked with a hint of a smile.

I returned it. I had not fed and I was hungry, oh so hungry.

She took me by the hand and led me from the club. I was acutely aware of Bronwyn's jealous eyes searching for me, and I hoped against hope that my young friend would stay away from me for a few minutes.

The young woman led me to the rear of the club, and we slipped out of the door, hand in hand, and found ourselves in deserted shadows.

She took my hands and gazed into my eyes.

I leaned forward and kissed her, gently at first and then with increasing hunger as my blood thirst made itself known. When we parted, her breathing was rapid, and she cupped my breast and teased the nipple. I sighed.

I pulled her in close, my hands traveling down her back to her behind as I nuzzled her neck. She began to pant.

I extended my fangs and plunged them into her neck, taking in great drafts of her sweet, feminine blood.

She was sick, so sick. She had a disease of the blood—leukemia. Her flavor told me she did not have long to live, even if I hadn't done what I just did.

As she lost strength, I cradled her in my arms and we sank to the ground.

"You're not human, are you?" she whispered, stroking my face, eyes glazing with shock and blood loss.

I shook my head. "No." I smiled at her.

"What are you?"

"It doesn't matter. What do you want?"

"There's no hope for me. I hurt all the time and I'm dying. I want to die while I can still walk."

I nodded.

Her eyes flickered with a little fear, a little anticipation, and a great deal of relief and peace.

"Is it going to hurt?" she asked, breath hitching.

"No. No more than it did last time," I whispered, kissing her eyes, her cheeks, and then her lips.

She slipped her arms around my neck and returned my kiss of farewell.

I kissed her along the line of her jaw, ending at her jugular. My hands roamed her body, tracing the muscles of her smooth thighs, reaching up to her hot, sweet womanhood. She gave a shuddery breath, chest heaving with arousal and swallowed convulsively.

I plunged my fangs into her neck, taking the last of her diseased blood.

She went limp in my arms. I held her lifeless body close to me, resting my cheek on her head and sighing.

I felt eyes on me.

I looked up, and Bronwyn was standing there with a wide-eyed stare.

Fuck.

The pain and betrayal in her eyes made my heart twist.

I gently put the young woman on the ground. "Bronwyn," I said, looking up at my mortal friend. "It's not what—"

It was too late. Bronwyn gave a strangled cry and ran down the darkened alleyway between the club and the sex shops beside it.

I swore under my breath and ran after her, onto the crowded footpath in front of the club, but it was too late.

She was gone.

I sighed. My heart felt heavy, and guilt weighed down my shoulders. I walked up and down the street, hoping for some sign of her, but she was gone. I went into a few of the other clubs along Darlinghurst Road, but she was nowhere to be found.

Close to dawn, I gave up and went to my car with a heavy heart.

CHAPTER FIVE

I awoke the next evening and bounded into the kitchen. It was empty, and I felt my heart sink.

I ran upstairs to her room and quietly knocked, but there was no answer. I opened the door and peered in. Her bed had not been slept in.

I leaned back against the wall and cursed.

It hurt me to think about her.

I felt unstoppably restless. I wanted to get out and go to city. If I was lucky, I would run into her there, and I would be able to explain. She would listen to me and would forgive me.

I got my bike and rode into the city at breakneck speed, cursing the traffic that slowed me down. I felt a flicker of anger, so I parked my Japanese bike in the Harley riders' spots and walked up Darlinghurst Road.

The pedestrian traffic teemed, and the cars crawled up and down the road.

I started toward one of the clubs, but then felt like being alone. I did not want to admit that I could barely go near a club without the ghost of golden hair and laughing green eyes showing their fond love by my side.

I was also hungry, so I had to feed. I went down one of back alleyways and found a young man passed out, the smell of alcohol thick around him.

I didn't bother with any niceties or gentleness as I grabbed him and took the blood from his body in a few swift drafts. I spilled my blood over the fang marks and got up with a sigh.

I could feel the blood racing through my system, and it should have thrilled me but it didn't. I still felt as though my heart had been torn out of my body.

I slipped out of the alleyway and went back to my bike.

As expected, there was Allenby, leaning against it and giving me a cold, furious stare.

"You just can't leave well enough alone, can you?" he said as I approached.

I smiled. He was alone, obviously waiting for his friends to arrive.

"Neither can you," I said, standing eye to eye with my arms crossed.

"You fucking bitch," he said, and punched my ribs.

I barely felt his hand bounce off my side. "You stupid, fucking cretin. You want to go another few rounds with me?"

"Cunt," he said and aimed another futile punch to my stomach.

It bounced off.

I knocked him over backward with a slap.

He gave a wordless snarl of rage, leapt to his feet, and raced toward me. I let him crash tackle me, and we went down in a tangle of arms and legs.

We pummeled each other like a pair of testosterone laden school-boys. I pulled all of my punches so he was bruised by them, but not too damaged.

Finally blood spilled down his face from a split lip and his chest heaved. I put a booted foot on his chest.

He struggled.

"No, I don't think so," I said. "Don't push me or I'll kill you."

"Fuck off, you bitch!"

"Thank you, I think I will," I said and removed my foot. Before he could blink I was on my bike and roaring off down the road.

I felt restless; the fight with Allenby had worked off some of my excess energy, but I still felt terrible. I wanted to go out, but I wanted to be alone.

Unable to decide what I wanted to do, I went home and slumped in my recliner, tortured by the pain I had seen in Bronwyn's beautiful, bright green eyes.

The following night, I went into the city to feed. Bronwyn had not come home. I was restless and aching. I wanted her. When I drove down Darlinghurst Road, I saw Allenby. He was with a group of rough-looking men, and he scanned the motorcycles that passed them. I pulled up into a side street and parked, and then quietly snuck back to them and hid so I could watch him.

His posture was tense, and he reminded me of a coiled snake. I thought he was looking for me but rejected the idea. He wasn't just looking at the Japanese bikes; he was looking at them all. A couple of riders even looked like me, but he didn't display any reaction to them.

Something about his savage demeanor set my teeth on edge. Even though I was in the shadows, I couldn't shake the feeling that he could see me. My skin crawled.

I quietly backed away from him and went back to my car. I wasn't in the least surprised to see a young man holding onto my car and puking into the gutter. I took him and left his unconscious body in the bushes.

I headed back toward Allenby, but stopped.

I could feel a presence, another vampire, in the street behind me. I could feel waves of anger and loathing radiating from it. I stared into the shadows, trying to find it, but I couldn't see anything. I stood still for a few minutes, but they kept their distance, despite the viciousness I could sense. I tried to push the feelings aside as I went back to Darlinghurst Road to watch Allenby.

I had almost reached him when it finally caught up with me. I was surprised it followed me. I stopped and turned, and felt it coming closer to me. I tensed, preparing myself to fight. I caught a blur of movement beside me and a shadowy figure grabbed me by the collar and hurled me backwards. I sailed through the air, landed with a thump, and skidded on my back almost all the way back to my car. I was immediately back on my feet, poised to fight, but the presence was gone.

I relaxed and sighed, hoping it was over. It wasn't the first time that I'd encountered a vampire like that, and I wasn't in the mood to deal with one now. All I wanted was Bronwyn.

I lost my interest in Allenby. I had done what I needed to do, I had fed, now I wanted to go home and wait.

I got into my car with a sigh, and thirty minutes later was sitting in my recliner, the strains of my favorite music in the background and tears stinging my eyes.

I stayed at home for the next two days. The city wasn't a safe haven for me. I spent my time wandering around my house, riding my bike, and waiting to see if she would come back.

On the fourth night, I ascended from my basement hideaway, steeling myself for another lonely night.

My eyes widened in shock as I took in her beautiful eyes, still and calm, watching me. She sat at the kitchen table, hands clenched, knuckles white with tension.

"Bronwyn," I breathed. "Bronwyn." I couldn't hide the relief in my tone or eyes, and both broke her.

In a second she crossed the kitchen and was in my arms, sobbing against me.

"Crowley," she said when she was able to muster some coherence.

"I'm sorry," I said.

She peered up at me, eyes red rimmed and aching. "I don't know why you're apologizing. I'm the one who needs to say sorry and that's what I'm doing."

"Don't do that to me again," I said. "Please."

"I can't help it," she said. "When I saw you with that girl . . . I . . . I . . . it hurt . . ."

"I know it did. I know. But—"

She put her finger to my lips. "I know we're not together," she whispered. "I know. I know you're a free woman. So am I. My head knows all of that. But my heart hasn't quite caught up yet."

I nodded. "That's why you came back, isn't it?"

She flinched. "I'm not here because I have no better option."

"You've found somewhere else to live?"

She hesitated. "Yes, I have. But I don't want to."

"You really should go. If I'm hurting you this much, what good am I to you?"

"You want me to go?"

I gazed into her green eyes and shook my head.

She let out a gusty breath and sank into my embrace. "I'm sorry."

My disobedient arms tightened around her, and I breathed in the scent of her beautiful, clean, sun-warmed hair, her recent arousal. "Forgiven, Bronnie. Forgiven."

We stayed tangled together for a few moments, simply taking animal comfort from one another.

Finally I was forced to pull back when I felt my stomach growl softly.

I gave her a crooked grin. "I have to go out for about an hour."

She nodded. "You want a bite to eat here?"

I shook my head.

"Be careful," she said.

I nodded. "I always am."

We gently disentangled. I wasted no time going out to feed close to home. I was anxious to get home and back to Bronwyn. When I got back, I closed my eyes and listened for her. I smiled when I picked up the soft sounds of the television in the master bedroom. I went upstairs and knocked softly.

"Come in," she said.

I went in and sat on the edge of the bed. She had schoolbooks resting on her knees and a pencil hanging out of her mouth.

"I'm studying for a test I have tomorrow," she said.

"Oh. I suppose I'd better let you get back to it, then."

"No. Stay." She patted the bed.

I sat beside her, and she closed her books and put them on the floor. She lay in my arms with a sigh.

"Where did you go?" I asked after a little while.

"I went to a friend's house and we talked." She looked up and caught my look of alarm. "Not about you specifically. I remember your rules. I'm not prepared to break them."

I nodded, relaxed.

"You feel something for me as well, don't you?"

I sighed.

"Don't deny it," she said. "Look at what we're doing."

"I just don't have room in my life for romance," I said. "Besides. Think about what you've been doing for the past few days. I can smell it on you. You've had your fill of a few men. And women."

"You can cheat on me but I can't cheat on you?"

"Neither one of us is cheating on the other, and you know it. But how can you keep telling me how much you love me when you can go and do what you're doing with other people? Say I wanted a relationship with you—what would you want me to think?"

She sat up and met my eyes. "I want you. I know you want me. I can see it in your eyes. I can see you're jealous. Don't try to hide it. What I don't understand is what's wrong with me? Why won't you take me? You're not overwhelmed with things you *have* to do, you just go and do what you want. Why do you say you have no time for me? Is it because you're really not interested or because you really have no time?"

I was silent for a moment. "I'm not lying to you. But that doesn't really matter. You're so young. You deserve a life with someone who really loves you and I can't give you that. All I can give you is a meaningless existence."

"I won't give up on you. Never. You're all I want. And meaningless?

Why are you so stalled in life? You're so young, so strong and so beautiful. You're rich. You could have it all if you wanted. Why aren't you moving forward?"

Her eyes glinted with tears and pain as she gazed at me, studying me. Her hand almost unwillingly traced the line of my jaw.

"You're so beautiful." She sighed. "There's so much I want to know about you. Like why you never come out during the day. Like why you always seem so sad. Like your family and your life. You, Crowley. I want to know all about you."

"Honestly, there isn't that much to know about me. You've pretty much seen all I have. You have some idea of what I'm like. I like darkness. It's my best friend."

She studied me for a moment or two. "It'll all come with time." She dropped her eyes and studied the cotton covering my stomach. "You asked me about fidelity. I believe in monogamy. I do. But it just makes me so crazy to know you love me and you're perfectly prepared to go out and fuck anything in a skirt. If you can do that, I can do that."

I narrowed my eyes. "Trust me, I don't fuck everything in a skirt. Haven't you heard of safe sex? Don't you practice it?"

"How I have sex is none of your concern, angel. And yes, of course I know how to take care of myself."

We glared at each other for a moment, and then the fight went out of me.

"This is such a strange conversation," I muttered.

"I know," Bronwyn said, much to my surprise. "But nothing seems to work on you but oblique."

I laughed.

We were quiet for a moment.

"You know," she said. "Today's my birthday."

"Is it?" I asked, arching an eyebrow. "Why didn't you mention it earlier?"

"It slipped my mind. I was more worried about you than anything else."

"Don't worry about me," I said. "You'll only get gray hair."

She joined my soft laughter.

Her eyes flashed, and her beautiful face broke all of my resolution.

"How about a birthday kiss?" I asked, and claimed her lips in a deep and gentle kiss before she had a chance to protest.

Burning shock traveled up and down my body at the touch of her soft lips and her unmistakable response. When we broke, she lay on my chest, trying to catch her breath.

I was glad I was lying down. I knew that my knees wouldn't support me if I was standing.

"Whoa," she said, voice cracking. She cleared her throat. "Um . . . that's the best present I got all day."

"Um," I responded.

She gazed into my eyes. "Thank you, friend."

"Ahem . . . you're welcome," I said, trying to muster a cocky grin and failing miserably.

"You know what I want to spend my night doing?" she asked, blushing.

"What?"

"Dancing with you."

"I think that can be arranged," I said, standing and holding out my hand.

She took it, and I led her downstairs. I put on the music, and we danced.

Around midnight we went back to her room, and I held her as she fell asleep, whispering sweet words of love to me that almost tore me apart.

When dawn forced me to my own bed, I brushed her forehead with my lips.

"Sleep well, beloved mortal," I said and left her.

ℰᴏ

Life continued quietly for the next week. She had exams and studied for them under my watchful eye. I helped her as best I was able.

It was after midnight on a Thursday night. We went into the Test Tube Factory and found our usual table. Our waitress gave me her normal, hungry stare. Bronwyn glared at her, consistent as always, and then dragged me out onto the dance floor, more crowded than usual.

I was unable to stop a pair of young men cutting in and blocking me off from Bronwyn. She looked surprised but kept dancing. I allowed myself to be swept off the dance floor and went back to our table.

The waitress came over, and her eyes lit up when she saw I was alone. She leaned over me. "Want to have some fun?"

I smiled. I was hungry. I had not feasted. Bronwyn wanted to go out for a ride, and I had taken her. My stomach called for food.

I allowed her to take my hand and lead me out into the alleyway behind the club.

As soon as we were outside, she pushed me back against the wall and claimed my lips in a ravenous kiss, massaging my breasts and teasing my nipples as her thigh slipped between my legs.

I moaned in frustration, and it drove her wild. She loosened her dress and her beautiful breasts tumbled into my waiting hands. We sank to the ground as she pulled up her skirts, her hands roaming my bare skin beneath my shirt.

I pushed her onto her back and parted her legs. She moaned and tangled her hands in my hair as I kissed my way down the front of her body, studiously avoiding her breasts.

I kissed her parted thighs, senses filled with the sweet scent of her arousal.

She moaned softly.

I hated her and hated myself.

I sank my fangs, hard and fast, into her thigh, sighing as I was instantly filled with her life giving blood. I felt her slow and still, her passion ashes as she lost consciousness.

I pulled out and covered the fang marks with my blood, erasing them. I covered her breasts and left her there.

When I stood and turned, I saw Bronwyn.

This time she didn't just look hurt. She had tears pouring down her face, and she looked devastated. She gave vent to a strangled, animal cry of pain and sprinted away from me. Despite my greater speed and strength, I couldn't catch her, and she was lost as I burst out into the street, startling a few drunk patrons of Kings Cross.

My shoulders slumped as I gave up and walked back to my car. The pain cut into me like a knife. I immersed myself in it as I viciously crushed the reason for it.

CHAPTER SIX

She was not there when I woke up the next evening, and I knew from bitter experience that she would stay away from me for a few days if I left her to her own devices.

I went out looking for her, and purely by chance I found her in the Kings Cross Hotel. I went out onto the dance floor and smoothly took her into my arms.

"Well, well, well, and how are we this evening, my succulent young charge?" My voice was just loud enough to carry over the noise in the hot and smelly nightclub. Her warm body settled against mine with the ease of gentle familiarity. I pulled her in close, relishing the chance to feel her warm, living body against my cold, dead one.

"Fuck, Crowley, what are you doing here?" Bronwyn was clearly drunk as a skunk, and her eyes were bloodshot as she shook her head to clear out some of the cobwebs.

Dawn was far too close for my liking. I had to get under cover in very short order, so my patience was just a tad strained.

"Brat. I was looking for you to take you home." My eyes bored into hers, and she slipped closer into my cold embrace and held me tight as we whirled around the dance floor in time to the raucous music. Her face rested against my chest, and I felt the breath of her sigh against my skin. I winced as I took us through a pall of smoke and flashing lights.

"I don't want to go home." She glared at me, eyes unfocused, and hiccupped.

I wondered if she was going to throw up. I was quite sick of watching mortals do that. A drunken girl, younger than Bronwyn, brushed past us, spilling half of her precious drink. She glared at me and drew in breath to abuse me, but whatever she wanted to say died on her lips when she looked closer at my pale skin and burning eyes. She scurried off to her equally drunk friends, holding themselves up on a small table close by.

"Untrue. Yes, yes you do. Remember our bargain? You do what I tell you to do when I tell you to do it." My tone and fierce eyes allowed no room for argument. "Don't you remember you have exams starting on Monday? You need to study." In other words, I wanted my playmate around.

"Yes, Mum." She looked down at my clean shirt and grumbled softly, forgetting how good my hearing was. She drew my disapproval with that remark. I was a vampire, an unwholesome creature of the night, not someone's mama bear.

"You have your whole life ahead of you to do this sort of shit. If you want to go out and get laid, I don't care, but do it after your exams." Actually, I was lying. I cared very deeply about who she was sleeping with. I took her hand and led her out of the club, trying to avoid the stranger's fingers that always reached out to touch me.

Behind us, the girl who had spilled her drink and all her friends followed us with their jealous eyes. Although the club was packed almost to capacity, we managed to avoid being jostled, thanks to my silent signal to the drunken humans around us to watch where they were going. The song that had been playing finally finished in a crescendo of electronic squealing, and there was blessed silence for a second or so until another song, louder than the last, began. When we were outside in the relatively fresh air, I breathed a sigh of relief that my eardrums were no longer being perforated by bad music.

Bronwyn pulled me to a halt, moved around to stand in front of me, and forced me to look at her. "Why don't you care? Why don't you care about me?" Beseeching, teary green eyes stared up at me. "I love you." The outside world slipped away from us. I wiped the tears from her eyes in the middle of the busy footpath as people bustled all around us.

"Actually, I think you're drunk as all hell and a pole would look like a good score if it had the right pointy bits. Besides, I never said I didn't care. I care a lot about making sure you're all right." There was no way in hell I was going to tell her I really hated it when she got laid. Coupled with that, why did she get all mushy on me when she was drunk?

"Why won't you get it? I really do love you." She pulled herself from my grip and turned away from me. I watched her in despair. Why couldn't she get past the ridiculous idea of loving me? If she really meant it, we were both in big trouble. If she was asking for sex, it wasn't working, and wasn't the best approach to use on an adult anyway. Perhaps it would be best to show her who I really was, to knock some of the sparkle off my armor, so she could see past beautiful features and arresting blue eyes to my true, dark nature.

I gently touched her shoulder, but she tore away from me and walked down the street. Heaving a deep sigh, I tried to calm my emotions, and quick as a flash I was standing in front of her. All around me the world awakened. I had to get back to my basement, safe from the morning sun, as fast as I could.

Blindly, she walked right into my chest and grunted. I caught her and spun around so I was by her side. I kept my arm around her shoulder, steering her toward my freshly washed car before she had a chance to realize what was really happening to her.

"Bronwyn." My voice caressed her. "We have to talk, but we can't do it here. I have to get home now. Come with me."

She looked up at me, defiance in her eyes, and I willed her to see my unease. A war between curiosity and anger battled behind those normally calm green eyes. She was so close to telling me to fuck off again and meaning it, but the enamored part of her heart wouldn't let her. Finally she heaved a deep sigh and waved a hand. "Fine. Whatever."

I took her hand, and we walked down the busy street for a short distance and then turned right down a dark side street. The pedestrian traffic was sparse because it was the street most murders were normally committed on. Bronwyn drew in close to me, tightening her hand in mine, drunkenness thrown off by the adrenalin in her system. I sighed with relief when we made it back to the car. I had parked illegally, close to the club I had guessed she was at, in too much of a hurry to worry about the parking police. A sulky Bronwyn stood next to the passenger side door and waited for me to unlock it with uncharacteristically shaky fingers.

The hair on the back of my neck prickled as a deep man's voice sounded behind us. "Well, well, well, if it isn't the fucking bitch who keeps kicking over my bike."

I turned.

Bronwyn's eyes widened as she hid behind my back and fumbled with the car door, and climbed into the vehicle.

"Well, well, well, if it isn't the fucking bitch who keeps parking her half-arsed excuse for a motorcycle in my path." I mimicked his tone exactly, while my spirits sank.

Allenby stood by us, hatred in his eyes. I hated him—the ratty brown eyes were psychopathic and dangerously intelligent. I wanted the pleasure of seeing him grow old and frail. I would kill him much later on in his life when he was completely defenseless, just so he knew exactly how it felt to be picked on by a stronger opponent.

He stood before me with his arms crossed in a posture of supreme arrogance, a smug smile playing about his thin lips. He shifted to rest his weight on his back foot, and his tattoos appeared to snake and ripple up and down an unusually clean arm. Something about him had changed, but in my anxiety to be under cover before dawn, I could not see what it was.

His hand shot out and grabbed the front of my white shirt, and I looked down with mild alarm when I saw the knuckles. I had not expected such speed from a mortal. From a mortal. I studied the hand with rising shock. The knuckles gleamed with their snowy skin, the hair clearly outlined on the back of the hand. I followed the white hand up the white arm to his equally white face and looked deep into unfathomable burning brown eyes, shining in the predawn hour, the lustrous, graying, dark hair.

Oh my deary me. He was one of us now. A vampire. What idiot had been responsible for that?

"Okay, so you're one of us now." My voice was cold as I leaned forward to glare at him. "Remember this: You are nothing but a novice compared to me, and I do not have time to waste on you. If you ever come near me again I can and will kill you."

Faster than the eye could catch, I wrapped my strong fingers around his throat. He swallowed convulsively and clawed at my arm with iron fingers as I picked him up and hurled him against the nearest brick wall. There was an ugly crunching sound, and a small spray of blood on impact, and he slid down the wall to collapse in a still, crumpled heap.

From behind me, I heard Bronwyn give vent to a sobbing, moaning scream and fumble for the car door. Quick as a flash I was behind the steering wheel, punching the central locking button, and on my way out into the traffic, looking anxiously up into the brightening sky. Cursing, hoping I was going to get home in time, I took a quick look at Bronwyn.

She was curled up in the seat as far away as possible from me. Her eyes were wide with horror and the wariness that had taken me so long to extinguish flared up again in full force.

"Bronwyn?"

"You killed that man."

"Actually, no I didn't."

"Oh really? So what was that back there?"

"Something I never wanted you to see." It was true. I was a killer and did enjoy drinking blood—that much was true—but did not enjoy doing it with an audience. I also realized I had lost her, whatever regard she may have had for me, and that hurt like hell.

"When were you going to kill me?"

I cast an anxious eye at the steadily lightening sky and struggled to remain awake. I weaved in and out of slower traffic, suppressing a curse. When I got clear again, I put my foot down on the accelerator and turned to her. "I'm not going to kill you, Bronwyn. That's the truth."

She stared at me, face inscrutable. "Oooh yeah, right. You never wanted me around anyway." It took all of my considerable restraint not to flinch at the sarcastic tone and barefaced directness.

"Bronnie, I don't really have time for this now, but I will answer all of your questions this evening." I was most of the way toward being unconscious and was rapidly losing my coordination. Before I caused a massive accident, I pulled over to the side of the road, in front of an abandoned park that was so overgrown it was almost a wilderness. Traffic blared horns past us at my unscheduled stop.

"Hey! What are you doing?" Bronwyn stared at me, alarmed despite herself. She reached for me, but I avoided her grasp.

I staggered out of the car and leaned heavily back in the window. "I don't have time to explain now. Wait for me this evening at home. Please?" I was begging. I didn't want to lose her.

Bronwyn's wide green eyes were suddenly sober. I could see she was fighting herself. One half of her still saw a beautiful woman, the other half thought she saw an unpredictable, cold-blooded murderer. There was also a glimmer of courage in her eyes as she realized the power she had resting in her hands. "How does it feel to have the tables turned on you? Why does my opinion matter to you so much? Ask yourself that."

She was right. Why didn't I want to lose her? Was it because she was a friend? Was it because I could finally say to someone what I really was? Was it because I needed to tell my story, to justify myself to her? I didn't really want to lose the sheen she had put on me, did I? "Please? Wait for me? Please?"

Bronwyn smiled a cold smile and nodded decisively. "I still owe you one for taking me in, I suppose. All right, then, I'll wait for you."

"Thank you." Never had my words been more heartfelt, and I let everything I was feeling show in my eyes. Her eyes widened in surprise. "This evening." She had seen me at my most vulnerable. Now I could only hope that she kept up her end of the bargain and be waiting for me . . . alone.

I stumbled into the ragged bushes, barely functioning, as the first rays of dawn lit up the sky. I found a dark place between two bushes and fell to my knees. My conscious mind was almost gone, pushed aside by the deepening paralysis that was rapidly claiming me. I allowed my pure animal instinct to take over and dug myself into the forgiving earth before sleep claimed me.

I was rare for a vampire. I did not need to rest in my mother earth. Vampire history had it that those who had been made willingly were not bound to the earth that had once housed their moral remains. Those who were made unwillingly did have to remain in their mother earth. It seemed somehow cosmic justice—those who thought that being undead was a prison sentence were kept confined; those who didn't were free to roam the earth. Naturally, I was free to roam the earth.

As always, when I slept I did not dream, and I never woke up stiff and sore as humans do. It was the one real blessing about being a vampire. I could do what I wanted and I never hurt myself; the blood was a wonderful restorative. That night was no different, but when I woke up the next evening, it was with a groan. I clawed myself out of the ground, with no small amount of disgust at the filthy state I found myself in. I blew a sod of dirt out of my mouth, and coughed and spluttered against the unwelcome, coarse taste.

It'd been quite some time since I'd been out under the stars far away from civilization, trying to sleep like that just to see if I could do it.

Now I remembered why I didn't like doing it.

I rubbed the back of my neck and sighed at the gritty feeling. After pulling myself to my feet, I stretched and looked down at my ruined clothes. Dirt did not stick to my skin so I would be clean in no time, but my cool and stylish apparel wasn't cool and stylish anymore.

I walked to the edge of the road and took a good look around. Traffic was light, as I suspected it would be. It was exactly why I'd chosen this route. No one would really be around to see the Cave Creature of Borneo emerge from the ground. Of course, it wasn't the most direct route home, but if I ran I could make it back there in about half an hour.

Resigned to my fate, I began to run down the road. My body settled into a comfortable rhythm, stomach loudly mentioning its neglect. I would have to feed before I spoke to Bronwyn; I suspected it would be a long night of intense conversation with her.

About ten minutes from home, I stopped off for a quick bite. It was a filthy, hallucinating, homeless young man, and I made sure I did my usual trick of healing his wounds with my blood, so people would think he'd had a heart attack.

As I approached my house, I felt a slight tremor of apprehension. Would Bronwyn have called the police? What would be waiting for me when I got home? The question that really twisted my gut was whether Bronwyn would still be there. Would she give me the chance to explain? Had I lost my young mortal friend?

It was time to face the music. The gates stood wide open, and I walked through them. I made my way up the asphalt driveway, wondering how I was going to tell Bronwyn what I needed to tell her. With a steady hand I put my key in the front door, twisted the knobs, and opened them.

"Bronwyn?" I heard the unsteadiness, the aching question in my voice and cursed myself for my weakness. "Bronwyn?"

I noticed the dribbles of earth that were coming off me and landing on the clean, white tiles of the foyer. I was too melancholy to think clearly, so I wandered down to my basement hideaway to change my clothes, resolving to clean up after myself once that was done, if Bronwyn was still not in the house. I had no idea where she would have gone, other than the police. Being a vampire, I was quite lucky because I never had to follow human laws. If I ended up in custody, it would be a novel experience I could snack my way out of, rather than a huge drama.

In the shower I soaked luxuriously in the hot water, trying not to think about my young friend. After I was done, and I threw my soiled clothes into the trash, I stopped and extended my keen hearing to cover the house. There was the ticking of a clock, mindlessly marching through eternity; the scrape of tree branches against the windows of the upstairs spare bedroom; the gurgling and crunching sounds of the refrigerator turning itself on and off. There was no sign of life, I realized after several moments.

I slowly and listlessly went up darkened stairs to check the master bedroom. Bronwyn's bed had been slept in and some of the clothes were missing from the wardrobe. It was odd; even after I'd brought her clothes in, she still insisted on wearing mine, claiming she liked mine better than hers. That thought brought a wry grin with it, and I shook my head.

I walked out to my tidy garage. The car was resting askew in it. I idly promised myself for the millionth time that if I ever saw her again I would teach her how to park. I put my hand on the smooth, silver bonnet—the engine was cold.

She'd taken off. On foot, so it would seem. If so, she had to be close by somewhere. If I wanted to, I could find her. If she didn't want to be with me, I would not force her to stay by my side.

None of it really surprised me. In one evening all her illusions about me had been shattered.

Why did that hurt so much?

I made my way back into the dark house and wandered into the Spartan and fanatically neat living room. I sat down on the recliner, trying to calm my emotions. I liked Bronwyn, that was certain, and I found her hellishly attractive. Did it go any further for me? My heart shied away from the question. It didn't matter one way or another for a number of reasons. First and most important, I was one hell of a lot older than her. I may have not looked very old, but I most certainly was not a child. Second, I was dead and she was alive. Alive. That brought such an unexpected stab of pain that I winced. She couldn't love me, and I certainly couldn't love her. It would be ruination for us both. I also could not understand why she said she loved me so much. I wasn't one of the cuddliest people I'd ever met.

I heard the front door open and close. I took a deep breath and closed my eyes, trying to calm my jangling nerves. Soft, almost hesitant, footsteps came toward me and stopped at the foot of my chair.

"Bronwyn." My voice was soft and gentle, and I'm afraid it was the most heartfelt word I'd ever spoken. So much emotion betrayed me.

I could feel her move up beside me and touch my face with feather light fingers.

I opened my eyes and looked up at her, only to be ensnared in her pained green gaze. Her hand left my face as she moved closer to me, and my senses were teased by the smell of warm, feminine mortal as she drew me in close, and I buried my face in her chest. I slipped my arms around her and held her as closely as she held me. I took a deep breath, pulling the clean scent of her clothes, the dim fragrance of her perfume, and light sweat into my lungs.

It was the most wonderful thing I'd ever smelt.

"Crowley." I pulled away and looked up at her, allowing all the sorrow I felt to show in my eyes as her gentle gaze reassured me. "Are you going to tell me what happened?"

"Where were you?" Had she gotten the police?

"I keep telling you I love you, and I still mean it. Why won't you believe me?" I gave no answer. She sighed and shook her head. "I went for a walk after I had my dinner. No cops. This is about you and me." She sat on my lap so we were eye to eye. I slipped my arms around her waist.

"It really is, isn't it?" I smiled slightly and took a deep breath. "Why do you insist on saying you love me? You hardly know me."

A small wry grin teased her red lips. "You have to keep asking that don't you? One day you'll get it. Start talking—you owe me an explanation."

"That's a very dissatisfying thing to say. I honestly don't get it." I gazed at her, but all she did was give me her enigmatic, maddening, sphinx-like smile.

She shifted in my lap so she was more comfortable and caressed my shoulder, and then pulled her hand back with obvious regret. "Stop changing the subject. We have a small matter of grievous bodily harm to talk about before we start spouting Shakespearean love sonnets at each other."

"Okay, okay." I matched her smile. It was best just to give her the bland truth. No matter what I said, what excuse I gave, I always had the same chance of her believing me. Either she would or she wouldn't. "I didn't kill him." She looked at me as though I'd lost my mind, so I held up my hand before she could speak. "There is no easy way to say this and not sound stupid. I'm a vampire."

Her eyes twinkled with mirth. "Tell me something I don't know."

I raised an eyebrow, giving her my best doubtful look. "Huh? What do you mean? How on earth do you know?"

A gentle finger traced my eyebrow. "I'm not stupid. You're always cold. Your skin is an almost unattractive shade of white. You only appear at night because you obviously can't stand sunlight. For God's sake, Ms Undead, half the time you bloody well forget to breathe. Last night just took me by surprise. I assume you are tactfully trying to tell me he's a vampire as well?"

I had to laugh. Busted. "Okay and yes."

"Now I'm going to strike terror into your heart." She grinned as I looked at her in real alarm. She laughed. "Relax." She ran a finger down my throat and onto my chest, eyes soaking up the view. Her next words were a whisper. "So unbelievably beautiful. My living statue." Her gaze met mine, raw emotion pouring from her and through me. "Us. We have to talk about us."

Inwardly I winced and sighed. She looked at me, dazed, as she suddenly found herself cradled in my arms. I held her soft gaze as I put her on her feet, and she slipped her arms around my neck.

"Us? Sorry, kid, that's not a word that strikes terror into my heart. That only works on the unfaithful."

"I thought it was undead too?"

"Sorry, lovey, wrong kind of 'un.'"

"Well, that's just a major pain in the arse, isn't it?"

"Not for me it isn't." I smiled, fuzzily sensing that I was only seconds away from kissing her. I struggled mightily with myself and finally managed to rein in my tangled and tumultuous emotions. She seemed to sense the change in me and pulled back.

"Look," I said, sighing. "There's more to it than just the blood sucking factor. There's also quite an age difference. Do you have any idea how much older than you I am? I'm old enough to be your grandmother."

She colored slightly. "You don't look it." She shrugged. "You don't look much older than me. I don't understand how someone who doesn't have the limits of an aging body can actually be old on the inside? Don't old people always say that they never feel old, they feel young?"

I chuckled and pulled her close again, slow dancing with easy familiarity. "Yes. That's true, they do say that. Age isn't only about what you are and aren't physically capable of doing, it's also about how much experience you have. You don't have as much as me and it shows."

Bronwyn pulled back from me and gaped. "You patronizing–patronizing–patronizing—"

"No, no name calling. It's true."

She pulled out of my arms and peered at me closely, all traces of good humor vanished. I could tell by the set of her shoulders and the clenching and unclenching of her hands that she was furious.

"So what you're telling me is that you couldn't possibly love me because I'm a child. We have nothing in common and never will."

I thought about it for a moment. Did she have a point? "No, I do think we have things in common. But we're not only talking about a fifty-eight year age difference, we're also talking about a species difference. You're young and you have your whole life ahead of you. You're alive and I'm not."

She crossed her arms and glared at me for several moments, during which I struggled not to fidget. "God, what a cop out. You know what your problem is? You have no faith."

"If I had faith I'd probably be burned to a crisp by now." It was a lame joke that failed miserably, judging by the anger in Bronwyn's eyes. "Look, nothing is ever that simple. Your view of the world is amazingly naïve if you really think that we could wave a magic wand and make some kind of stunningly beautiful couple living a stable life in a perfect world. What do you think would happen? Do you really think I'm going to pick you up from school—during the day, mind you—on my gargoyle so we can go lurching off into the sunset?"

"No, what I'm saying is that people who have a flexible mind aren't afraid to try new things." Her voice rose in volume. "It doesn't matter how old you are, it matters how you react to situations and what kind of a person you are on the inside. It's not always about age and looks. You're a coward, Crowley."

I looked at her closely. Her face was red, and she was breathing hard. I took a moment to calm myself. She simply could not understand what I was saying to her. I could see her point, but there were other things that she hadn't considered. Did she want children? Did she want to get married? What did she want for her future? We were so different on fundamental levels that a relationship would never work, even if I had been of a mind to pursue one.

She turned her back to me, and her shoulders were hunched.

"Bronwyn."

She almost kicked the carpet like a small child having a tantrum.

"Bronwyn."

Her shoulders stiffened, so I knew she heard me. I took a step toward her and laid a hand on her shoulder.

"Bronwyn, look at me." I gave her a gentle nudge, and she finally turned around to face me, eyes brimming with tears and misery. "What about if I agree to keep an open mind?" I knew it was just plain stupid to pretend that there was nothing going on between us.

Her eyebrows contracted, and she wiped away the unshed tears from her eyes. "What do you mean?"

"It means we'll talk about this more, but there's something I have to show you first."

A dim spark of hope flared in her eyes. My heart lightened almost unwillingly. I could not stand to see her upset and I felt no small amount of disgust with myself for causing it. I could not help it; there were things we needed to say. If we were to have any kind of relationship at all—even friendship—we would have to be on an even footing. There could be no gross imbalance of power.

Did I even want any of this? Once I would have said no, but now I was not so sure. It was such a relief to be able to declare my nature to another being and not to be judged badly for it.

She took a step forward, her bloodshot green eyes locked onto my burning blue ones. We stood a hairsbreadth apart for a second. She sank into my embrace, oddly drawing comfort from me, the person who was hurting her the worst.

I stroked her hair, feeling the soft stir of her breath against the smooth, sensitive skin of my throat, and then I pulled back, gazed at her, and held her small hands in my large ones.

I could not bear to tear my eyes away from her beautiful face. "Yes, we do need to talk, but I want you to come with me first. I have to show you something. You game?"

She pulled away from me, slipped her hand into mine, and tangled our fingers together. "I'm game if you are. Lead the way." She gestured before us.

It took every ounce of will power I had not to kiss her as I led the way to my car.

CHAPTER SEVEN

"Where the hell are we?" Bronwyn wrinkled her nose in disgust as we pulled into the old and weedy parking lot of a private hospital.

I shook my head, unwilling, as yet, to say anything. The trip here through the light traffic had been a quiet one, as we preferred the company of our own thoughts. With each second that passed, the twin urges of grim determination to get here and to run as fast as I could in the opposite direction warred with one another. Finally, the visiting won out, but only by a hair.

Finding parking was easy. Although the small, single level hospital was full of patients, most of them never got that many visitors. I always hated coming here. I turned off the engine with a decisive twist of the key and sat for a moment or so as Bronwyn watched me closely.

Okay. Let's do this.

With a leaden hand, I opened the door, got out of the car, and gave the dark parking lot an automatic quick scan for any signs of trouble. Bronwyn followed me out of the car a second later, still unable to take her eyes off me. I saw the wheels turning behind her eyes mingled with concern. I gave her a brief smile, knowing it didn't touch my eyes, to reassure her. She hesitantly returned it.

I gazed at the building in front of us. She was right—it was pretty gross, but the facility had an outstanding reputation and an equally outstandingly stupid name: Sunnybank Long Term Care Facility. Why the fuck couldn't they just call it an old peoples' home and be done with it? No name could hide the way its appearance broadcasted its function. The outside looked as though it had seen better days. The brickwork was faded, the windows scratched and a little dirty, the writing almost obliterated from the signs. Overall, the place was a bit like the people who called it home—it had seen better days but still stubbornly powered on.

"Just come with me." I gestured and led the way toward the doors, nestled under a crumbling and somehow cancer riddled awning. She slipped her hand into mine, and I squeezed it reassuringly. "It's okay. I'd like you to meet someone."

I walked through the front doors. Most of the facility was deserted, and the ultra clean antiseptic smell hit my senses, warring uneasily with the smell of old shit and age, almost making me gag. Crepe paper streamers hung listlessly on the walls, and in between the bends were crayon pictures, most hanging askew, drawn by the kids in the local schools as if trying to instill almost desperate cheer. Bronwyn wrinkled her nose in disgust as she surveyed the wide, deserted hallways.

This place had always made my skin crawl, but it honestly was one of the best of its kind. The staff was genuinely attentive and caring of both the people they tended and the visitors.

Steeling myself, I led the way past a nurse's station, deserted at the moment. If the nurse had been there, I would have waved in greeting. They were used to seeing me here at this time.

We went down the corridor, past another empty station and beyond two darkened doorways, into a small ward. It was as dark as the other rooms had been, the sole light source being the dim illumination from the hallway. Bronwyn's hand tightened in mine. She trusted me to guide her past obstacles because I knew her eyes were adjusting to the change in light, and mine didn't need to. Two of the beds in the room were deserted, but the last was the home of an old woman. I smiled sadly when I saw her. I glanced at Bronwyn to make sure she was watching. I gestured to her to sit on the metal and plastic visitor's chair by the bed, while I sat on the edge of the bed so I could face the occupant.

The lady in the bed was wrinkled, sleeping soundly, mouth slightly open to show her toothless, pink gums. Her wisps of white hair had been brushed away from her forehead. Her flannelette nightgown was sensibly done up all the way to her ancient, wrinkled neck. Her liver-spotted hands lay on the greenish hospital blanket, sheets beneath it white and starched. With the utmost care, blinking back tears, I took the frail, arthritic hand and once again looked at a well-loved face. At one time, it had been youthful and vibrant; now it was just a pale, sick shadow of what it had once been. The years had been so unkind to her. I remembered everything, all that she had been to me: mother, teacher, friend. There had been so many good times and all so long ago.

As though for the first time, I drank in every change that time had forced upon her—the almost non-existent white eyelashes, the paper thin skin, sparse white eyebrows, wrinkled lips. I could still see her, as she was so long ago: the sunset hair shining in the brightness of noon, full red lips, twinkling blue eyes, and straight white teeth as she flashed her beautiful smile. Once young and strong, she was now aged and failing. She had not known that this was what fate had dictated for her. She had always believed that she would go in her prime, or die old and frail in her bed, surrounded by her grandchildren. In reality, her children had deserted her, and she had not met her grandchildren. I was the only person who really came to see her, and that was as often as I could, usually once a week.

I sat there for the longest time, lost in pain for her and everything she meant to me, until Bronwyn's hands found my broad shoulders, and she gave me a reassuring squeeze. The salty tears slipped almost unnoticed down my cheeks as I kissed those soft, wrinkled lips.

"I won't say goodbye. Until we meet again." I knew my whisper would never wake this old woman.

I was shocked when the lips moved to form words, and I put my ear close to her. "Thank you, Little One. Until we meet again." It was the endearment she had always used for me, and the pain of just hearing it tore through my insides. The shadow of the voice I had once known sank a wickedly sharp dagger into my heart, bringing more unwanted, bittersweet memory with it. I felt myself break a little more.

My self control vanished, and tears ran down my face unchecked as I nodded. "Yes."

With regret I stroked the cool, fragile skin of her forehead, silently telling her farewell and I still loved her and would never stop. No matter what my path was, she would always hold a private corner of my heart that no one would ever break into.

Bronwyn sensed that I was done and slipped her arm through mine and led me out of the hospital. My protective, young mortal and I walked in privacy through the deserted hospital hallways. No one saw my tears. I was still crying when we hit the semi-deserted parking lot, and Bronwyn pulled me into her arms to soothe me. Quite frankly, that just made things worse.

I didn't want to hurt my mortal friend, so I disentangled myself and led her to the car, gleaming dully under the insect encrusted fluorescent lights of the car park. I dug in my pocket for the keys and found them after a few shaky attempts. I opened the door for her to get in. I took a deep breath and got into the driver's seat.

"I need a moment." I saw her worried face and gave her a reassuring smile. "We're going home."

"Okay, Crowley." She sat with her hands in her lap, looking straight ahead.

Heart heavy, I turned the key in the ignition and started the engine. Without a backward glance, I pulled out of the space and onto the dark road. Bronwyn was silent for the entire uneventful trip.

What to tell her? How much to tell her? Had I fallen in love with Bronwyn? Was I able to love Bronwyn? What to do next? The questions consumed me right up until I pulled into my garage. I didn't have answers to any of them.

We got out of the car, and she slipped her fingers into mine as she led me to the house. I had given her a spare set of keys, and she unlocked the door and pushed me through it. She dropped her keys on the marble hall table and took us into the living room. She left me standing there in the deep shadows as she selected my favorite CD. After pushing me into my chair, she sat on my footstool and made sure we were eye to eye.

She took my cold hands into her gentle, warm ones. "Who was she?"

The silence stretched out as memory of my youth, both good and bad, teased me. "Rose Carter McDonald. She was my best friend when I was a child and we became lovers just before and then after this happened to me."

"I thought that might have been your mother or something."

I gave a rueful snort of laugher. If only it were that simple. "No, that most certainly wasn't my mother."

"How often do you go and see her?"

"As often as I can." I was silent for a moment, collecting my thoughts. I was still buffeted by my memories of Rose and made a solid effort to push the yammering voices back so Bronwyn and I could seriously talk. "All the nurses think it's hilarious that she talks to me like I'm her best friend. They don't know that I really am, and I'm the only one she still recognizes. Her family doesn't bother visiting much anymore because she's not at all what she once was. She's pretty much incapable of functioning as they want her to. I take care of her."

I had known her children but had distanced myself from all of them, partially because Rose had wanted me to, partially because I didn't want to attract any of their unwanted attention. We had not gotten on for quite some time, and they had abandoned her a long time ago. I paid all the bills for the home she was in, and they didn't know it. They had all but forgotten about her, content to leave her as a whispered rumor of a crazy, great grandmother. There was no big inheritance for them, and she had lost more than one of her marbles.

"That's horrible." Bronwyn's eyes showed her empathy for my beloved Rose and her disgust at Rose's family.

I squeezed her hands. "Yes, it is. Do you want to know how old she is?"

"Let me guess. About eighty?" Bronwyn sounded distracted.

I gave a small, bitter smile. "No, try ninety-eight years old. She's just a bit older than me."

Bronwyn stared at me, gobsmacked. "Huh?"

"That's right, Bronnie, she's fifteen years older than me. That's what I really look like. That's what you think you're in love with." I drew a deep breath. "As I've been telling you all along, there's a lot you don't know about me. I have been a vampire for more than sixty years. I am now at the time when all my human friends are dying of old age."

Bronwyn said nothing, just stared at me, realization flooding her eyes. "Is that why you took me to meet her?"

"I am a vampire and I will not age," I said. "There are so few things that can kill me—and no, a stake through the heart won't do it—that I'm virtually immortal. I will never change. I do not have a human body, and not breathing is only where the fun begins. Let's just say that I did love you." That was the hardest thing I ever forced from my lips, and it was a struggle to continue. "Let's also say that we became lovers. Do you really want to watch me stay the same while you grow old? Do you really want to see me dying inside every moment knowing that you are but an eye blink in my life? If you really loved me, would you want me to take up the same death watch with you as I'm doing with Rose? Do you want me to show up at your death bed with a new lover?"

She tried to look away, tears beginning, but I cupped her face so she was forced to meet my blazing eyes. "Can't handle it, can you, kid?"

Bronwyn snarled and pushed me savagely back, her hands on my chest. Then she grabbed me by my shirt and pulled me forward so I had to face her furious green eyes. "Then make me one of you!"

With the speed born of fury and my vampire's reflexes, I pinned her against the wall, my white knuckled hand grasping the lapels of her shirt, my body holding her in place. "Have you learnt nothing, mortal? We are unchanging in a changing world. We are emotional creatures. Of necessity we live a solitary life. You know why that is? It's because a relationship between vampires is truly forever, much longer than any mortal marriage. Okay, so you want to be a vampire because you love me. Fine. But what happens in fifty years time when you decide you're sick of me? Everyone you knew and loved will be either dead or dying. You can't form any other relationships with mortals because they are just that—mortals. You've met a bunch of other vampires and after such a long association they make you sick as well. What are you going to do? Make more vampires? I hate to tell you this, but we tend to keep clear of one another because we fight and kill each other. Think human with an endless life span. It's a ruthless and lonely life, Bronwyn Hunter."

She punched me in the ribs, and the fight went out of me and I put her down. What an arsehole I was. I could have been much gentler with her. What made it all so much worse was that I finally admitted to myself that I was falling in love with her, against my better judgment.

She sat against the wall, knees pulled up to her chin, face cradled in her hands. "So that's it—friends or strangers. Fine, I chose strangers. I'll leave you to wallow in your own loneliness after next week. *You* still don't get it do you? Life is a dynamic thing and even though you don't breathe like I do, and your blood is cold, you are *still alive*. The very emotions that make you a vampire also make you a human being. Things *can* and *do* work *if you at least try*." She studied me with cold, angry eyes. "By the way, I don't *think* I love you, I *know* I love you." She waved a hand at me, a curt gesture. "I also know that you love me every bit as much as I love you, you stubborn fuck."

She levered herself to her feet and stalked off, leaving me standing there, all alone, in my living room.

It didn't matter that we felt the same types of emotions. It didn't matter that we were probably quite passionately in love with each other. She couldn't even begin to comprehend the idea of eternity and not dying. I couldn't make her a vampire, because I knew what lay in store for her. Other vampires I had met were quite cavalier about adding numbers to our ranks. I was not one of them. I would not wish it on my worst enemy. That was why I didn't even want to try.

If I allowed myself to love her that way, then I would be opening myself to heartbreak. She would move on from me in perhaps weeks, and I would be left mourning her loss. My life was complicated enough without adding that to it.

I had to hand it to myself, really. It was a wonderful justification. I could sit behind the barriers of age and adult emotion, writing her off as a foolish, young woman. The problem was that it was pure bullshit. Bronwyn's emotions were not so cut-and-dry and I could not really dismiss them out of hand. I was back at square one of confusion.

Okay. So why was she moving out next week and not sooner? Her final exams were done at the end of the week.

Oh. Her formal was next week, and I'd agreed to go to it as her partner. Besides, I was looking after her, and it was up to me to make sure she was okay, right? And her parents certainly weren't going to make an appearance, given that they had severed ties with her, right?

Right.

Bugger.

I didn't really want to go to the thing, but I'd promised her. It had seemed like a good idea at the time.

Despite my rationalizations, and my resolve not to let anything happen between us, my feelings for her were slipping from my grasp to invade my every thought and action. I simply could not get her out of my mind and my heart, no matter how hard I tried. I always listened for her soft footfalls, searched for the gentle smell of her perfume, longed for her light, teasing touch on my cold body.

I was alone for the rest of that night. Bronwyn stayed away from me and was still up when I was forced to go to ground. She unnecessarily locked herself in her bedroom. She needn't have bothered. I needed some time alone to think, partly because of our conversation, and partly because visits to Rose always took me down memory lane and put one of my feet into the land of depression.

That pretty much set the tone for the rest of the week. We didn't talk at all, and we didn't see one another, even canceling our standing

Friday night horror movie date. I did my best to avoid her as each of us was locked in her own private hell of misery. It was a horrible experience, at least for me, because I had gotten used to her presence and I missed her a great deal.

I went out in the evenings, looking for trouble and drinking it all in. I even went looking for Allenby just to beat the shit out of him and his accursed bike. As I did so, I could almost feel her worried green eyes boring into my back, waiting for me to come home, even though she had no idea what I was doing with myself. I could feel her almost sigh with relief when I walked through the front door unscathed. She went out drinking, and I would sit up waiting for her until dawn, wanting her to come home before the sun forced me to ground, but she never did. Every time she did it, I wondered if that evening would be the last evening, but it never was. She contented herself with torturing me, teasing me with her just out of reach presence.

She couldn't leave me any more than I could leave her.

I had time to think. Lots of time. Did not telling someone you loved them mean you loved them any less? What would cause more pain, traveling through immortality aloof and alone, or opening myself up to Bronwyn and having what may be years of fun?

Finally, after one of the longest weeks of my life, the evening of the formal arrived.

Just after sundown, I waited at the bottom of the stairs for her to come down, aware that we were already late. We hadn't been together since that night I'd taken her to the nursing home, and I wondered what we would say to each other.

I hadn't feasted due to our time constraints, as we had to get to the venue before she technically graduated.

I glanced at the grandfather clock. I was glad, for once, for its slow, measured ticking. We really were cutting it quite close.

I heard her footsteps at the top of the stairs and made the fatal mistake of looking up at her. She was dressed in a long, black evening gown, electing to leave her hair down because I think she knew I loved it that way. She wore only the slightest hint of makeup and for that I was grateful. Normally, when she went out, she tended to look a little like a raccoon, and that always annoyed the hell out of me. Why cover such natural, unconscious beauty with war paint?

The whole effect was designed to drive me wild, and it did. I made sure she didn't know how wild. Unfortunately, I think the knowledge that I was a vampire and what it meant for us both overwhelmed the other, simple fact of my existence: I was a grown woman, young in body, and just because I sometimes didn't follow through on my urges didn't mean I didn't have them and didn't want to do something about them. On the other hand, she was probably banking on the fact that I would find her irresistible, simply to wear down my resolve. She sadly underestimated my self control.

"Bronnie, you look stunning." I was quiet and awed and the easy familiarity slipped out past my defenses.

"Thanks, my dear angel. You look pretty hot yourself." She smirked, and her eyes locked onto mine. Although she tried to hide it, she could not quell the spark in her eyes at seeing me, confirming she knew what she was doing to me, and what I was doing to her.

I looked down at my attire and snorted. "Well, at least it doesn't show too much skin."

She laughed and took my arm, and our bodies touched. "I don't think it shows enough," she whispered. "Well, let's make this evening memorable since it's probably going to be our last one."

I struggled to hide the bolt of pain. "Mmmm, but I think yours does." I made my intimate, leisurely study of her beautiful, young body last long enough for her to squirm. I waved a hand. "Okay, fine, let's be on our way. But I have to stop for a quick bite before we get there." I took a step toward the door.

She smiled up at me and pulled me to a halt. She traced my cheekbone with her finger, and my flesh betrayed me as I swallowed. Every nerve ending sprang to attention, and my skin tingled in the wake of her electric touch. "Sure, gorgeous, whatever you say."

I slipped an arm around the small of her back, pulled her in close, and nibbled her ear. I planted a small kiss, an intimate caress, on the soft skin under her jawbone. "I say."

She trembled and wriggled out of my grasp, but not before she sank into me for a second or so. I struggled to hide my triumphant smirk.

It was nice to see a crusty old shit like me still had it in her.

I held out my hand, and she slipped her hand into mine, and our fingers tangled together. I gave her hand a gentle squeeze, and she moved closer to me. I escorted her to the doors, shortening my stride to match hers, and on the way out I scooped up my hat off the hall table with a flourish. She gave a gentle laugh, but didn't comment, and she tried not to look at me.

She linked her arm through mine, and like the perfect companion, I led her out to the car.

I helped her into the sports car, getting a good dose of cleavage in the process. I averted my eyes, not wanting to start down the path of trouble that started there and led to her almost haunted eyes.

I chose a route that took us through the worst part of town so I could find what I was looking for. Bronwyn started when I pulled over next to an inner city park, populated with homeless people and young men wanting to do bad deeds to unsuspecting passers by.

I leapt out of the car and ran noiselessly to a shadowy figure. I crash tackled him almost soundlessly, with something less than my usual finesse. I had to feed quickly and was in no mood to be subtle about it.

"C'mon, Crowley, we don't have all night." Bronwyn leant by the side of the car and tapped her foot impatiently. She glanced at her watch. She was used to me feeding, having had plenty of time to adjust to it when we had gone romping in the city before I had confirmed her suspicion that I was a vampire.

"Okay, okay, I'm here." I emerged from the bushes, giving myself a quick check to make sure I still looked all right.

"You look wonderful as always, sweetie. Now can we go please?"

I had to grin at her. The blood was making me feel light-headed. I have no idea what that young man had taken before I took him, but I could already see this would make for an interesting evening. Well, if worst came to worst I would just go home and sleep it off while Bronwyn went to her after formal party.

"Patience, youngling, we'll get there." I wagged a finger and smiled.

She smirked and gave me a kiss on the end of my nose. "What was in that person's blood? You look very strange."

I shook my head and kissed her back on the nose. "I have no idea. Just pull me out of there if things get well . . . you know . . ."

She giggled. "Okay, I think I can do that. But you better let me drive there."

"Well, you know where the keys are." Lucky for me they were in the ignition and not my pocket.

"Okay, my beloved angel, get in the car." She opened the door for me. Much to my embarrassment, my feet didn't quite understand what I was asking them to do, and I tripped forward and fell into her arms. They tightened around me for a moment, and then she helped me to my feet, grinning evilly the whole time. "Yeah, good on ya, Crowley."

She helped me into the car, and we set off with a great squealing of tires.

CHAPTER EIGHT

"Shit, they're starting to hand out the diplomas." Bronwyn strained her neck to see over the throng of people the snakelike line of young people in the upper gallery. They went up one set of stairs, all along the top and down the other set of stairs. The master of ceremonies had reached the D's and was rapidly heading toward the H's.

Bronwyn grabbed my hand and tugged me toward her schoolmates. We bolted up the wide, carpeted stairs, miraculously missing all the other traffic using them, and then ran along the line looking for her classmates. She garnered a couple of stares, some greetings, and several snarled curses as we brushed against people and the half empty tables on the upper levels.

"Oops, sorry." She gasped and apologized to the kids around us as she found her place in line. I sauntered up behind her and seated myself on the metal railing, arms crossed.

She sidled up to me. "What the hell are you doing?"

I looked down at her, wondering what the fuss was all about. "I'm sitting down. What's the problem?"

"What happens if you fall?"

I shrugged and threw my hands into the air, balance wobbling slightly. "So I fall. So what? I can play dead quite well, so they take me to the morgue. I bust out. Case closed." I smiled, thinking that she was amazingly beautiful when furious with me. Her classmates tried not to stare at me.

"Has it ever occurred to you that I might not want—" She sighed, avoiding my eyes. "That I maybe I couldn't—" She shook her head, threw up her hands, and turned away. "Never mind. You sit there."

I slid off the railing, turned her to face me, standing so close our bodies were almost touching. "Look at me." She refused, studying the buttons and smooth white of my shirt with intense interest. "Look at me." I lifted her chin with my forefinger so I caught her anguished green eyes and held them. "That's better. I'll be fine. I'm a survivor."

Her shadowed, pained green eyes locked onto mine. "It doesn't matter if you're a survivor or not, what matters is whether or not I see you splattered all over the ground. I can tell you right now, that's something I simply can't see." She dropped her eyes and fiddled with my shirt buttons. I was only dimly aware that the kids around us had snuck back an inch or two, sensing that we were having a very private conversation in a very public place.

I lifted her chin and held it as gently as I could so she would have to keep looking at me. "I'm sorry if it upsets you, but you have to realize that I'm impervious to things that would hurt a mortal. There are a lot of things I'm not afraid of anymore, and falling and hurting myself is one of them. On top of that, this will all be a memory to you when you're sitting in your rocking chair next to your old goat of a husband, wishing to God the kid you have dangling on your knee would just burp and be done with it."

She glared and drew in breath to answer. Just as she opened her mouth, a tall, pimply boy with carefully brushed dark hair ran up to us. "Bronwyn. I've been looking all over for you." His anxious puppy dog blue eyes stared soulfully at her. One of the girls close to us gave him a glare that would have turned him to stone if she had been a medusa. I raised an internal set of eyebrows, and then turned my attention back to Bronwyn and the young man.

"Robbie." Bronwyn looked as if she wished she were somewhere else, and both of us let him know by our twin glares that his intrusion was not welcome.

His puppy dog eyes remained unchanged as he put on a half smile to try and attract her. "I just wanted to say you look terrific. Will you dance with me later?" The girl who glared at him now rolled her eyes in disgust.

Bronwyn sighed, clearly struggling to find something nice to say that would get rid of him. "Robbie, we broke up months ago. Get over it. And no, I don't want to dance with you." There was a gleam of triumph in the girl's eyes that went unnoticed by both Bronwyn and Robbie.

"Just once." The pleading in his voice was terrible, and the other kids were giving us more attention than I really wanted. "You don't really mean it's over? Couldn't we just try again?" The other kids were staring at us now, some with sympathy, some with disgust.

She looked as if she was about to give in to him. I felt

an unexpected stab of intense jealousy. For this one, final evening, Bronwyn Hunter was mine, and I was in no mood to share her with anyone.

I leaned around Bronwyn's back and touched her. "Look. I hate to tell you this, but her dance card's full." My voice was gentle but my eyes were not.

Bronwyn turned to me, brushing me with her body, and put a restraining hand on my chest. She turned back to Robbie. "Sorry, Robbie, looks like I'm taken."

Robbie glared at us with hatred in his eyes. "Everything was lies, then, about why you broke up with me. I didn't stress you out, and we weren't too different. You broke up with me so you could go out with her, didn't you? You're one of those, aren't you, and you always were? And you didn't have the guts to tell me the truth, did you?"

Bronwyn said nothing, just held his gaze, expressionless.

Since I'd won this round, I could afford to laugh and did so. Bronwyn had never broken up with him because of us—there was, after all, no "us." He just figured now that he wasn't man enough for her. His ignorance astounded and disgusted me. Now the other kids were gaping at us.

"Kid, just go back to your place in line." We shuffled up one as another person's name was read out.

"Just who the hell do you think you are, pervert?" He stood so he was almost nose to nose with me, glaring at me, shaking a finger in my face.

My temper, already on shaky ground because of my interrupted exchange with Bronwyn, slipped another notch. "Move your finger, son, or I'll bite it off." My voice was silken, and he paled slightly.

"Don't tell me what to do."

I leaned forward, tense, and jumped a little when I felt Bronwyn's soft, hesitant touch.

She looked at me anxiously. "Don't hurt him." In the distance, I was dimly aware that her name had been called. The girl who had been glaring at Robbie nudged Bronwyn and earned her own glare as Bronwyn let her know that the intrusion was not welcome.

I felt a kind of sad surprise at her words, and a sliver of hurt filtered through into my eyes. The boy was a kid. Did my loose morals really look that bad to her? Did she really think I would hurt a poor, defenseless child? "I'll meet you on the other side." I took her arm awkwardly and led her down the stairs as Robbie fumed behind us, the girl grabbing his arm and pulling him in for a few well chosen words. "Don't worry about him, and no I won't hurt him." I smiled as I gave her hand a quick, reassuring squeeze and took off to the other side of the highly polished dance floor.

I watched her confidently walk across the dance floor, her heels clicking on the wood. She shook the Bishop's hand as he gave her the diploma and laughed softly at his undoubtedly sub standard joke. The men standing around him, the school principal and counselor, I guessed, watched her for any signs of disrespect. Bronwyn ignored them, no doubt relieved she could finally do so without fear of reprisal.

She walked back across the slippery floor with ease, shoulders straight and head held high, incredibly beautiful in the artificial light and her sensual evening dress. I felt a shot of possessiveness and a quick sinking feeling that no matter what I did, I probably would not be able to escape the gentle snare of her incredible inner and outer beauty. I knew I was losing the fight with myself, but all I had to do was make it through the night and it would be done. Bronwyn would leave my life, and I could continue on, gasping in shaky relief at the mistake I could have made.

Perfumed adults in lovingly kept and infrequently worn evening wear, clutching a multitude of different alcoholic drinks, milled around me. The servers and some of the girls and boys brushed too close by me, unable to resist the predatory pull I had over them. I willed them to not notice me with anything other than the most cursory of interest, but I was only partially successful. People glanced at me, stroked me, and whispered about me. I did my best to ignore them, focusing solely on my lovely, young charge.

Bronwyn held her diploma in a white knuckled grip. She marched up to me, lips pressed in a straight line. "Outside. Now."

"Who the hell was that girl who kept glaring at Robbie? The one who nudged you in the back?"

Bronwyn stared at me, storm clouds gathering on her brow. "She's been in love with Robbie forever, and now he's a single man she still can't get him to look at her. She hates me. Don't change the subject."

I held out my hands in denial. "I didn't. We don't have a subject yet." People brushed around us, trying not to stare. She glanced around, noticing apparently for the first time the number of eyes on us, slavering for details of our disagreement.

I allowed her to take my hand and tug me outdoors. Out in the smooth blackness of the night, she shoved me back and poked a finger in my chest. "For fuck's sake, what the hell are you playing at? You already told me I'm a free woman. If I want to dance with him and try to resurrect my relationship, you can't stop me."

God that hurt. The fact that it was true made it hurt worse. "Look, he's an idiot. You can do better than that."

"Yes, well, I tried. And that didn't work." She turned away to hide her pain. The tense set of her shoulders said more than anything else ever could. I touched her and watched her melt and turn to me. She was bravely struggling with her tears. A feather light touch to her beautiful green eyes made her smile.

"We have one night. One night." I reached for her, but she was already in my arms, warm body against mine, heart aching in time with mine. I was grateful she couldn't see me. My ability to fight the battle against myself to hold her at arm's length slipped another notch. I closed my eyes, not allowing the outside world to see the love I had for her.

"One night is all I ever asked for. No promises from you—I'm not stupid. I realized that early on." Her forlorn voice was muffled against my chest as she breathed deeply of my nonexistent scent.

We stood for the longest time, holding one another, simply basking in the warmth of our shared existence. I drew in a breath to tell her we had to talk, when the music started. It was the dance of the debutants.

Bronwyn pulled back and stared at me with carefully masked features. I could still see the turmoil inside her and felt my own. It was shredding us. "That's our cue, my beautiful angel."

I smiled ruefully and gestured toward the brightly lit room with all the laughing people. "Lead on, MacDuff."

She slipped her arm through mine, and we went to the dance floor. I made sure the people parted before us. Not that it took much effort. Most people couldn't take their eyes off us—we did make a gorgeous couple. Ebony and ivory, carefully entwined. The fact that we were also both beautiful women certainly didn't hurt.

We took our place, gazes locking as all others around us disappeared. We were more natural a couple than the schoolgirls and schoolboys with their mothers and fathers all around us. We knew each other in a way that none of them ever could.

I led her around the dance floor, and she held me tight. I can say

I enjoyed the dancing experience. Even with the partner changes that had me stuck with a whole load of gangling, uncoordinated school-girls who got even worse when I held them. Through it all, I could not take my eyes off her. Her natural good spirits reasserted themselves, and she whirled in time to the music, laughing with her dance partners. I was amazed at her ability to remain calm and enjoy the evening, even with the uncertainties of her life.

Finally, the music stopped, and she caught my stare. I'm afraid my eyes may have said much more than I wanted them to because when she walked toward me, it was as though the entire world faded away, leaving just the two of us.

Together.

I liked the sound of that more than I cared to admit.

The energy between us crackled as the music started up again, and we began to dance. I held her in my arms and spun her around the room, and we both laughed wildly. She was one of the best sixties dancers I'd ever seen, swimming, snorkeling, and generally wiggling and waving all over the room with gay abandon, causing a lot of the people to laugh, me included. A few people tried to take my partner from me, but I stopped that from happening. She had me transfixed with her wild energy and full acceptance of the demands the music made of us.

Some time later, I led her off the crowded dance floor and past the sparsely populated tables, to the outside of the circular building. She was breathing hard, and I made sure I remembered to do at least that for her. I didn't, after all, want to freak out any of the human folk inside the hall.

In the welcoming darkness, I led her to a dark corner and took her into my arms. I had loosened my tie and undone the top two buttons on my shirt and she stared at my snowy skin, hesitantly drew her finger down the parts she could see, to the start of my cleavage. I willed myself to remain still under her gentle touch as I watched her, unable to tear my eyes away.

"You haven't even worked up a sweat." She felt the tip of her finger with her thumb and then made the fatal mistake of looking into my eyes.

I knew there was raw desire blazing in them, and I couldn't hide it. "It's something you don't want to see. I'm dead, after all."

She smiled ruefully and put her palm on the side of my face. "No.

You're alive." She stared at me intently. "One night." Her voice was a whisper.

My arms betrayed me as they tightened around her body, pulling her ever closer, head bowing almost against my will as I kissed her, long and deep.

I think it was shock that caused her hesitation in responding to my touch. When she did, it drove me wild, and I ran my hands over the bare skin of her back. She moaned softly as her hands reached up to tangle in my hair.

She was breathing hard, her face flushed, when we broke for air. I gazed at her, love shining bright in my eyes. "I really want to get out of here."

"We never even found our table," Bronwyn said.

"So? Do you really think either one of us truly gives a rat's arse about trying to be nice to human adults?" I laughed. "Let's go."

Her whisper was so soft I almost missed it in the noise coming from the inside of the building. "I love you, Crowley."

I tightened my arms around her. I kissed her hair and sighed, loving the clean scent, the slim body, the warmth and fire of her. "You ready?"

She kissed the exposed skin of my chest, tasting it, and nodded.

"Okay then, let's go." I pulled her in close and led her along the cobblestone path that encircled the building, dodging couples having some private time outside of the throng inside. The groups of adults also standing around tried not to notice them or us as we made our way toward the parking lot. We had parked all the way at the back because we were so late, and Bronwyn hung onto my arm as I led her between tightly packed cars to my sports car. As I unlocked the door she gazed at me, eyes unfocused. She pulled my head down for another hungry kiss, and I took advantage of the proximity to run my hands along her back, down to her hips. It was not enough for her, and she groaned as she got into the car.

"Take us home."

I nodded, jogged around to my side, and slipped behind the wheel. The ride home was pure torture. She could not keep her eyes or hands off me, and I did my best to reciprocate. Unlike my usual precautionary custom, I chose the most direct route back to our home. I couldn't stand to have her so close to my fingertips and not able to touch her. I'm sure we put on quite a respectable, immoral show for our fellow motorists, but I was beyond caring. All I cared about was Bronwyn and tasting more of her beautiful kisses in private.

An eternity later we finally pulled into our street. I shrieked into the driveway, the car scarcely under my control. I only just waited for the gates to open before I put us back in motion and took us into the darkened garage with smooth precision. We got out, and she was in my arms before I had a chance to blink. I smiled when she kissed me, and fell back against the car as her starving hands roamed my cool body.

"Slow . . . easy . . ." I stilled her hands and scooped her up into my arms before claiming her lips in another deep kiss. Her response left me struggling to co-ordinate myself properly. I carried her up the dark front path to the unlit front door. I took us through the unlit dining room into the kitchen, then downstairs to my basement hideaway. I did not bother to lock the door behind us. The idea was pointless, now that she knew I was a vampire and needed the darkness. I carried her down the rickety steps toward my room, and she closed her eyes, stroking my cheek, trusting me to keep us safe.

When we got to my room, I put her back on her feet, in front of my neatly made bed, and pulled away from her, but kept a gentle hold of her hands. "Are you really, really sure about this?" I certainly wasn't sure about it, but I could not stop myself.

She smiled, eyes radiating passion and uncontrollable longing that mirrored my own. She slowly and deliberately pulled my jacket and pants off. I reciprocated by removing the annoying dress that hid her from my view. She moved her hands up my body, under my shirt, to cup my breasts.

Sighing, she undid the last buttons of my shirt and gazed at what had been teasing her so mercilessly. "My God, you're so beautiful. So beautiful."

My skin had always been pale, despite my jet-black hair, and death had given it an almost eerie, snowy shade. I had taken care of myself in life, and all the muscle I'd built up over the years stood out in gentle relief beneath my smooth woman's skin. The dark hair, full breasts, and sculpted, classic features were courtesy of my long dead mother's genes, and I thanked them nightly for making it so easy to find prey. My blue eyes that had once been bright, now burned flame blue, and snow-white teeth were gifts of my father.

"So are you," I breathed.

I looked at Bronwyn's mortal, living perfection. Although I had never admitted it to myself, the creamy skin, green eyes, shining blonde hair, gentle swell of her breasts and pervasive femininity had always driven me wild. Sometimes I'd wanted more, but swiftly denied and stifled those impulses.

She moved to me, and I felt her lips on my nipple. With a soft sigh I gently pulled up her head, cupped her face, and claimed her beautiful lips once more. "Oh no, young one, me first."

I pushed her into the bed and worked my way down her body, nibbling and kissing every inch of exposed skin I could find. I paused with a grin to tease her womanhood with a feather-light kiss, while she moaned and begged me to end the torture.

I used every tool in my arsenal to tease her: skin, lips, teeth, tongue, hands, body. I had her every way I could dream up. She rode me savagely, and I tasted long and deep of her as she called my name into the benevolent night; she begged, demanded, and forced her releases from me. As we lay tangled together, temporarily sated, she uttered gentle admissions of love.

We lay in the bed, and I idly ran my fingers through her pubic hair, teasing her as she stiffened with the aftershocks of her most recent orgasm.

Breathing heavily, she nibbled my lips, tasting herself on me. "Why? Why now?"

I smiled, the anguish in my eyes causing her to pull back slightly. "I can't help myself. I'm tired of fighting."

She sighed. "You were right. I don't want to be a vampire."

I could not stop the single sticky tear that trickled down my face. "An eye blink."

She brushed my tear away with gentle fingers. "We have to work this out. You know perfectly well that if we split up, neither one of us will be able to live with it. Besides, who's to say you're not going to get sick of me in a couple of years?"

I hadn't thought about that. The problem was, what I felt for her was different from what I'd ever felt for anyone else. I wouldn't get sick of her in a couple of years, just like she wouldn't get sick of me. Somehow this was much deeper than any school girl crush or vampire's flight of fancy. "I'm making you the same promise I should have made to another—as long as you live, Bronnie. As long as you live."

For the first time I was completely honest with her, and those simple words promised so much more than I had done for Rose. I had always been passionately in love with Rose, but the era we had come from was so different to the way things were now. We could not acknowledge the love that we had guilt free, so we had not been able to explore it fully. I had remained for decades on the fringes of Rose's life, ready to step in and take care of her when she had gotten old. It had not been something we had planned; it had been something I had fallen into.

It had been a horrible shock to see her hair turn gray, then white, and the gradual slide of her youth into harsh age. The last time I had seen her moving around on her own, I had known that if I had had any kind of respect for her I would have ended it, but it was the same respect that stopped me from doing it. She knew I was a vampire, but did not want to sample any of the gifts I could offer her. In her eyes I went against the natural order of things, pure and simple.

Bronwyn was a totally different creature. She was from a more open age, and her reasoning for wanting what she wanted was different. Yet I knew she too was going to get old and die, and that thought brought such pain my mind shut down from the prospect of it.

With tears in her eyes, she cupped my face with a hand. "Ask me about immortality in a few more years. I can't bear to be without you. I love you."

Could I adjust to the time I was in? Could I do this, guilt free? What good were the lies I told her and myself about my lack of feelings for her? What did they accomplish, other than misery and pain? I closed my eyes and leant into her touch. When I peeked at her, she was watching me with a tender and gentle expression. I smiled and met her eyes. "I love you too, Bronwyn Hunter."

The pure joy in her eyes was incredible, and she rolled over to kiss me—not designed to ignite, but to share love. When she pulled back, the grin became feral. "Now it's my turn."

I felt a stab of pain and couldn't hide the sorrow in my eyes. "Not breathing is just where the fun of being a vampire begins."

Her eyes widened. "You mean you can't—"

I shook my head and smiled ruefully. "No, I can't."

"Are you sure?"

I raised an eyebrow. "Oh, you're most welcome to try." I gestured elegantly and lay back with my fingers entwined on my stomach, teasing grin on my lips.

She kissed her way down my body and pulled my nipples into her mouth causing me to arch my back, tangle my fingers in her blonde hair and sigh at the almost forgotten sensation. She continued down my body with slow deliberation and then stopped.

She gazed up at me. "You're not—"

I shook my head with a rueful grin. "No, I'm not. I can't do it anymore." This one thing had eventually destroyed my relationship with Rose.

"The problem is, I still want to taste you." The feral grin was back as she made good on her words.

I laughed and growled as she suddenly found herself flat on her back, my face a bare inch above hers. "You mean like this?"

I tasted her thoroughly, and as she came she cried out and collapsed back onto the sheets, heart hammering. I lay next to her, cupping a breast and idly playing with a pink nipple, head resting on my free hand.

"This is why this is so much worse for me. It's all about emotion since sex doesn't really enter into the equation anymore." Vampire relationships were founded on emotion, and I personally thought it was the one reason we fought so much. We had nothing, really, on a physical plane that separated us, or allowed us to come closer together.

She gently chided me. "Hello, Crowley? Hello? It works the same for me. I'm so desperately in love with you that it almost scares me. You were always my knight in shining armor, and I guess in some ways you still are, but I know what you're really like now. You like teasing people with that beautiful body of yours. How do I know you're not going to do that to anyone else?"

I was stung. "Hey, I'm a vampire. It goes with the territory. But I'm not that shallow and I'm also not that easy to get rid of. What about you? You've taken every opportunity you can to go into the city for a quick tumble with strangers. How do I know you're not going to do that anymore? I hate to tell you this, but I'm the jealous type and I won't take kindly to sharing you."

She glared at me. "God, you're such an idiot. The reason I took off from my parents' place so much was because I was looking for you. When I finally found you, I thought you didn't want me, so I tried to get on with the rest of my life. I tried to make you jealous, but it didn't work." Her voice thickened as her eyes filled with tears. "It didn't work."

I pulled her close, and she fought me. I kissed her hair as her struggles ceased. "Yes, I'm a complete idiot, but no, I'm not stupid or blind. I hate to tell you this, but it did work. It used to drive me nuts but I would never admit it." I pulled her face up so she was forced to meet my eyes. "You own me body and nonexistent soul. I'm not going anywhere. And I think we've just proven I'm not expecting you to be a nun—just don't do it with anyone else apart from me."

Despite herself, she grinned. "Idiot. As if I would want to."

She kissed me until her breathing went ragged.

We lay back in my bed, and my body began to feel it was almost dawn. "Bronnie, it's almost dawn. I'm going to sleep."

"I want to see you sleep."

Sleeping was the one thing I'd never shared with anyone, not even Rose. Humans that knew of my nature only had an intellectual grasp of the difference between life and death. Sleep changed most people who saw it. If Bronwyn loved me as much as I loved her, that it was no crush, then she had to witness this facet of me.

I winced and sighed. "Please remember I'm really and truly dead. You don't want to see this, believe me. Above all, don't freak out on me."

She cupped my face in her hands and kissed me. "Oh ye of little faith. Actually, lover, I do want to see this. Trust me. I want to know you. *All* of you."

I cursed under my breath as sleep took hold of me. My last thoughts were sorrowful. I really didn't think she could handle this. I only hoped I didn't accidentally kill her while I slept. If she did anything that my sleeping form interpreted as harmful to me, she would suffer the consequences. I would literally pick up the pieces. My last thought before I sank into oblivion was that it really didn't matter, and that I couldn't stop her. It was done.

CHAPTER NINE

The surface I was lying on moved gently up and down, and I wondered for a second what the hell was going on.

I had a splitting headache for starters. What the hell did that dratted boy have in his blood when I'd taken him last night? I vowed never to take an unaccompanied youngster squatting in an inner city park again. They were more trouble than they were worth.

That thought led on to memories of the formal, and what had happened afterwards.

Then it hit me.

I was in bed and I'd slept with Bronwyn.

Ouch.

Would she still want to have anything to do with me after the day's sleep? When I slept I knew I looked more than a little like a corpse. The more dangerous side of the coin was that I had on occasion woken up with a dead human lying close by my sleeping form, and in this case I was damn lucky the same fate had not befallen Bronwyn.

Bronwyn. What she had done was so dangerous I couldn't do much but wince at the sheer foolhardiness of it.

The arms that had been encircling my body tightened, and there was the soft sensation of skin on skin as she moved around to kiss the top of my head. "Evening, beloved angel."

I couldn't help myself; I smiled, partly from relief, partly from soft wonder that she still wanted to be with me at all. "Evening, Bronnie." We shifted around so she could settle comfortably in my arms, head on my chest. "I'm sorry. I never really wanted you to see that."

She looked up at me, mostly with affection, with a dose of amusement thrown in for good measure. "It's okay. I do really want to know all there is to know about you, the good, the bad and the just plain weird. The first night after you took me in I had plenty of time to notice you weren't breathing. You look like a statue more than anything else."

"Well, thank God for that. It's sorta nice to know nothing hangs out or looks gross while my eyes are closed." I was teasing her, and she tried to tickle me in retaliation, but I didn't respond.

"Not ticklish, huh? Is that another side effect?"

"Nope. Was never ticklish while I was alive either."

She laughed and punched me in the chest, and I mock groaned and tickled her. After a brief tumbling of limbs, I allowed her to straddle my hips, my hands teasing her sensitive nipples. I felt the moisture gathering between her thighs, and I chuckled. "My insatiable mortal." My frustrating lust and primal urge for blood battled in my blood stream. On the other hand, Bronwyn was clearly enjoying herself too much to be interrupted. Before long, she was calling my name at the height of her passion, clutching me with a strength that surprised both of us.

We lay tangled together afterwards, and my stomach made itself known.

Bronwyn stared at my disobedient midsection. "Hey." She slapped my stomach, and I laughed. "Knock it off. That's no way to conduct a warm afterglow."

I pinned her to the bed. "Uh, sorry." I gave a sheepish grin. "Perhaps not the best manners, but when it wants blood it wants blood. I have to go and feed." I tried not to notice the pulsing arteries in her neck. They were always something I registered, but the urge to explore became much more difficult when I was hungry for blood.

I didn't need to tell her what could happen if she tried to keep me there, so she sighed. "Okay, fine, let's go out for a bite. I'm hungry myself." She was hungry all right, but by the look in her eyes it was not for food.

I couldn't help myself; I kissed her again. "Don't worry, this won't take long and then you can do what you like with me."

She laughed, holding me tight. "Is that a promise?"

"Oh yeah, that's a promise."

෨

Bronwyn's arms tightened around me as we rode through the inner city streets of Newtown. There was a pub on almost every street corner, and I scanned the small clusters of people walking up and down the main road.

I saw a single, staggering young man break off to the left toward a dimly lit side street. Bronwyn's weight shifted as she leaned forward.

"Hey!" she said. "You see something?"

I nodded and glanced back at her, my stomach growling. "Yes. I'll be back in a sec."

"If it's a woman I'm going to have to put a stake through your heart, you know that, right?"

I laughed as I pushed down the kickstand. "I won't be more than five minutes. Try to stay out of trouble, will you?"

She gave me a light slap and mock growled as I took off running behind the young man. I stopped and scanned the street for him, and saw him staggering drunkenly up the road.

I feasted without my usual finesse, and barely remembered to dribble my blood over the fang marks in his neck. I left him lying in someone's hedge and turned around. Bronwyn was leaning against the bike, and three young, male predators were standing before her.

Her body language was tense.

I jogged back up the street and stood behind them. Bronwyn saw me, and her shoulders sagged in relief.

"Can I help you with something?" I asked them politely.

The tallest of them, a good inch or two shorter than me, turned around and eyed me appreciatively from top to bottom. He was stylishly dressed in designer ripped jeans, and had two days of stubble on his handsome face.

"I don't know, love," he said, taking a step closer to me as the second young man who'd been trying to interest Bronwyn took a step closer to her. "You interested in going into the pub for a couple of drinks?"

The second young man put his hand high on Bronwyn's thigh, and my temper snapped. I took a step toward the Ken doll. "No, I'm not, and neither is she. Hands off."

Ken Doll's face turned into Darth Vader's. "No need to be like that, love. I was just asking you for a friendly drink."

"I said, hands off."

"Playing hard to get?"

I pulled myself up to my full height and glared at him. "No, I'm not playing at all. Go away and leave us both alone." I growled, low and deep in my throat, and even Bronwyn looked as though she wanted to take a step back.

Ken Doll looked up into my eyes, his own dark and angry. We exchanged glares for a moment, and he walked away.

"Fucking bitch." His soft voice came back to me as they retreated into the pub.

Bronwyn sank into my arms, sighing. "Thanks, angel. I love you."

I tightened my arms around her and breathed in the gentle scent of her clean hair. "You're welcome. I love you too."

She pulled back and smiled. "Okay, what do you want to do now?"

An idea came to me, and I grinned. "When was the last time you went to the zoo?"

"I haven't been since I was a kid."

"You want to go now?"

She giggled. "Sure. With you around I'm sure it's going to be a unique experience."

I joined in her laughter. "I hope you meant that in a good way."

A minute later, we were on the bike again. As I pulled into the traffic, I saw Ken Doll come out of the pub, his cold eyes boring holes into us.

I took us to the zoo, and we parked in the darkness of a narrow side street, close to one of the walls. It was simple for me to scale the wall and take her with me, clinging to my back with her arms around my neck, although it did garner me a peculiar stare. After I had told her of my true nature, I behaved a little less like a normal human and more like a normal blood sucker, but only in small doses. She needed time to adjust to each new thing about me.

We wandered through the enclosures, my unnatural presence upsetting some of the animals. It drew the attention of the security guards, whom I found to be a bit of a hindrance, but easy to avoid. They had to rely on their flashlights to see the path in front of them; I did not. Each time they investigated a noise, I made sure that we hid not more than two feet from where they were. After a while, avoiding the guards became irritating, so I finally stole a kiss from Bronwyn while we perched on the edge of the wolf enclosure. We struggled not to giggle as we watched the security guards tramping clumsily before us, looking for signs of things that should not be there. I closed my eyes and gave a quick nod to the wolves, and they obeyed my request to begin an eerie howling. The guards rushed to bright lights and warm, enclosed spaces. I thanked the wolves as courteously as I could, and they accepted this, wishing us well with baleful, yellow stares and lupine bows.

Bronwyn stared at me, taken aback, and I shrugged. What was I supposed to say? So I could talk to wolves, who knew? They were interesting creatures. Some were nice and some weren't, but wasn't that true of every other living creature on the planet?

I took her to the lion enclosure. The big cats stared at us with baleful, untamed eyes.

I picked the largest one because we knew each other well. Calm and unafraid, I met his malevolent, yellow stare.

"Watch this." I ran up to the top of the enclosure, Bronwyn's hiss of surprise following me. I strolled along the narrow edge, arms outstretched so Bronwyn could see where I was going.

"Christ!" Bronwyn said. "Come back! You're gonna bring down every security guard on us."

I grinned. "No I won't. The only thing I'm sorry for is that the glass is too thick for you to hear my little kitties purring. They sound like they have holes in their mufflers."

"What? Purring?" she said. "You're not going in there."

I looked down into the darkness. It was easily a drop of about fifteen feet.

Child's play.

I jumped down, landed lightly, and bent my knees to cushion the blow. I gazed out at my round-eyed lover and smiled at her alarmed, hissing intake of breath. I stood still, allowing the cats to become used to me, to approach me, and to decide whether I was predator or prey.

While they were like oversized housecats and sort of cute, they certainly smelt quite bad. God, hadn't their keepers ever heard of a bath? Weren't lions supposed to like water?

Finally I saw the one I played with the most. "Come here."

He was half-grown, with a scruffy, coarse ruff and an unusually active, playful disposition. Well, as much as could be had for an animal that spent more than half its life asleep.

The look on his face was rather funny. *Oh fuck, not* you *again.* I hid my smile and met him eye to eye. It was an action that cats normally hated, but this young male seemed to enjoy the challenge.

With his most regal air, he sighed, dipped his head, and came up to me for a scratch behind the ears, just like a nice little kitty. I could never understand why they did this for me, since it was so out of keeping with the normal behavior of wild animals. I could think of two possible reasons, either of which could be wrong. First, they were not truly wild animals because they had been born in captivity. Second, I honestly don't think they knew what to make of me. I didn't have the scent of prey the way humans had, but I didn't smell like an inanimate object, either. I think in the end they finally decided I was a nice, mobile scratching pole for them to use.

His fur was warm, the texture amazingly beautiful to my cold fingers.

"Nice to see you again, old friend." He closed his eyes and sighed, leaning into my touch.

I looked up at Bronwyn. She was staring at me, transfixed, a healthy dose of fear and wonder on her face. She was pale, and every time one of the cats moved, she jumped.

"Crowley! Can you hear me? Be careful!"

"I'm fine. They won't hurt me." I smiled at her, while the cat gave me a bit of chest to tickle.

"How do you know?"

"They already tried it once or twice. Didn't work so I reckon they've given up." I grinned, ruffling his thick hair. He purred, enjoying the attention.

Bronwyn rolled her eyes. "Please? Please? I only just found you."

I grinned. "Okay, okay, I'm outta here."

It took me less than two minutes to climb up the side of the enclosure and dash down to be by her side. She smiled and then poked me in the chest with an unforgiving forefinger.

"Don't. Ever. Do. That. Again. You scared the fuck out of me." Each word was punctuated with a stab. "I thought they were going to rip you to shreds. Ah, ah, before you say anything—" she held up her hand "—I know, I know you'll be fine. But what about me? What makes you think I want to see you ripped to pieces?"

I gave her a sheepish grin, captured her exasperated gaze, and kissed her on her soft lips. She responded after a moment, and my knees felt a trifle weak. "I'm sorry, it's just that I haven't had to worry about much for so long that I forget what I'm doing is just plain weird or dangerous at times."

"I love you and I think you know what I'm gonna say next, don't you?" She kept her arms around my waist and looked into my eyes. The vestiges of fear lurked in her steady, gentle regard.

"I'm an idiot?"

Her soft laughter matched mine. "Yes, beloved, you're an idiot."

I kissed her soundly, and she stared intently at me, pupils heavily dilated. I took her hand and tugged her along before her scrambled senses had time to react. "Let's go. Want an ice cream?"

She knew I couldn't have any, but could not resist indulging. Her one great weakness was for ice cream. Almost any flavor would do, but she had a special passion for cookies and cream. I bargained with ice cream any time I wanted her to do something.

She sighed into my neck when I scooped her up into my arms so we could run faster.

ഔ

We sat by the old fountain in Kings Cross, bodies touching, Bronwyn delicately licking her ice cream. It was a few hours from dawn, and mortals, more and more inebriated, staggered past us, steadfastly ignoring us. I did not want to attract any more attention than I needed to, so I silently told them all to leave us alone. For once, my magic worked as it should, mainly because most of them were more concerned with either getting home to sleep it off or finding some quiet corner to be sick in.

I don't know why we kept ending up in Kings Cross; more than likely it was my stomach dictating my actions though it wasn't giving me any trouble now. The other reason was that I loved its anonymity, warring with the small town feel it had about it. It had been renovated to look like a tourist area rather than a red light district, but the veneer of cleanliness could not hide its true nature. Overall, it was a bit like a brothel or an opium den disguised as the play area at a children's restaurant.

I could smell the decadent night air, but something on it spoke to me of oddity, of things just out of my reach. I felt something that was almost an interruption to the flow of life around my supernatural senses. I cast my sharp gaze around the park to see what was causing it.

"I'm not here to fight you, Crowley." The voice was soft, well below the hearing of the mortals around me. I could not tell what gender it was, and that was a warning in and of itself. Brownyn sensed the change in me and glanced at me in concern, ice cream almost forgotten, when she saw me straighten.

"Where are you?" I matched its low tone perfectly. Bronwyn gave me an odd look when she saw my lips move but no sound emerge.

"It doesn't matter. They are watching you."

"Tell them to fuck off and mind their own bloody business."

The last words were spoken to the empty, still night air. The speaker was gone. I was uncomfortable and defensive. Not seeing the owner of a voice coming or going rarely happened to me. I had a greater ability than normal to tune into my surroundings, direct my prey, and keep track of the species near to me, and it only failed me in times of extreme danger or when the perpetrator was extremely stealthy.

I stood up and scanned the crowd, trying to pinpoint the source of the message, but it was too late. Humans bustled all around us, and there were no flashes of white skin that signaled the presence of another vampire. The speaker was truly gone, whoever he or she may have been. I toyed with the idea of it being Allenby, but I had not seen him for quite a while. Maybe he had moved on to other pastures. His eye color told me that he was not confined to the city.

Bronwyn got up and forced me to look at her, ice cream abandoned. "What is it?"

I smiled down at her, hiding my trepidation. "Nothing. C'mon let's get out of here." Although the sinking feeling coursing through me soured my night, I kept it well hidden from this defenseless girl. She didn't need to know what had happened, or what the warning had meant. I would keep her safe from harm to the best of my abilities, without alarming her. "I want you in a much more private place."

Her gentle eyes swept through me, and the outside world ceased to exist as I got lost in her quiet, affectionate regard.

I had really fallen very, very hard for this young mortal.

We went home and spent what was left to us of the night tangled together in passion.

The next evening when I woke up, I was snuggled in Bronwyn's arms. She cupped my breasts as I stretched, and I stole a quick kiss from her.

"Evening, Bronnie."

"Beloved angel." Her arms tightened around me as my stomach grumbled. "I suppose you're going to have to go out for a bite to eat?"

"Well, I don't exactly have humans stored in my refrigerator, so yes, I'm going to have to duck out for a quick bite."

"I'd be okay with you storing them in the fridge."

"Good."

"Just not under the bed."

"There's no need to worry about that. They just won't fit."

She laughed, and I soon joined in.

"I love that you've loosened up so much, beloved angel," she said. "I'm going to miss you."

I sat up and stared at her. "You're going to miss me? Where on earth are you going?"

She stroked my face. "Relax. I'm not really going anywhere. Just for a week. It's a week in Queensland. You know, after school finishes." She smiled. "We arranged it about ten months ago. I'm sorry I can't bring you with me."

"Oh," I said. "When are you out of here?"

"I'm leaving on Sunday night," she said, blushing. "I don't suppose you'd take me to the airport?"

"I can do that," I said. "I'm going to miss you."

My stomach grumbled.

She grinned. "I recognize the signs. Why don't we go into the city? It's been a while since I saw Kings Cross."

"You saw Kings Cross last night," I said, slipping out of bed and heading toward the shower. Bronwyn came with me, and it took us quite some time to get moving.

☙

An hour and a half later I emerged from the thick bushes in a back street of Kings Cross. Bronwyn waited for me, but was looking around anxiously at the shadowed figures that haunted the same place we did.

"Relax, my young mortal," I said. "You have nothing to worry about while I'm here."

She took my arm and hugged me. "Are you sure about that?"

I pulled her to a halt and gazed into her eyes. "I'm extremely hardy, and I'm also strong and fast. You have nothing to fear."

She gazed at me, eyes flickering, and I sighed.

"Look." I extended a wrist so she could see the unblemished, white skin, and then gently nicked it with a fang. Blood poured from the wound as I held it out to her.

She gasped and then quieted as the skin closed, and the blood flow ceased in seconds.

"See?" I said. "It takes a lot to damage me. I'll heal before anyone has the chance."

"Wow," she said, finally finding her voice. She studied my face with disquiet eyes. "You look like a normal woman, and I know intellectually that you aren't one . . . and then . . . this . . . wow . . ."

"Does it frighten you?"

"I don't know," she said. "I think I finally know that I'm safe around you, but some of this stuff is very hard to take in stride."

I smiled. "I know. But believe me when I tell you I love you and I would *never* intentionally hurt you. You really *are* safe around me."

"Okay," she said. She took my hand and pulled me forward. "I think I just need a little time."

"I have nothing but time," I said with the ghost of a grin.

"Why so sad, angel?" she asked, pulling me to a halt. She stroked my cheek.

I gazed at her beautiful face, a frozen moment in time. "Nothing. I'm fine. I love you."

She gave me a sad smile. "I love you too and I don't think you're ever going to know how much."

I held her so our entire bodies touched. "I think I do."

She pulled away from me, and we walked again. I cleared my throat. "So, my beloved mortal, where are we going?"

"I want to go to the Test Tube Factory," she said with an evil grin.

"Don't you like any other watering holes in this place?"

"They play pretty good music."

"That waitress we keep getting just drives you insane, doesn't she?"

"Not anymore. Now I know there's no way in hell that you would ever have slept with her, I'm good." Bronwyn glanced at me and braced herself. "What did you do to her? And that girl I saw you with the first time—what was that about?"

"The waitress . . . don't worry about her. I didn't touch her with anything other than my teeth." I sighed. "The girl, Bronnie, she was sick. Very sick. She didn't have much time left, and I gave her what she wanted."

Bronwyn flinched. "What was wrong with her?"

"She had cancer."

Bronwyn grimaced. "Beloved angel. I'm sorry for ever doubting you."

I shook my head. "It's okay. How were you to know?"

We arrived at the Test Tube Factory. There weren't many people around, so we got in quickly and sat at our table. Bronwyn and I exchanged a glance at the waitress who came to our table. Our normal waitress was nowhere to be seen.

This waitress was as beautiful as the last one, and as full breasted, if not a little more so. She bent over, almost spilling out of her dress. Bronwyn and I exchanged a glance and sighed.

ଛ

For the next two nights, until Bronwyn was to leave on her vacation, we settled into an easy rhythm. I got up in the evening and went out to feed, and when I came back, we either went out for a ride on the bike, or I took her to bed and loved her for all I was worth. She slept with me during the day and we stayed together all night.

On the third night, I took her to the airport. The trip was silent for the most part. Bronwyn sat in the passenger seat, nibbling her lip.

"Hey, lover, why are you nibbling?" I asked, glancing at her.

"I'm going to miss you. Isn't that obvious?"

"And I'm going to miss you, and I sincerely hope you go nuts and enjoy yourself."

"I'll enjoy myself, I know that, but I just worry about you, that's all."

I raised an eyebrow. "Why on earth are you worried about me? I'll be here when you get back, and you're only gone for a week."

"I just don't want you to be sad, that's all."

"I won't be. You're always with me, beloved mortal, even when you're not standing beside me."

She squeezed my thigh and smiled.

We drove along in silence for a few moments. As we got closer to the airport, she shifted in her seat.

"What gives, my beloved mortal?" I asked.

"I don't want you to wait with me. Can you drop me off?"

"I don't mind dropping you off, but why don't you want me to wait with you?"

"This is already hard enough. I hate goodbyes."

I nodded. "So do I."

We pulled up at the departure drop off. It was busy; the cars were parked two deep but by some miracle I got a spot at the back against the curb.

We got out, and I opened the boot and pulled out her luggage one handed. She fidgeted as she waited for me.

She lunged into my arms and squeezed me for all she was worth. I gazed down at her, and she kissed me, tasting me, running her hands over my back. When we broke, she was gasping for air, and I was silent, staring at her with wide eyes.

"Oh, God, I'm going to miss you so much," she said.

"Easy, lover," I whispered, pulling her in close again. "What time does your flight get in? Do you want me to pick you up?"

I felt her nod.

"You can always call me, you know," I said.

"You have a phone?" she asked, shocked.

I burst out laughing. "Yes, I have a phone. Do you want the number? And don't forget I won't be answering it except after dark."

She dug in her pockets for paper and pen, but I was already reaching into my car and pulling out paper and pen from my cluttered center console.

I wrote quickly and neatly, and handed her the paper. She studied it with wide eyes.

"I had no idea you had a phone," she said.

"I think I must have gotten it specifically for you."

"Did you?" she asked, wide-eyed.

I laughed. "No, sorry, love. I didn't get it for you. I got it so I could keep tabs on Rose."

"Ah," she said.

Two girls burst out of the glass doors and ran toward us.

"Bronnie!" The dark-haired taller of the two was waving at us. They skidded to a halt when they saw me.

"I'd better go." Bronwyn sighed.

"Take care of yourself," I said, giving her a gentle hug.

"I will, and I'll call you as often as I can," she said, kissing me gently.

She grabbed her luggage and walked toward her whispering friends. They stared at me, but I did not acknowledge them. I got into my car and maneuvered out into the traffic, headed for the city and Kings Cross.

I was hungry, restless, and already missed my beloved mortal.

Twenty minutes later I was sitting by the old fountain in Kings Cross. I ignored the teeming mass of humanity all around me. I remembered the message I had gotten and wanted to see if there really were any vampires watching over me.

I closed my eyes and extended my senses. Most of what I felt was raw emotion, but it was too hard for me to discern individual thoughts. The general gist of it was a desire for drink and sex, which did not surprise me.

I could not feel any other vampires, and was surprised Allenby was not there.

Finally, with disquiet in my heart, I got up off the old bench, neatly side-stepped an unconscious drunk, and headed back to my car. I wanted to go home and watch old horror movies, and try to forget how much I wanted Bronwyn by my side.

When I got home, the message light on my answering machine was blinking. I gave it a brief smile and hit the replay button.

It was Bronwyn. "Hey, lover, you really do have an answering machine, and you recorded a message and everything. I'm proud of you." There was a slight rustling sound and indistinct voices. "I just wanted to let you know that I arrived safely and that I love you. I'll give you a call the night after tomorrow. Bye."

I hit the stop button. I didn't want to erase the message.

I went to my basement and lay back on the suddenly too large bed with a sigh. I picked up the remote, flicked on the television, and channel surfed until dawn when sleep overtook me.

80

The next night I left the house with the rosy glow of dusk still in the sky.

I wanted to go into the city to feed. I was feeling restless and toyed with the idea of visiting my old friends the lions in the zoo.

I took my bike into the city and purposely parked in the Harley riders spots on Darlinghurst Road. I walked the streets, looking for my next victim.

I saw a woman in her thirties leaving a bar. She was well-dressed but rumpled and drunk. She had a hint of cruelty about her eyes and mouth, and clothing that spoke of expensive taste and money.

I wanted her badly.

I trailed her down the back streets of Kings Cross as she weaved toward her car. After five minutes of searching, she staggered up to an old Holden, fumbling in her purse for the keys. Finally she found them, and after the second attempt to get the key into the driver's side lock, I was by her side with my hand on hers, steadying it.

She screwed up her face and stared at me, trying desperately to focus her eyes. "Thanks," she said, as though nothing were wrong with a perfect stranger standing so close to her that they almost touched.

"You're welcome," I whispered. "Do you want me to take you home?"

She frowned. "I'm not that way, muff muncher."

I smiled. "I am."

Before she had any idea of what was happening to her, I had her in a strong embrace, and my drooling fangs were headed toward her hot and throbbing neck.

She screamed as my teeth broke her skin, but it died as I pulled the precious blood from her body.

I caught her as she collapsed, near death. I did my usual trick of covering the fang marks, and carefully put her in the car, tossed the keys onto the seat beside her, and locked the door.

I straightened, and was grabbed from behind around the chest, my arms pinned to my sides. I tried to break the grip, but to my dismay I couldn't.

"Hello, you fucking bitch," Allenby said in my ear. He kissed the lobe.

I snarled and pulled forward, hoping shock would loosen his grasp. There was a solid clunk as the side of the car buckled from the force of my lunge. Allenby squeezed me, trying to break my arms.

I levered myself up so my feet were resting on the battered door of the car and pushed back with all my might. Allenby fell backward onto the deserted road, with me on top of him.

His grip loosened, and I leaped off him and twisted so we faced one another. He climbed halfway to his feet. I growled and took him with a flying tackle so his head cracked against the dirty asphalt of the road. I sat on him and held his shoulders down with my knees as I pummeled him with my fists.

I felt the satisfying crunch of bone beneath my knuckles, and he went limp, his eyes fluttering closed.

"Hello, you fucking bitch," I said as I glared at his misshapen face and dusted my hands off on my tee shirt.

I curled my lip and growled again, watching him for any signs of movement.

He remained still.

I got up, shaking, and walked away. He would not be out for long, and I wanted to go out for a ride through the National Park south of Sydney and to sit on the cliffs and watch the moonlight play over the ocean.

I heard the whisper of cloth behind me and half-turned and braced myself for another of Allenby's tiresome attacks.

Something connected with the side of my face and tore my flesh to the bone, washing me with precious blood. Dazed, I sank to my knees, and the scrap piece of wood descended again, crushing my temple. My head screamed in pain as I toppled over. I had no power of resistance as the wood snapped my ribs, my sternum, and my left arm.

Shock stilled me, mercifully blanking some of it out, and I collapsed, unconscious.

The next time I opened my eyes my damaged body told me it was close to dawn. I could barely move. Allenby had taken the time to break my legs. The skin on my face had mercifully closed but my temple throbbed, and I could still feel a slight dimple from the break.

I was lying up against the fence of a nearby town house, just another drunk in Kings Cross. In the distance there was the sound of life from drunken revelers but I was too far away from them to take any blood that would heal me enough to find a hiding place for the day.

Dawn was brightening the sky, and my eyes teared in the light. I heard footsteps coming down the footpath toward me. It looked like someone was heading toward their car. I closed my eyes, waiting for them to approach.

The footsteps got louder.

"Yeah, so all she did was whinge about her ex-boyfriend from the second I picked her up. She began to cry about two minutes later, so I pulled over—"

"What the fuck?" a second male voice asked, and the footsteps rapidly approached me.

"Holy Jesus," the first man said. "I reckon she's dead." I heard him drop to his knees beside me, felt the heat from his body, and smelt the bourbon on his breath.

My eyes opened and burned blue fire as they bent over me. Faster than they could blink I sat up and sank my fangs into the closer of them. He was young, all of about twenty, with beautiful, kind brown eyes.

I held his larger, chubby, blonde friend in an iron grip as I drained the brown-eyed man's body as quickly as I could. I felt an instant of regret as the life left his body.

I gave a slight smile as I felt his blood coursing through my body, giving me strength. It was not enough to knit my bones, but it was enough to make me feel less groggy.

Predawn burned down on us as I took the fat man. His blood gave me sweet strength, removing the pain from my broken bones and giving me the strength to look for a place to sleep the day away. I flexed the arm that had been broken. It had healed but was weak.

I left the bodies lying near the fence, flinching at the cause of death. Kings Cross would undoubtedly be a bad place to hunt for the coming weeks as the police trawled the streets for the serial killer taking young men.

I blinked and winced, and slowly and painfully dragged myself over the curb and onto the narrow nature strip beside the footpath. I looked at the first gate and swore. Behind it was a field of concrete. I took in the next house and dragged myself toward it with my good arm.

The brick fence was seven feet high and there was a faded "For Lease" sign in a dirty front window. There were no curtains, so I could see it was deserted. Better than that, it had a thick, overgrown front yard.

I dragged myself back with both arms, favoring the one that had been broken. I reached for the gate and gave it a gentle tug, and it opened for me. I breathed a sigh of relief, eyes heavily tearing and my skin burning from the approaching sunlight. My limbs were starting to feel leaden as sleep crept up on me. I fought with every ounce of my strength to sink into the cool, damp and fragrant earth. I fumbled with the leaves and bark in the little alcove that was to be my hiding place for the day, with barely enough time to cover my face before sleep took me.

☙

I woke up the next evening ravenous and tingling from top to toe. It was not exactly pain but not far from it, and I knew that I had been exposed to sunlight. My legs were still hurt, and by the jagged, crooked look of them I knew they were still broken.

I flexed my arms. They were fine. They had healed.

I dragged myself out of the undergrowth and peered down at my body. I had taken on an alarming shade of pink and wondered how close I had come to being burnt to a crisp by the sun's purifying rays.

My stomach growled.

I forced myself up the footpath toward the sounds of humans and life in the main street of Kings Cross. I made my way as quietly as I could down a darkened alleyway, peering into the shadows for my next victim.

I saw her kneeling in the shadows, pale and sick, a steaming puddle of waste before her. Her face was wet with tears and her shoulders slumped.

She was so distracted, I was beside her before she knew I was coming, and her gaze was half-puzzled, half-horrified as she realized I was there.

I took her before she had a chance to move, and this time I was able to cover my marks.

I waited for what seemed an eternity as her blood roared through my system, further healing the damage to my body. My skin lost its alarming pink shade, and my legs looked whole and straight again, but were not strong enough to support me.

I sank back against the brick building that formed one side of the alleyway and grimaced. It was much easier to catch victims if one could at least walk.

I stayed there for hours in the darkness, wondering what Bronwyn was doing, disgusted with myself that Allenby had actually managed to hurt me and hoping against hope that he would not come back looking for me.

Through most of the night clusters of two and three and sometimes more wandered down the alleyway, unable to see me in the dense shadows. I let them all go. I needed a lone victim. I could not fight a group of them.

Finally, at around three o'clock in the morning, a young man strode down the alleyway. He was in a singlet and baggy jeans, heavily tattooed and with a shaven head. His dark eyes had a coldness about them that was disturbing.

I lunged toward him, grabbed his ankle, and pulled him to the ground. He slid a knife between my ribs before I had the chance to pin both arms, and I felt the precious blood flowing from my damaged body. I pulled him down, pinned his arms by his sides, and took him as quickly as I could.

When I was done I tested my limbs. My arms had fully healed, as had the deep cut between my ribs. My legs had straightened, and I slowly stood, hoping that they would be strong enough to support me.

I toppled over with a sigh. I would have to wait it out for another day in my hiding place and try to go home the next night.

Bronwyn would be panicking, I thought with a sinking heart as I staggered and crawled back to my deserted house.

This time I dug myself into the cool earth before sleep took me.

ဢ

I was stuck in Kings Cross for another night before I finally healed enough to go to my bike so I could get home.

I cautiously walked to the Harley riders' spots, looking for my bike, but it was missing.

I scanned the ground and found shards from a shattered side mirror. I winced and walked down the side street off Darlinghurst Road. There was a chunk of rubber from a footpeg and broken plastic from the fairings.

The trail of wreckage led to the rear of a pub.

My bike had been demolished, I could see. Parts of it lay scattered all through the pub's filthy yard, amidst empty beer kegs and over-flowing garbage cans. There wasn't enough of it left to scoop up into a dumpster.

"Hello, cunt," Allenby said in a smooth voice.

I whipped around. He leaned against the fence behind the alleyway.

I glared at him. "I'd say the same to you but I'm just not in the mood. What the fucking hell did you do that for, you rabid mother-fucker?"

I grabbed him by the front of his tee shirt and slammed him into the fence. He looked at me and laughed.

"Bitch," he said. "I'm only sorry I couldn't do it with you watching. When you die, mine is the last face you're going to see."

I dragged him along the road and into the backyard of the pub, away from prying eyes, and slammed him to the ground. I glanced around and grabbed the shattered remains of the front forks of my bike. I ground my teeth, rammed the first one through his chest with exquisite slowness, and twisted as I went. He grunted in pain as it pierced his cold, unfeeling heart. I sank it into the concrete beneath his body. I took the other fork and hit him as hard as I could across his face so he lost consciousness.

I felt sick and needed to leave, so I turned and made my way toward Kings Cross station. All I wanted was the comfort of my home.

ॐ

I walked into my kitchen about an hour and a half later. My legs were sore. I had been forced to walk home. I would be going out to buy myself another bike tomorrow. The silence and darkness surrounded me, and I closed my eyes and sighed. The house was not the same without Bronwyn in it, and I wondered why I had ever contemplated not allowing her to stay with me.

I made my way downstairs, intending to have a nice, warm shower and to spend the night heckling bad movies on television. As I got to my room downstairs, I saw that I had seven messages waiting for me and I flinched.

I hit the play button, knowing it would be Bronwyn.

"Hi, angel, it's me with my promised call. I'll call you later . . . Angel, still not home? Okay, no worries, I know you're a night owl . . . Angel, you know I wanted to call you, where are you? Okay, I'll try again later. I love you . . . Crowley? Where are you? If you wanted to break up with me, couldn't you have had the courtesy to do it to my face? I'll call you later . . . Crowley, I'm sorry about what I said before. I love you. I'm starting to get worried here, so please pick up next time I call, okay? . . . Angel, where are you? I can't get home any quicker than Sunday night, all the flights are booked up until then. If I don't see you at my arrival gate, I'm going to make my own way home. I love you so much and I miss you really badly. I'll find my way to you again . . . Please, beloved angel, where are you? Please be all right . . ." Her soft sounds of distress cut off as she hung up.

I walked into the bathroom and looked at my face. I had a thick, twisting scar down my cheek. I could not hide it from Bronwyn, and I prayed that she would not ask about it.

I sighed. I had no hope of hiding it. The best I could hope for was for it to fade in the two days I had left before I picked Bronwyn up from the airport.

CHAPTER TEN

"Crowley!"

I stood at Bronwyn's arrival gate as she came running up the jetway toward me. Her eyes were bloodshot, and I knew she had been crying. I held open my arms, and she flew into them.

"I missed you," I whispered, kissing her head.

She pulled back and kissed me as people poured around us.

The world slipped away as we gazed into each other's eyes.

"God, I was so worried about you, angel. Why didn't you—Why do you have a big scar on the side of your face?" Bronwyn touched it with a shaky hand. "You got hurt, didn't you?"

"It's nothing, lover," I said.

I heard a throat cleared close to us and looked up to see two of Bronwyn's friends staring at us.

"Are you all right now?" one of them asked.

"I'm better now," Bronwyn said from the safety of my arms.

The second of the two treated me to an unwavering stare. "She's been miserable, and if you don't start treating her right we're going to have to hurt you." She followed this up with a glare.

"Right. Gotcha," I said.

This time they both glared at me before walking off.

I pulled Bronwyn into motion so we headed toward the baggage carousel.

"Seriously, beloved angel, what happened to you?"

"Nothing," I said. "I just got knocked silly. It's nothing that a little blood won't fix."

She pulled me to a halt and gazed deep into my eyes, her own anguished. "Understand this. I love you more than life itself. If anything happened to you I honestly don't think I'd make it. I wouldn't kill myself but I'd be living a half life. Promise me, please, that you'll always do your best to stay alive? Just for me? Please?" She nibbled her lip.

"I promise you, BronwynHunter, that I will always find a way to stay alive."

Her green eyes were turbulent, but they had a peace in them that had been lacking when she got off the plane. We collected her luggage and then headed off to the car. It was only about ten o'clock, so I took her into Newtown. We parked in the back streets and then walked down King Street. I found a crowded ice cream parlor and got her a double scoop of cookies and cream, and we headed to a small, suburban park and sat down to enjoy the evening.

I crept my arm around her and pulled her in close as she licked contentedly on the cone.

"Beautiful, isn't it?" she asked, breaking the comfortable silence.

"Yes, it is. I always loved the night," I said.

"Do you ever miss sunlight?"

I gave her an amused look. "In my present condition, no. But yes, sometimes I wish I could see the ocean in full daylight. It's been a long time for me."

She nodded. "I've been thinking."

"About?"

She nibbled her lip. "About this. I love spending all night with you, but I'm not sure I can give up being able to walk around in daylight."

"I know," I said, cupping her chin. "No nibbling."

She looked guilty and troubled, but stopped nibbling.

"Better," I said, despite the pain that went through me at her words. "Look, you're young. I understand that. I haven't asked you about immortality again because I know what it's like. I'm not sure I would do it if I was given the choice again. But why think about it now? Why worry about it? If it's a gift you really want in a few years time I'll give it to you. I love you."

She let out a gusty sigh. "There's more."

I nodded and waited.

"I love you but I want to be someone outside you," she said.

"What do you mean?" I asked as she settled herself against my shoulder.

"I love you so much it hurts and I always want to come home to your beautiful face, angel, and know that you're mine. But I want some kind of life outside you. This last week was really important for me because it reminded me that I am someone outside us."

"Oh, God, I'm so sorry. I never realized I'd done that to you."

"You didn't do it to me, I did it to me," she said, capturing my gaze and holding it, her faith in me and in us firming her voice. "I got thrown out of my parents' house because I was being a stupid child. I clung to you because I was frightened. I'm not frightened anymore."

I smiled. "Now that's a good thing."

"I applied to university because that's what I thought I had to do. I'm not so sure I want it anymore, but I also don't want to give up on it yet."

"Yes, I should have gone to university when I had the chance," I said. "I didn't go and I've spent a long time regretting it."

"Why didn't you go?"

"It wasn't as important in my day, and I just didn't want to go," I said. "When I finally did it was just a bit too late for me."

"Why not go now if you really want to?"

"I'm technically dead," I said with a grin. "So I can't just enroll in school and get a degree. Plus I don't really need to, anyway. What knowledge I need I can always get from a book."

Bronwyn shook her head. "I want to go to uni so I can get a career and a life—so to speak—but I don't want to do more study because quite frankly I'm fed up with it."

I shifted and rested my head in my hand. "Look, why don't you go and see what it's like and if you really want to do it, keep going. If not, then just take a year off or something until you do want to go back. Either way, I'm going to be here for you. I'm not going anywhere. I love you as much as you love me. We're together for the long haul. I've lived a long time, and I can wait for you to do what you need to do."

She stared at me, ice cream forgotten.

I smiled. "You're dripping, my beloved mortal. Surprised?"

She cursed softly and licked the dripping ice cream. "Yes, I guess I am a bit surprised," she said after a few thoughtful moments. "I don't know what I was expecting, but it wasn't this. It reminds me of why I love you so much."

"I've made my mark in this world, so I understand why you want to make yours. We're together because we *want* to be together, not because we *have* to. Remember that and keep living your life. Forget immortality. If you actually want it we can talk again when you're ready, all right?"

She nodded and kissed me, tasting me. She dropped her ice cream and climbed into my lap. I crept my hand up her thigh to her soft, wet heat, and her back arched as she tried to lean into my touch, wanting me to take her.

I teased her, nuzzling her neck as she moaned.

"Jesus," she gasped, tearing herself away. "Let's go home. I've been without and without you for long enough."

I stood and scooped her up into my arms.

Wish granted.

∞

Life continued peacefully for the next two weeks.

It was close to Christmas, and darkness of the evening was thick with heat when we emerged from our basement hideaway. Bronwyn smiled at me and went to check the mail. I stayed in the kitchen, torn between suggesting we go out so we could both eat or preparing dinner for her.

Going out won, and I sat on the kitchen counter waiting for her to come back.

She came into the kitchen slowly, jaw working.

"What's the matter, love?" I asked, jumping off the counter and taking her into my arms.

"I think you should hear this," she said, taking my hand and leading me to the answering machine.

She hit the play button.

"Hello, Ms. Crowley, this is Rebecca Ferris, director of nursing from Sunnybank Long Term Care Facility. We regret to inform you that Mrs. McDonald passed away this morning . . ."

Her voice faded away to nothingness as burning shock drove me to my knees.

Bronwyn slipped her arms around me and cradled me as the worst of my tears erupted. She stroked my hair and held me, and all I could do was sink into her soft, feminine warmth. Finally, when I had quieted a little, she gazed into my eyes, her own stained with tears as she shared my pain.

"We have to go there," I said. "I have to see her one last time."

"Do you want me to come with you?" she asked.

I nodded. "I need you with me."

"Okay," she whispered and hugged me again.

I was too upset to drive—or feed—so Bronwyn grabbed my car keys and drove us to Sunnybank. By the time we pulled into the parking lot, I had collected myself enough to face Rebecca Ferris without breaking down in tears.

We went to the front desk, and I flinched as memories came crashing down on me, and a disconnected feeling began. After tonight, I knew I would never see this place again, and it hurt. Although it depressed me, I had also taken comfort from it because my beloved Rose was there.

"Ms. Crowley?" a middle-aged woman with gentle, kind eyes asked. She held out her hand. "I'm Rebecca Ferris."

I felt an instant of surprise, and Bronwyn squeezed my hand. I gave her a grateful smile. I had not heard her ask to see Ms. Ferris.

"Carlisle Crowley," I said, automatically shaking her hand. My jaw worked. "May I . . . may I . . . ?"

"Yes, I'll take you to her," she said.

"Do you want me to come with you, angel?" Bronwyn asked.

I shook my head, unable to speak.

"I'll wait for you," Bronwyn said, gesturing toward the tiny waiting room near the front desk.

I nodded.

Rebecca led me away toward the bowels of the hospital.

"We'll hold her here until you've made arrangements," she said as we headed down the fire stairs to the lower levels.

"All right," I said, finally finding my voice. "Either I or my companion, Bronwyn Hunter, will give you details."

Rebecca nodded and pushed open the door to a small waiting room. "We can't let you in there with her. It's against government regulations. You can see her through the monitor." She gestured toward a small television in the upper corner of the room.

"All right," I said.

Rebecca nodded and left me. A few moments later, I was looking at what once had been my lover.

I couldn't stop my tears. She looked so peaceful and husked out. I loved her still.

I *never* wanted to see Bronwyn like this, and thought for a second or two about pulling away from her, but the pain that brought made me cry harder. I could no more leave Bronwyn than I could Rose.

Fifteen minutes later, I went to the waiting room, and gazed at

Bronwyn, her fair head bent over a tattered magazine I could see she wasn't reading.

"Bronwyn," I said quietly.

She looked up, and I was struck by her sculpted features and youthful beauty. My heart twisted at the gentle sympathy I saw in her vivid, green eyes.

"Angel?" she asked uncertainly.

"I'm feeling a little better," I said. "I have to go and make arrangements for Rose. Will you come with me?"

She stood, giving me a sad, half smile. "I won't leave your side unless you send me away."

"And I never will." I took her hand, and we went back to the front desk. Rebecca Ferris looked up at me the same gentle sympathy in her eyes that Bronwyn had in hers.

I told her I would give her details the next day, and we left.

We went to a mortuary close to home. I knew they would be open after dark. I had bought Rose's plot there, close to my empty one. Bronwyn stood by me as we planned out Rose's funeral service.

It hurt me more than ever to know that I would not be able to attend.

After it was done, we went home. I spent the night in Bronwyn's arms, unable to voice my grief, cradled by her gentle sympathy and soft tears.

ॐ

Two nights later, Bronwyn and I stood by Rose's grave. The headstone had not been placed and would not be for another two weeks. They had to wait for the ground to settle, said the morticians who had taken care of Rose.

Bronwyn stood a little behind me and off to one side as I gazed at the disturbed earth. There was a single rose lying on the dirt, and I looked back at her.

"This is from you, isn't it?" I asked.

She gazed at me warily and nodded.

"Thank you," I said and held out my hand to her.

She came to me, her eyes wide and body stiff. Her gaze shot between Rose's fresh grave and the headstone on mine. I felt as though I were spinning out of control again and pushed the feeling back.

Death had not taken me, not yesterday, not today and it would not take me tomorrow. I would continue to walk the earth, and I was no longer tied to this place because Rose was there. I was truly free.

I was also isolated and alone, except for Bronwyn.

It felt awful.

I was beginning to understand what she meant by moving with the times. Despite her gentle presence, this was no life for her or for me. We had to move on.

"Thank you, Bronnie," I said with a crooked smile. "I think she would have liked that."

Bronwyn let out a gusty sigh. "Thank God. I was afraid I was interfering."

I laughed softly, despite myself. "Oh, no. Not at all. You never had the privilege of meeting Rose in her prime. She was very beautiful with a laugh that made everyone laugh along with her. Roses were her favorite flower. She inherited her love for them from her mother."

"I think I would have liked to have met her, even though I'm sure I would have been jealous," Bronwyn said, half smiling. "What did she like doing the most?"

I raised an eyebrow. "You really want to know?"

"Yes, angel. I really want to know."

I held out my hand. "All right, then. I'll show you. Come with me."

She took my hand, a question in her eyes that I did not answer.

I drove us to an abandoned house close to my home. The gates across the drive were rusted and leaned precariously on broken hinges. We went to a vine encrusted, cracked brick wall, and I helped her over, then followed her with lithe grace that made her roll her eyes. We went past the dilapidated wooden house to a forgotten, overgrown garden at the rear.

"Where the hell are we?" Bronwyn asked, peering into the darkness, the sounds of the river running close to us in the background.

"This was once Rose's house. She signed it over to me before she went into Sunnybank. She lived here until then, but she wouldn't let me fix it. It was her parents' home." I turned and looked at the house. "It was a beautiful showpiece during its prime, but when Rose and I were together, her family turned their backs on her, and it fell apart. I always wanted her to live with me but she wouldn't give it up." I winced at the unexpected pain the admission brought. "This is where she was most alive. And this is what she loved doing most of all with me."

I reached out a trembling hand and slowly stripped Bronwyn. Her eyes burned with desire as she reciprocated, and her full breasts pressed against mine, and I moaned softly as she claimed my lips.

"Not yet," I whispered as I grabbed her by the hand and ran down to a rock by the water. I slid behind her and took her in my arms. I leapt into the air with her, turned a neat summersault, and landed in the cool water with a solid splash.

We both came up, Bronwyn gasping for air and grinning wildly.

"Oh my God," she said. "My body wants one thing and my head wants another and something else wants both!"

I smiled and swam over to her, then held her close and tread water as I teased her body.

"Oh, God, if you keep doing that I'm going to drown," she said.

I laughed, ducked under the water, and replaced my hands with my lips. She clutched at me, stiffened, and shuddered, and I came up laughing.

"Fuck," she gasped, "you're so lucky you don't have to breathe."

"Yes, thanks," I said. We gazed at each other, and my heart ached for her and for Rose. "You ever swung off a rope into the water?"

She shook her head.

"Follow me," I said, swimming away from her toward the shore.

Soon she followed me back into the water, swinging from an old rope under my watchful eye, laughing wildly.

We went several more times, and finally lay back on the bank of the river, staring up at the stars. She kissed every inch of my body, and I saw my frustration mirrored in her eyes. No matter how much I wanted to, I would never quicken.

Finally, close to dawn, we dressed, and I led her into Rose's house.

The deserted rooms tugged at my heart strings, as did the dust and the decay. With the ease of long experience, I led her down to the basement that I had once shared with Rose, and fell asleep with Bronwyn's golden head resting on my chest.

CHAPTER ELEVEN

We awoke the next evening and left the old house. I didn't think either one of us would ever be back there. As we drove away, headed to Newtown so I could feed, I promised myself for what felt like the millionth time that I would fix the house up, to the way Rose had always loved and remembered it.

After we both ate, we walked into the city and found ourselves sitting on the concourse around the Opera House, watching sleeping birds riding the currents of air coming from the Harbor Tunnel.

Bronwyn thoughtfully ate her ice cream, watching them. "I start university next week."

"What are you going to enroll in?" I asked.

"I got into Arts Law," she said. "I don't know what I'm going to do with the Arts part. Probably do mostly science subjects. I'm going to leave off physics. I hate physics."

"I was never much for math or science when I was in school," I said. "I much preferred English."

"Yikes, how could you stand doing all that reading?" she asked with a grimace.

"I liked it when I was young," I said, watching a flying fox swoop over our heads. "It also gave me a good sense of the world and the places I wanted to go when I got older."

"Have you done much traveling?" she asked.

"Enough," I said. "I haven't traveled the entire world, and now it's more difficult to do. I think I'd probably have to travel by sea, these days."

"Do you want to go anywhere? There's somewhere I've never seen but I really want to go."

I sighed. "Now, with Rose gone, I'm not tied to Sydney anymore. I think I'd like to move around a little."

"Really? Would you go somewhere with me?"

"Where do you want to go, my mortal?"

"I want to see the States."

I grinned. "I was there when I was young." I schooled my features into impassivity. "When would you like to go and how do you propose to finance this little venture?"

She blushed, and I relented.

"All right," I said. "I can finance things quite easily. When do you want to go for a visit to the States?"

"Are you going to come with me?"

"Yes, I'll come with you, but you're going to have to promise not to argue with my choice of conveyance," I said.

Her eyes lit up with suspicion. "How do you propose to get to the U.S.?"

I laughed. "You're either going to have to fly me over in a coffin, or we're going to have to go by sea. I can't be out in sunlight."

Her jaw dropped. "You're kidding me."

"No," I said. "Those are my only practical choices."

She nodded. "Let me think about it." She cocked her head and gazed at me. "You really mean it? You'd go with me?"

I brushed her cheek with my fingers. "I mean it. I'll go with you."

She leant into my caress. "Good. I don't want to do this without you. I think you need it more than I do."

"How so?" I asked.

"Because Rose's passing has got me thinking. We may not have a tomorrow, and I don't want to waste any today I have with you." She paused, collecting her thoughts. "It's the reason I've decided I'm going to accept my offer to uni but not go this year. I want to spend more time with you. I want to build up memories with you. If you die tomorrow then I want to be able to look back on my time with you and know that I have enough memories to last me until I can finally join you."

I put an arm around her. "I'm not going to die."

"Really? When I came back from my week off I saw the scar on your face. I know you won't tell me what happened, but I know it was enough to stop you from going home for a few nights. You came close, I know that, and I half want to stay ignorant and half want to know how close. I don't want you to die, my love."

I remained silent.

"So," she said. "What do you think about my taking the time off?"

"If it's really what you want to do, I'm okay with it. But always remember, I'm not going anywhere. I won't leave you."

"I'm sorry," she said. "I feel like I've found the perfect woman for me, and that you're going to slip through my fingers, or that it's going to just vanish before my eyes."

I kissed the crown of her golden head. "I think I understand. You're going to have to do the same thing you're always telling me to do. You're going to have to just let go and live for the moment. In the end, it's all you have."

"I know," she said. "But that's just it. I don't want this to be an isolated moment in time. I want every tomorrow you have."

"But you're afraid of immortality and love sunshine too much to give it up?" I asked. "Relax. Just let it go for a while. Enjoy it all while you can, lover."

She was silent for a long moment. "Thank you, Crowley."

"For what?"

"Being you."

She slipped her arms around me and tightened them.

"When was the last time you were in The Rocks, angel?" she asked, peering up at me with a grin.

I smiled. "It's been a while. You want to go for a walk?"

"Yes, please." She slipped out from the railing and held out her hand. I took it, and we strolled past the other lovers on the concourse, headed toward The Rocks.

"Have you ever thought about marriage?" she asked as we walked past the buskers at Circular Quay.

I tripped over my own feet. "Not for a long time."

"Geez, are you all right?"

I cleared my throat. "Yes, I'm fine. Just stumbled. I do that on occasion."

"Sure you do. You're the most graceful woman I've ever seen. You just don't want to marry me, do you?"

"Hey!" I said, pulling her to a halt. "Stop doing that, will you?"

"Doing what?" she asked, nibbling her lip.

"Assuming the worst," I said, smoothing her chin. "Don't just assume I'm going to say no to something like that."

She blushed. "What does that mean?"

"It means you still seem to have lingering doubts about where my heart lies. It's with you. No one else."

"I'm sorry," she said, blushing. "I can't help it. It's just that you're criminally beautiful and people keep coming onto you."

I shook my head. "It's just something we both have to live with. I'm not necessarily attractive because humans want to screw my socks off, I'm attractive because I draw them to me so I can feed more easily."

Curiosity blazed in her eyes. "Are you calling them, somehow?"

"Something like that," I said. "I'm a predator. A little bit like a pitcher plant but much taller."

She gaped at me for a few seconds and burst out laughing.

I laughed with her.

"I didn't answer your question," I said when we both quieted. "I'd love to marry you, but there are two problems. First, I'm legally dead. I can't. Second, even if I wasn't, there's still the small problem of gay marriage being illegal."

"I know both of those things. But couldn't we have some kind of ceremony?"

"How about a compromise?" I asked. "Consider this an engagement. After all, you've proposed to me, and I'm accepting. My only request is that we wait a few years before doing the deed. Have some freedom and life first."

"It won't change the way I feel," she said with some asperity.

"I know," I said, knowing nothing at all. "But you told me that you need to feel like a whole person outside of me and us. I *want* you to do that. Marriage won't give you that freedom."

She studied me for a few moments, a question in her eyes. "I'd ask, but I know you won't tell me."

"I'd answer if I thought it was important," I said. "It's not. My past is my past and my future is yours, beloved mortal."

"I'll accept that for now," she said. "But it won't always be that way. Let's keep walking."

We spent the evening wandering around The Rocks. We went into all the tourist traps and looked at the souvenirs. I bought her a beautiful hologram of a heart with an arrow through it, and she bought me one of a knight astride a fierce eyed charger.

I took her home and made passionate love to her. We fell asleep at dawn, tangled together.

છ

Things were quiet for us between Christmas and New Year. She wanted to see the fireworks in the city and we went, standing in the milling crowd, as transfixed as all the humans around us. I could feel we were being watched, but I could not see who was doing it. I felt an uneasiness I could not shake, so one night I took Bronwyn with me, and we arranged our overseas trip.

After we were finished, I took her to the fair that had arrived in our little suburb. It was not the same one that was there around the time of her birthday, it was another, and I liked the look of it more than the other one. The rides were cleaner, the carnival crew less leery.

We roamed through the crowd and saw some of her old friends, and she stopped to talk to them briefly. They were all headed to university, looking shell-shocked and somehow non-comprehending. They did not seem to want to go, they seemed to think they had to go.

I had my arm around her shoulders as we cut through the crowd. I had my eye on the Ferris wheel. I knew it was much tamer than the rides she normally liked to go on, but I thought she would enjoy it. Only those afraid of heights seemed not to.

"You ever been on a Ferris wheel before?" I asked.

"Huh?" she said, pulling her attention away from the crowd. "No, I haven't. And yes, I'd love to try it with you."

I smiled. "What gives, lover?"

She pulled me to a halt and looked around. "I feel like there's someone watching me." She shivered.

I frowned. "Hold on a moment." I closed my eyes and focused on my senses. I could hear the crowd all around me, the catcalls, the conversations, the whisper of cloth from their clothes. Nothing was out of the ordinary, I thought as I scanned the crowd. My vision traveled over the teeming mass of hot and throbbing humanity, almost passing over the lone, young man at the edge of the trees bordering the carnival.

I narrowed my eyes.

"What?" Bronwyn asked, shaking me from my reverie.

"I see it. Wait for me here and don't move," I said, moving away from her.

"Crowley? What the—?"

"I'll be back in a minute," I said.

She threw up her hands and crossed her arms, looking miffed.

I hurried to the outsider who stood and watched me approach with malevolence in his eyes.

"Chris Carlton," I said as I approached him.

"Are you so sure?" he asked in a cold voice.

"A minion," I said, standing a foot from him and crossing my arms.

He said nothing, and the malice in his eyes washed over me in cold waves.

"What do you want?" I said, slowly and clearly.

"You. I want you. I'm coming for you."

"Come to me and die," I said coldly. "Leave me alone."

I had already fed, but I wanted the hold on this young man broken. I charged at him and sank my fangs into his neck before he knew what hit him. He pawed at me for a moment or so and then went limp in my arms as I took half of his blood.

I dragged him into the bushes to let him sleep it off. He would wake the following day, hopefully free of the mind that had seized him.

I went back to Bronwyn. She was leaning against the railing around a small roller coaster, watching the kids in it scream with delight.

"Bronwyn," I said softly as I approached her.

She turned to gaze at me and smiled. "Where did you go?"

"Do you still feel like you're being watched?" I asked.

"No. You took care of it, didn't you?"

"Chris Carlton still seems to find you eternally interesting," I said, giving her a crooked grin. "He won't be bothering you anymore."

"You didn't kill him, did you?"

"Um, no. Of course not. I don't run around murdering humans, thanks." I tilted my head. "Why is he so enamored of you?"

She blushed a deep and fiery red.

"Oh, Lord," I breathed. "You slept with him? You've gotta be kidding me."

"Well? So what if I did?"

"He's got such cold eyes," I said. "He's probably not a very nice man."

"I didn't look into his eyes that much," Bronwyn mumbled.

"Shit. I really don't want to know, all right?" I said, wincing.

We got in the queue for the Ferris wheel.

"You can't talk," Bronwyn said, a spark building in her eyes. "You and that bloody waitress from the Test Tube Factory. That was visual overload, lover."

I laughed. "I swear to you, I never touched her."

"Just like I'd never admit to swallowing."

I gaped at her, unable to speak.

She grinned and tapped my chest. "Gotcha, lover. Let's just drop the conversation, shall we?"

I nodded and wordlessly followed her.

We got in the queue for the Ferris wheel, and after waiting long enough to almost get bored, found ourselves stationary on top of the world, gazing out at the milling people far below us.

Bronwyn took my hand and kissed the knuckles. "I want to get out of here. I want to see more of the world with you beside me."

"We're out of here in few days," I said. "And I'll be glad when we do. I need a break."

She nodded. "So do I."

We went home at around midnight and danced until the sun forced us back under the cover of darkness.

෨

The following night was still and warm. The smell of her shampoo teased me, and the warmth of her body heated me as she restlessly traced the muscles of my back. She could not get enough of my body, and nightly I used it to take her to new heights of passion.

"Crowley." Her voice was soft as she kissed the rosy skin of my throat. I fed earlier in the evening, and we had stopped back here just in time to pick up some luggage before taking off into the night.

That proved to be a fatal mistake.

My sharp hearing detected the sound of footsteps coming toward the house, and I disentangled myself from her, held her close and behind me as they sped up the path with unnatural speed and stealth.

Suddenly, they stopped.

My heart sank as my senses strained to catch more. Bronwyn stiffened beside me, senses on alert, deeply alarmed.

"Crowley."

I silenced the soft question with a long finger to her lips.

There was silence for several more minutes, while I tried to use my senses to locate my visitor. Was it Allenby? If it were, I would kill him this time. No one invaded the sanctity of my home.

I saw a shadow flit past the window and whirled to face it, making sure Bronwyn was hidden by my back.

My bay window broke, and Bronwyn was torn screaming from behind me.

My tormentor continued on toward me, barreling me back against the wall hard enough to dent the brickwork. I was stunned, and my opportunity to fight back vanished as a male vampire lifted me off the floor by the neck.

I gave a squealing intake of breath. I did not try to break the hold he had over me, as I was unwilling to give away what level of physical strength I had. "Ahhhh, Lucien. This is a pleasure." So much for dignified strangulation. Not needing to breath came in handy.

Lucien was a tall man, approximately six and a half feet, one of the prettiest men I had ever seen. Long, shoulder length ash blond hair framed a perfectly sculpted face; laugh lines creased the perfect mouth, grey eyes burned from under thick, blond lashes. Broad shoulders, slim hips, muscles standing out beneath silky skin, he was every mortal woman's wet dream.

Pity he was not interested in any woman's flesh, beyond the problem of removing it from muscle and sinew, plus he was dead to boot.

I felt another presence come up to stand behind him, arms crossed, self-satisfied smirk firmly in place. This middle-aged, dark-haired man with blazing red eyes and good-natured features tapped Lucien on the arm and gestured for him to let me go.

Lucien did so with grotesque obedience, and I fell to the ground with a crash.

As I rubbed my throat I glared up at him. "Thanks ever so much, meat head."

Lucien growled, and only the restraining hand of the newcomer on his arm stopped him from bouncing me around the room. From behind me, Bronwyn drew a hissing, strangled breath, as she struggled against Allenby, of all people.

The look in my eyes promised lethal injury if he harmed her. To his credit, he took me seriously and contented himself with just holding her, refraining from the lewd whispered comments and boasts of his amazing sexual endeavors. What a moron—Bronwyn would have known that whatever was true of me physically would also have been true of him. He would never again fuck so much as a blow-up sheep.

A hand touched my arm, and I shied away from it, knowing it belonged to the man with burning red eyes, demonic in aspect. His voice caressed me in a way that I'd always hated. "Eleanor. It's truly a pleasure to see you again."

I looked at him, jaw clenched as Bronwyn stared at us wide-eyed. "David, you sorry bastard, why the hell don't you just leave me the fuck alone?" I shied away from his grotesque, intimate touch and the quick, cold peck on my cheek.

He ran a finger along my jaw as Lucien grabbed my arms in a bone-crushing grip. I struggled in his grasp and pulled my face away from the offensive David.

"No matter." His voice was a gentle whisper, and he truly looked offended by my lack of regard. "Our master is here now."

I snarled at him, pulling back my lips to reveal my fangs. "I have no master."

If Aristotle were here, it could mean only one thing. Bronwyn and I had to get away before he truly ended my existence.

I struggled harder. Lucien laughed at my efforts, and David looked on with grotesque, unwanted sympathy. A figure appeared in the shattered glass of the bay window. It glanced at the destruction in distaste, then sniffed in disapproval, and walked through with a kind of prissy daintiness that made me almost grind my teeth in frustration.

Just as I remembered him.

Tall and athletic, slicked down brown hair, burning, brown eyes hidden behind gold John Lennon spectacles that he didn't need. In his long-fingered, soft-looking hand, of course, he carried a book.

I could never figure out why he insisted on looking like that. He looked like a turn of the century dweeb. Jerk.

He finished reading his paragraph and then fussily marked his place in the book with a bookmark.

"Ah, Eleanor. It's good to see you." He was the picture of smiling congeniality.

"Aristotle. The pleasure is not mine, nor will it ever be." I gave him a bright, sunny smile. Bronwyn looked at me, wide-eyed, tense.

He smiled briefly, studying me as one would study an insect under a magnifying glass. I wondered if he'd fried lots of ants in the sunlight as a youngster.

"Tsk, tsk, no need for such bitterness." His lips puckered in displeasure at my disrespect. Then he leaned forward, voice low and dangerously soft. "You've been a very, very, very bad little girl, Eleanor."

"So spank me." My voice dripped with sarcasm as malevolence shone bright in my eyes.

He regarded me with icy cold eyes, and then he snorted. "I believe I'll leave that up to your sadly ignored spouse."

Lucien and Allenby tittered, as David's stony face remained expressionless. I heard a hissing intake of breath behind me as Bronwyn registered what he'd just said.

Aristotle turned to her swift as a striking snake, and my heart sank to somewhere below floor level. I had hoped we could escape this—that I could tell her of it in my own way. Oh, hell, who was I kidding? I'd hoped to avoid them until after she was gone from old age, and then let them have their wicked way with me, if they could find me. The arseholes had just blown all my carefully constructed plans all to hell.

"Didn't you know, little mortal girl?" His words were calm and inexorable. He shook his head in disgust. "What a way to find out. You are truly a mutant, Eleanor."

With that, he flicked his coat tails, and left the destruction of the house as carefully as he'd entered it, leaving his eager henchmen behind.

David turned and exchanged a meaningful glance with Lucien and Allenby. Lucien tightened his grip on me as Allenby threw Bronwyn into David's arms.

Holding her gently as she struggled, he turned and raised an eyebrow at me.

I already knew what he was going to do, and I prayed wildly to whatever god would listen that a bolt of lightning hit them all where they stood. I struggled mightily against Lucien's iron grip.

It was not to be.

Slowly, inexorably, David's fangs extended and plunged deep into Bronwyn's throat, and matching screams emerged from both of us.

Her struggles ceased by slow inches as he drained her of her blood. As she became still, so did I, losing my will to live, to fight. Lucien released me.

David dropped her, rudely smacking his lips, and nonchalantly picked a tooth as I barreled past him to cradle Bronwyn's still form in my arms.

Every nerve ending screamed in shock and pain, the salty, bitter tears flowed down my face, soaking my shirt front as my cries of anguish sounded throughout the night. "No, Bronwyn, No!"

My keen hearing picked up her faint heartbeat. The blessed sound filtered through my system, and I felt myself slipping to shock.

"Take them downstairs. We'll finish it this evening. It's too close to dawn for my liking." David nodded and walked out, but not before his casual, congenial air was broken by the savage kick he aimed at my ribs.

"We can't leave them together." Allenby looked at Lucien, then at us.

Lucien shrugged. "Who cares? Do you really think Crowley here is going to do anything?"

"If she does . . ." Allenby's voice trailed off with a smirk.

With none too gentle arms, they tore us apart and dragged our unresisting bodies through our house to the door to my lair. They threw us downstairs into my basement hideaway, and we tumbled down the steep, protesting stairs, Bronwyn's dead weight landing on top of me. Lucien giggled—a cold, triumphant, grotesque sound. He exchanged a quick, superior smirk with his buddies and locked the door behind them.

I paid only half a mind to it, knowing only Bronwyn, her mortal life nearing its close.

I held her tenderly, numb with shock and pain. Slowly her soft voice filtered into my consciousness.

"Eleanor? Pretty."

I smiled gently, trying to control my tears. "Eleanor Carlisle Crowley."

"David is your husband."

"Was. Technically he's a widower since I died before him. So no, I'm not married." The tears ran out of both of our eyes, unchecked.

The look of pure betrayal in her eyes was heartbreaking. "Why didn't you ever tell me?"

I hung my head in shame. For that inexcusable lapse there was no answer.

"I love you."

"I love you too, my beloved mortal."

"It's time. It's time."

She meant she was dying.

I could not live without her. I just couldn't do it. Life without her sweet smile, gentle green eyes, and playful spirit? Her cries of passion and love would haunt me to the end of time.

My voice was a whisper, impulse and selfishness driving me forward. "It doesn't have to be."

Her dazed and dimming eyes met mine, and I could see that she knew exactly what I was saying. She was grasping at the line I held out to her.

"You love me now. You probably won't after I've done it."

"Please. I want you. It's all I ever wanted." The beseeching whisper strained my battered and aching heart even more. "In death."

"Until life do us part." My lover lay dying, and I was still being me.

"Now, Crowley."

I sighed and kissed her goodbye for what would probably be the last time. Like most vampire marriages, we were probably not going to respect each other in the morning. The grief caused fresh tears to come to my eyes. At least she would still be alive, and I could still see her, even if she wanted nothing to do with me anymore.

Steeling myself, I nicked a wrist with a sharp fang.

"Drink. When you wake up you'll be just like me."

I yelped in pain as the blood flowed out of my body and into hers, leaving my nerve endings seared and jangling.

"Stop." As the blood hit her stomach, beginning the transformation, she sucked harder on my life force, bringing me to the point of death. I pulled my wrist away and slumped as she moaned at the loss of contact.

Weak almost to the point of immobility, I reached for her. I was so much older than her, so it was relatively easy, even in my weakened condition, to hold her steady as I plunged my ravenous fangs into her neck, almost shaking with need.

As her blood filled my stomach, some of the life returned, and I was able to control myself before I drained her to the last drop.

"Again." I nicked my wrist. She lunged for it and sucked the sweet blood into her starving body. Again I had to stop her as the pain became intense and the weakness set in.

"Please." She had had enough blood from me, and I was almost incapacitated. I could help her through the transformation, but I needed more of her sweet life force.

With trembling arms I embraced her, and took half of what she had taken from me. It left me a little stronger but hungry. It would have to be enough until I could feed again, show her how to do it.

I pulled her into my arms as she yelped softly. Ahhh, her first fang. What vampire had not accidentally nicked their tongue on their first fang? She stiffened and stared around the room in wonder. I could see what she saw, the powerful shadows in the room, the dust motes floating lazily in the air.

Her hair, a glorious blaze of sunshine during her life, increased in luster and beauty a thousand fold, and her skin faded to the same white as mine as my blood worked its magic on her. She turned to me, smiling, revealing her new born fangs, luminous, crystalline green eyes staring at me as though for the first time.

Beautiful in life, she had crossed the boundaries into absolute radiance in death.

Her face twisted in pain. "What's happening to me?" She twitched and gasped.

I grabbed her and stumbled to my feet. I ran for the bathroom, and put us both in the shower as her muscles convulsed. "I have you, I have you. Your body is dying. It's natural, but it'll last a few minutes. Try to relax."

I held her for the few hours left to us before dawn, as her body discarded all its waste, and she truly became dead. When it was done, I stripped us both and threw away our soiled, stinking clothes. I put her under the hot water with me, holding her, as she still appeared to not quite have the hang of supporting herself.

She stared at my naked body, transfixed, apparently, by a nipple. I looked down in amusement, my apprehensiveness hidden by my slight smile. "Hey, you all right there?"

"I can see everything." Her voice was soft wonder. I knew exactly what she was talking about. The eyesight we both shared was incredible, intense, electrifying. It was as though we could see every molecule of skin, every pore.

"You'll get used to it." I wondered if she still saw me the same way. Would she still love me or would she be drunk on her newfound power? Had she really wanted the gift I had just given her? The next evening would tell. Her eyes would either burn green or red.

She looked at me, and it was with the same lust she had always had in life. How long would that last?

I could feel the pull of dawn on my body, and I watched her eyes go glassy under the same spell.

"It's dawn. Time to sleep." I pulled her into my arms and took her to my bed. Naked, we lay wrapped around one another, her head on my chest. It felt so darned odd, but then I realized it was because she wasn't breathing.

She wasn't breathing because I'd just made her into a vampire.

Could she still love me? Worse, did I still love her?

CHAPTER TWELVE

When I opened my eyes the next evening, it took me a moment to remember what had happened to us. I felt the cool weight of Bronwyn's body, still in my arms, and I gazed down at her. I wondered how long it would take before she woke up.

I was starving, as I knew she would be when she woke, and almost desperately wanted to leave the shattered remains of our house.

I felt her muscles tighten in my arms and smiled as her eyes fluttered open.

She was truly beautiful—the smooth white skin, lustrous blonde hair, and vibrant green eyes that seemed to want to remain green, and ,in fact, looked as though a fire that was just beginning to smolder in them. Luckily, she didn't look like she was going to sink into the same mental mire of immobility or psychopathy that other fledgling vampires were prone to. Her eyes, while still a trifle distracted, were as sharp as ever, and she did not appear drunk on the power of life and death she now had over mortals. When she looked at me, I could see the same Bronwyn I had always known looking out at me. I ached to show her more of the beauty of the world around us, but I knew that we simply didn't have time to do it. In fact, there was no certainty at all that we would still exist by dawn.

The expression in her eyes made my heart skip a beat. It was a mixture of childlike wonder and desperate love for me.

"Good evening, lover," I whispered, giving her a gentle kiss.

She tightened her arms around me as she kissed me back.

"My beloved angel."

I held onto her. I loved the feel of her body in my arms, the soft sensation of her breasts against mine.

I pulled back, sighing. "We have to get out of here."

She nodded. "I know." She nibbled her lip, gazing at me. If she had been human, I thought she would have been blushing.

"I know." I grinned. "You're starving."

She nodded.

"Well," I said, getting out of bed. "We'll feed and then we'll head out of the city. I have a house we can go to."

"Oh." Bronwyn got out of bed and put on the shorts and tee shirt I had left out for her.

I pulled on my own shorts and tee shirt, careful to put my car keys in my pocket. I led her to the door Lucien had locked, and she peered over my shoulder at it.

"How are we going to get out of here?" she said.

I gave her a neutral stare. "I'm going to unlock the door and let us out."

"You're kidding?"

"No. It's my house, and the keys are in my pocket."

She blinked at me, nonplussed. "They locked us in here and left the keys with you?"

I nodded. "I don't think they were expecting me to make you into . . . ah . . ."

"A vampire?" she asked, flashing me a grin.

"Yes, all right, then, a vampire. I think they thought you would choose death, and I would be so distraught that I'd just be sitting there waiting for them to come back."

"That was pretty stupid on all scores."

"David always was a moron, and Lucien was always too arrogant for his own good." I snorted. "And Allenby? Well, he's just . . . Allenby. A fucking psycopathic idiot for all eternity."

We went into the living room and took in the damaged house. I felt a sick quiver of disgust at the carnage that had once been our home. Allenby had obviously taken the time before he left to smash as much as he could, and to slash as much cloth as he could lay his disrespectful hands on. It was, quite frankly, a miracle that the police had not come, that no one had investigated the racket the destruction had to have made, and that looters had not visited us during the day. The house was gone; it needed major repair work.

"Unlivable," I said.

"What does it matter if it's unlivable?" Bronwyn said, eyes flashing. Her arms were crossed in her classic pose of anger. "In case you hadn't noticed, they're coming to kill us for some reason I have yet to drag out of you."

I nodded. "Let's get out of here and go feed."

The car, I noticed as I started it with a dull roar, was undamaged. I thanked my lucky stars as I gunned the engine. We roared down the street toward a place I knew would have mortals for us to feed on and would be in the opposite direction to Aristotle, Lucien, and Allenby.

I tried not to let the pain of starvation show on my face as I stood with Bronwyn in the park close to our home. I gestured patiently to the couple making out in the bushes. I wasn't really keen on interrupting them, but it was necessary because I had to show Bronwyn some of the basics of being a vampire. She could watch me and learn.

Bronwyn stared at the night all around her, transfixed by her enhanced sensory input. She seemed to lack the ability to focus, but I knew that would pass as she adjusted to her new existence.

I held her and pointed toward the bushes, steeling myself. It was no use being embarrassed now, we both had to feed, and at least I knew I could be graceful when plunging fangs into a human neck. "You have to feed. I can't feed you any of my blood because I'm starving."

She looked at me questioningly.

I sighed inwardly. "It's not hard, really. Your strength is much greater than theirs. If you chose, you can be swift and gentle. It's up to you. Silly as it sounds, your senses will do the work for you, so you don't even have to consciously decide where to put your fangs."

She nodded and moved toward the couple enjoying each other in the bushes. She did not hesitate. She picked the boy off the girl by his butt and plunged her fangs gracelessly into his neck without any expression other than momentary confusion over which artery she wanted to bite. Amazed, hunger almost forgotten, I could only watch and wonder what was going through her mind. Distracted from my prey, I was dimly aware that the girl was struggling for her clothes. I reached out for her and held her arms by her sides with the ease of long familiarity. I gazed long and deep into her terrified brown eyes, willing her to relax. When she went limp in my grasp, I none too gently plunged my own teeth into her neck.

When it was done I showed Bronwyn how to spill drops of our blood onto the bite marks of our victims, so the wounds healed and looked less odd to the human authorities.

"Whoa." Bronwyn shook her head. "Now I understand why someone would want to be a vampire."

I gave her a sharp look as I tugged her by the hand toward my car.

"Well, you'll be doing it for the rest of eternity, so I should hope you enjoy it."

She studied the car. Then she took a couple of steps back and leapt clear over it to the passenger side.

I raised an eyebrow. "You all right there, Bronnie?" I had never seen Bronwyn during the day, so I had no idea what kind of an athlete she was, but I knew she was physically active, judging by the gorgeous, feminine body she had. I also knew that she enjoyed exploring her limits, judging by her nocturnal activities, but I had not expected her to adapt so quickly to the physical demands of being a vampire. She was going to test both of us, and she would have no trouble keeping up with me. That didn't really surprise me, actually; that was the way she had been when she was alive.

"I'm fine, believe it or not," she said as she gracefully leapt back over the car to me. "We have to talk. Why didn't you tell me you were married? Who were those guys?" She sounded quite matter of fact, but quite tired, as though she didn't want to face the mess we were in. I felt an instant of guilt. By rights, she really didn't have to—it was my problem, and she'd just been sucked along for the ride.

I wondered how much I should tell her, then settled for the truth. "Like I said before, technically I'm not married, because I'm legally dead and died before he did. He's a widower. I never told you I was once married because it's over and has been for a very long time. I don't even think about it or him because it's got nothing to do with my life right now."

Bronwyn glared at me in that way she had that made me love her all the more. "Look, I wanted you, and he wouldn't have been able to stop me. I still want you, and he definitely won't be able to stop me now."

I breathed a sigh of relief. From the moment she'd woken up, and I'd looked into her deep, radiant green eyes, I knew I was a goner all over again. Physically she pulled me toward her as hard as she had ever done. The blood I had given her had enhanced all of her wild beauty. It had changed her body in a fundamental way, but left her mind as sharp as it ever had been. When I looked at her, I saw my mortal lover at the peak of otherworldly beauty, the girl who had to have me at all costs.

"Go, girlie." I grinned.

She was silent for a moment. "I do have one final question, since you seem to have ignored the question of who they actually are. Why did Aristotle call you a bad girl?"

Oh dear. "Uhhh . . . because I am?"

"Crowley." Her voice was a sigh, and she shot me one of her patented looks with raised eyebrow that I'd come to know and dread. "We both know there's a hell of a lot more going on here. I'm not stupid. What are you not telling me?"

I threw up my hands, helpless. "Yes, of course there's more."

Without warning, I was flat on my back in the grass with her lying on top of me, nose to nose. Shit, that was quick—what else did she have hidden up her delectable sleeve?

I sighed, staring deep into her crystalline green eyes. "All right. Up until about ten years ago, Aristotle had a lover called Kilkenny. Beautiful, red-headed lady, deadly as hell. At the time, I was living as part of their little family. Someone burned her, one of the few ways we can die. Aristotle blamed me, as it was well known we hated one another. Aristotle hunted me, but I took off before he could find me."

"Did you kill Kilkenny?"

"Hey! I'm a killer not a murderer. No, I did *not* kill Kilkenny." I flipped Bronwyn onto her back and sat on her hard stomach, arms crossed, glaring down at her. My control over my temper slipped a little bit. I took blood because I needed to, not because I wanted to. I was at heart a gentle person.

"Then who did?"

"Oh, man, that one's so easy." I smiled slightly. "It was Sembur." I needed a moment or so to collect myself. She was going to be furious.

She stared at me expectantly and then glared when I took too long. "Well? Who's Sembur?"

"Stephen Masters Burr. S. M. Burr. Sembur. He's the one who transformed me into a vampire."

She flipped me over and sat on me. "C'mon, Crowley." She leaned down until there was only the barest of millimeters between us. "Don't make me drag it out of you. Why did Sembur murder her?"

I lay back and closed my eyes. "He burned her so they would think it was me and then murder me."

"What?" Bronwyn's voice thundered into the night.

I winced. "You wanna watch that volume, lover. You're going to make humans deaf."

"Do I look like I care?" Bronwyn's lip curled into a snarl. "Hello? This news is somewhat shocking to me. You just drop a fucking bomb-shell on me like that and expect me not to react? When you know perfectly well I love you to death? Will you please just tell me why all this is happening? My normally boundless patience with you is starting to wear thin."

Time to face the past and put it to rest. "Okay, okay, I'll tell you the rest of it." My voice was quiet and steady, much to my amazement.

Bronwyn kept her level stare, but smoothly slid to her feet and then held out a hand and helped me up. "We have to get moving. If we don't, the hit squad is going to find us before you tell me what you did."

She dragged me to my car as I tried to put my thoughts in order. I had to tell her what I knew devoid of as much emotion and judgment as possible, so she could make up her own mind about what was going on. Bronwyn climbed into the driver's side and carefully pulled out into the light traffic.

We were on the road for a while, headed nowhere.

"It's time to put your cards on the table. You have to tell me why you and Sembur are doing this." Bronwyn was quiet and serious, not exactly defeated, more accepting of the fact that something very nasty was about to happen to us.

I sighed. "All right. I told you once before I am at the time of my life when people all around me are dying of old age. I wanted to die with them, pure and simple." I glanced at her smooth, angular profile. "It all started with Rose. It wasn't until Rose went into hospital that I really realized what I'd let myself in for."

Bronwyn snorted after a moment of silence. "That's really stupid."

"Actually, no it's not. Look at you—you had me. No matter how you try to deny it, and I know you will, there's something very attractive about being in a relationship with someone that you know will never end. For you it's fine. For me, it's not. I knew that I was going to have to sit back and watch you die by slow inches. You also weren't going to stay young forever, and I was never going to get old. It would have torn us apart." The conversation felt quite stale. It didn't really matter, anyway. She wasn't going to age anymore. "I have been in free fall for the past fifteen years. I wanted to die."

She thought about this for a moment. "How do you know I would have turned down your offer of immortality if you made it again after a few years?"

"I didn't. I'm amazed you took it. Do you still love me? I mean really love me? If this was all about sex for you, then you can kiss that part of our relationship goodbye," I said. "You aren't going to be able to have sex with me anymore. If it was all some kind of romantic notion you had about vampires and humans, that's also over. You look at me now the same way I look at you, with a vampire's enhanced senses. We are truly equals. Now you're pretty much stuck with your crush for eternity."

Bronwyn pulled over by the side of the road, tires squealing, almost causing a major traffic accident. When the car was stationary, she faced me, eyes blazing, then the fight went out of her, and her shoulders sagged. "Fuck, what did I ever do to deserve your incredible lack of faith in me? It has never been about sex, although I must admit I'm going to miss that part, it's about love. Once I was a small child and an angel—you—rescued me from the side of the road. I never thought I would ever see you again after that night, and it hurt me quite badly, right up until I found you again last year, because I knew you were what I wanted for me. I got shy when we met again after all that time—I wondered if I would feel the same way about you that I once did, because I was an adult now. Yes, I'm an adult—I had dated and fucked a lot of people while I was out looking for you, so I have a hell of a lot of experience in the people and relationship department. I wondered if I'd badly distorted my memory of you, if I'd wasted my life looking for you. The bland truth was that I was older, and my love for you had changed, as it does. My feelings for you are an adult's feelings. Here it is, the honest truth: you make my knees weak with your incredible smile and your amazing blue eyes, but they aren't the only things I adore about you. I got to know you a little better and realized that I was in serious trouble—I fell very hard for your off beat sense of humor, gentleness, courage, and romantic spirit. They really got to me and made me yours. You cared for me, you protected me, and you loved me, even though you would never admit it. Okay, so we're physically on a more even footing, but you're still my beloved Crowley: my angel, my lover, and my friend. We can talk about sex, teens, and crushes some other time when vampires aren't trying to kill us."

I was embarrassed. I had misjudged her. She was no child, she was a grown woman.

Her green eyes were filled with anguish. "Please don't let them murder you. I don't really want this without you."

I pulled her toward me and wiped away her tears with feather light fingers. I gazed at her, willing her to know that I understood and would be by her side in eternity. I kissed her, long and deep. She responded with the same passion she always had in life, slipping her arms around my neck and pulling me in as close as she was able. I tasted her, and she leaned into my kiss, moaning softly.

When I finally broke it, my voice was a gentle whisper. "I love you, as much as I ever did. I've always loved your curiosity, compassion, and ability to roll with whatever situation you end up in. You took care of me, every bit as much as I took care of you. I stopped wanting to die very soon after you moved in with me."

She leaned into me, and we held one another for a while. Finally, she looked up at me, trust complete in her beautiful green eyes. "What's our next move?"

"We have to find Sembur. We have to get Aristotle to leave us alone, but we'll need Sembur for that."

Bronwyn looked at me, puzzled. "Why?"

"Something else I didn't tell you: Aristotle is six hundred years old. He could kill me with his little finger. Sembur, on the other hand, is five thousand years old, and Aristotle doesn't stand a chance against him. Sembur also promised me a small gift, and I want that gift now, to give to you."

She looked at me curiously, but did not ask, knowing full well I would not tell her what my gift was until I was ready. "How do we find him?"

"We don't." My grin was rueful. "He finds us. I can only hope he finds us before Aristotle does."

"Too late." A third voice, male, interrupted us.

I whipped around to stare at Allenby's ugly face, leaning into my window. At the same time, Bronwyn yelped in shock as Lucien pulled her bodily out of the driver's side window. She grabbed at the frame but to no avail; Lucien's grip was iron.

Without missing a beat, I matched Allenby's smile. Quick as a snake, I punched his smug face as hard as I could. I was rewarded with an ugly crack as I shattered his nose, with a satisfying spray of blood. I crushed a chunk of his face so he looked like raw hamburger. I smirked as I got out of the car and advanced toward him as he rolled on the ground in pain. I kicked him in the stomach almost as hard as I could. A set of steel arms grabbed me, knocking me slightly off balance. Slowly Aristotle appeared in my field of vision, burning eyes as cold as ever. As usual, his clothes and hair were pristine, much to my formless irritation. A wave of dislike crashed over me.

"Well, well, well, Eleanor. It looks like you tried to run from us." There was no sign of his ever-present book, and I knew we were in a great deal of trouble. He never traveled without the book.

He pulled my head back by my fringe and leaned in close with a casual, almost cultured, ferocity. He extended his fangs, and I felt an intentional cold wind and the drool from his fangs on my neck.

"Now, now, Aristotle." The voice came from the vampire holding me. It was David. I should have known. "Undamaged, if you please. You did, after all, say I could have her."

"I lied." Aristotle's voice was clipped. We were almost nose-to-nose, kissing distance. His eyes were ice cold, with a glint of something in them that I didn't like at all. There was not one trace of human compassion, only a rigidity of purpose and a stubborn clinging to old viciousness that didn't fit in a modern world. Happiness was an anathema to him, if it did not involve mangling other creatures. He saw me as a problem, requiring a long overdue fatal solution.

The dislike I had for him intensified, and I extended my own fangs to let him know that I would not be an easy meal. I had been bullied enough by him throughout my life as a vampire.

In the background, I could hear Bronwyn struggling against Lucien's powerful grasp. I felt a fleeting sick concern for her and hoped she survived long enough to escape, even if I couldn't.

"Kill me, Aristotle. Find out what happens to you if you do." Our eyes locked in mutual loathing.

The struggling behind me intensified, and I wriggled in David's arms. Aristotle looked up and frowned. "Lucien! No! She's not for you just yet."

I struggled from David's grasp and threw him back as hard as I could. He stumbled backward, and I whirled and lunged toward Bronwyn, skin crawling with horror at the spectacle of Lucien's sharp white fangs dimpling the tender, white skin of her throat. He grinned when he saw me moving toward him.

As my hands brushed Lucien's arm, I was slammed to the ground by the catlike Aristotle. I thrashed around ungracefully, trying to dislodge him.

"Not now, Eleanor. I have plans for you. For now, it's time for you to be more submissive," he whispered in my ear.

His old fangs slipped into my unprotected neck, and I felt the dreadful sucking as he pulled the life-blood from my body. My elbows collapsed beneath me so I lay unresisting under the heavy weight of his body. I grew ever weaker as the stream left my body, until I could not even twitch. My vision failed as the pain of his moving fangs and noisome sensation of his lips on my neck made me cough and retch in revulsion. I moaned in agony, and I heard Bronwyn's scream of horror coming from somewhere in the burning twilight.

It took no more than a minute for Aristotle to drain me enough for consciousness to desert me. He was greedy, even for a vampire.

I had no idea how long I was out for.

I was awake, but my body refused to move. I fuzzily wondered why that was. I had my arms and legs, I could even feel them, but they would not work. They felt like lead weights attached to an equally leaden torso.

I asked my eyes to open slowly and wondered if they would obey me. I was amazed at the feel of the smooth, cold stone beneath my cheek.

I heard a gentle voice from somewhere beside me. "Crowley?" The question in the voice was heartbreaking, so hesitant and frightened.

I groaned. "Oh. My. Aching. Body."

"You're alive." The relief was almost palatable.

"So it would seem." My eyes were functioning again, and I decided to push my strength to its limits by sitting up. My stomach screamed abuse at me, willing me to feed it. Slowly, protesting, my muscles responded to my strongly worded question to sit up.

I realized my eyes were not damaged, and that we were really in a dank and dark place. Completely devoid of any light. I realized, to my slowly dawning horror and despair, exactly where we were. Trying to pierce the gloom, I looked all around until I spotted Bronwyn chained to a wall. "Bronnie? Are you all right?"

"I'm okay. How about you? Aristotle drained you—I thought he killed you." I could see that she was forcing herself to say the words.

"I can't say I'm fine because I'm not, but at least I'm still alive." I crawled to her, and even that was a journey and a half. Ravenous as

I was, I craved her touch. It took most of my remaining strength, but I finally managed to sit up against the wall she was chained to and pulled her back so she was leaning more comfortably against me.

"I can't break the chains." She was apologetic and slightly abashed. "Do you know where we are?"

I could feel a clock ticking, signaling our ruination, but I pushed it aside. "We're in Aristotle's crypt. He and his mates live in an old church, and they've basically put us in the basement."

"A church!" Bronwyn sounded alarmed.

"Relax. Last time I looked I wasn't possessed by Satan, crosses don't upset me, and holy water has a rather nice flavor."

"You mean we're not—"

"No, we're not demons."

"Thank God for that. I wasn't terribly comfortable with the idea of having sold my soul to Satan."

I laughed softly. "I love you, Bronwyn. Don't ever forget that."

Salty tears dripped onto my body, wetting my shirt. "I love you too, Crowley." She sighed and leaned into me for comfort.

"Please don't cry." My voice was soft and slightly hesitant.

"I don't want you to die."

"No matter what happens, I will find a way for us to be together again. Trust me."

The salty, slightly bloody tears ran down my body, and I sighed.

We were saying goodbye to one another. It was too late for us to escape. Aristotle would keep draining me to the last drop of blood I had in my body, so I would be too weak to fight back. It was only a matter of time before he did to me what had been done to Kilkenny. I only hoped Bronwyn would not be forced to watch. Perhaps she would even be able to escape.

We sat like that for an hour or so, taking simple comfort from each other's presence, before the door to our cell opened and Lucien appeared.

He smirked when he saw us, and the best insult I could manage was a curled upper lip, much to my considerable frustration.

When he saw it, he laughed, and no matter how I willed my body to obey my impulse to kill him I just couldn't move enough to do it. Aristotle's fangs had done their job.

He grabbed me and hauled me into the air, as though I weighed no more than a pillow. I ground my teeth as I was slung with arrogant ease over his shoulder. With a casual flick of his wrist, he unchained Bronwyn and hauled her to her feet.

She struggled, but my night-old youngling was no match for his five hundred year old strength. He took us to the upper chambers of the open-roofed church to cast us before Aristotle. He sat in his comfortable, ostentatious throne, placed where the altar should have been. A light mist curled around his ankles, caressing them. I suppressed a shudder of revulsion at the intimate touch.

I sank to my knees, head bowed, and when Bronwyn tried to come to my side, Lucien pulled her back and hurled her against the wall. Aristotle pursed his lips in displeasure. I longed to rip both of their throats out.

"That was ill advised, Lucien. Now you're going to have to pick her back up."

I struggled to remain expressionless. Bronwyn lay still, too still. I feared the impact of her head against the wall, which had been sickening, had done her severe damage.

Lucien trotted to her like a good dog and picked her up. With that same shocking lack of concern, he dropped her onto the floor next to me, and I struggled to hide the dismay at the pool of blood that was expanding around her shattered head. Her life hung in the balance, but I could not think of that now. I held back tears, allowing myself a full moment of mind numbing panic that tugged and tore at me.

"Aristotle, you will pay." My eyes glittered with hatred as I held his gaze to let him know that if he killed me I would find some way to come back and destroy him. Death would never hold me back.

"That's no way to talk to your elders and betters, my dear." As always, David huffed in displeasure at my disrespect. Why on God's green earth had I ever married the moron? What had I ever seen in him? Why had Aristotle brought him into vampirism? Maybe I was really in hell, and we were the spawn of Satan.

Behind us, a huge pile of wood waited, and I wondered how long it would be before they lit it and threw me aboard. I only hoped that it would be quick and it wouldn't hurt too much.

"David? If you please?" Aristotle gestured elegantly to my ex-husband, who slipped back into the shadows, presumably to get some matches and a bucket of petrol for his barbecue.

"If you kill me it's only the start of your problems." I would make good on that promise to Aristotle.

Bronwyn lay discarded on the ground, too still. My beautiful, beloved Bronwyn, caught in the jet wash of my defunct master plan.

David had returned with his matches and lighter fluid. With practiced, accursed ease, he lit the base of the bonfire. The cheerful flames began to eat the abundant fuel.

I smiled, despite myself, and nodded toward the bonfire. "Aren't you afraid this might burn your precious church down?"

For the first time ever, Aristotle threw his head back and laughed—a deep, rich, joyful sound, and it made my skin crawl. Finally he quieted in fits and starts. He got off his throne and sat in front of me. "It's a horrible feeling, is it not? Is this what you did to Kilkenny? Did you enjoy her screams of pain and terror?" He appeared honestly interested, but it was the kind of interest you had when you ripped the wings off flies. Like he wanted me to tell him about flesh melting off bone.

I did not answer him.

"Did you enjoy the smell? Did you enjoy the victory over me?"

"Why can't you ever say something fucking original?" I snarled.

"Time to die." He got up and dusted off the seat of his brown trousers. Lucien and David walked toward me, both grinning in anticipation.

I shot a bitter smile at my ex-husband, watching the triumph in his burning, red eyes. "Enjoy this, David. You were a rotten and boring husband and I was always stronger than you." David hefted me to my feet, while Lucien cradled my beloved Bronwyn in his arms. "You used to beat the living shit out of me while we were alive. That's why I left you. It wasn't for Rose, it was because you used to torture me. The last time you did it I miscarried, and you lost your heir. The one that was so important to you, remember, David?" The slow march toward the crackling flames was inexorable. "Watch the flames well, David, and pray you never die. They are what await you in hell."

The mist thickened and blanketed the ground, shying delicately away from the roaring inferno before us. I was resigned as I watched the flames leap high into the air, hungry to consume my almost immortal flesh. I said goodbye to the things that I had loved in life and death, offering a silent prayer to my Bronwyn whom I had not been able to protect, and who did not deserve my fate.

CHAPTER THIRTEEN

The mist coalesced into a humanoid form, thickening until it had some substance. Aristotle and his merry misfits were so intent on being pyromaniacs that they failed to notice that an opaque male vampire had joined the party. As the figure gained in solidity, it became apparent that he was mighty pissed.

"And what do we have here?"

His smooth, gentle, deep voice stopped Lucien dead in his tracks, and David paled. The newcomer whipped out an arm and grabbed Aristotle so abruptly that he was unable to make a sound.

My entire soul sobbed in relief, and a single, bitter tear trickled down my face. "Sembur! You came."

His face remained stony, and his eyes ice cold, but his lips curved into the barest hint of a genuine grin for me.

David turned around, dropping me on the way. I looked at the vampire that could have been my twin brother with his fiery, ice blue eyes and shoulder length, pitch-black hair. A casual hand, almost boundless in strength, held Aristotle by the throat. Aristotle clawed at the fingers that held him in a crushing grip. I noted with mild interest that it was the first time I had ever seen him go pale and actually look a little bit frightened.

The turn of the century, sadistic jerk twitched and struggled under that cast iron grip. Lucien and David looked poised to strike, as though they expected the drama to last minutes instead of seconds. They didn't seem to realize that this didn't start out as a fair fight and certainly wasn't going to finish as one.

Sembur smiled at me, love shining bright in his beautiful, slightly demonic eyes. "I heard you, Crowley. I came."

With almost a casual gesture, he threw Aristotle into the flames, as Lucien and David watched, frozen with horror. Aristotle did not have time to scream as the volatile vampire's blood in his body caught fire. A white hot ball of flame roared and jetted into the cool night air above the sandstone building. Aristotle writhed and thrashed, no more than a matchstick man of flame, his skin melting and running down the remains of his body. He finally found his rapidly disappearing voice and screamed. It continued until he sounded thick and hoarse, and finally finished in a dry heaving of soot.

A pale and shaken Lucien recovered his strength. He gave David a desperate glance, and I knew he was about to do something incredibly stupid. David looked affronted, mixed with a kind of sick desperation, since he knew they were clutching at straws. They would not live beyond the next few seconds, let alone escape.

Lucien carelessly dropped my broken lover, and as one they lunged toward my maker.

Sembur smiled and shook his head. It was futile for them to even try it. Like me, Sembur did not like killing things, even ones as disgusting as that pair of morons, but they intended terrible harm to him if left unchecked, so his only option was self defense. I had no idea if Sembur would have let them escape if they hadn't lunged toward him, but in the end, that really didn't matter. Before either knew what hit them, they were sailing toward the bonfire, howling in terror.

I winced as a twin conflagration sprang into being. I crawled to my knees, stomach threatening to expel its very lining as the quiet of the night was shattered again by screams of agony as skin melted from bone. Finally, mercifully, cries were silenced as vocal cords were seared away, and bone was finally reduced to ash.

David was gone. Finally gone. Looking deep inside myself, I found nothing. Whatever he had done to me in life had been so long ago it was truly just a memory. All the dislike I'd felt for him after death came from him being simply himself, an arrogant, shallow, self-absorbed man.

I didn't hear or see Sembur come up behind me to pull me into his arms. He cradled me, holding me tight against his cool body as my sobs finally came. I slipped my arms around him and once again felt his hard muscle, smooth skin, and stubbly cheek resting against my head. I had been strong for so long, it felt good to let go a little. A small, nagging voice at the back of my head yammered about Brownyn, and I didn't want to quiet or soothe it anymore. I felt like she had—I could make it through eternity by myself, but it would be nowhere near as fun without her by my side.

"My beloved Crowley." Sembur's words were gentle and heartfelt.

I could not stop myself and did not want to. This was the only man I had ever really loved. I leant up, and we kissed long and deep, tasting one another.

"Sembur."

"Shhh, little one, don't speak." He paused for a moment. "I couldn't let them kill you. I still don't want you to die, nor will I help you do it to yourself ever again." He gestured toward Bronwyn, who lay on the ground not three feet from us. "There is time, but first I must help you."

He delicately nicked his wrist with his sharp fangs and held it to my lips.

The sheer fountain of power radiating from his blood was indescribable. Greedily, I lapped every last drop I could before the wound closed. The ancient blood, so powerful, so humbling in its purity, flowed into my system, and I moaned as every nerve ending sprang to attention. It was what was needed to heal my beloved Bronwyn.

I slumped to the floor, sighing, allowing the dizziness to pass. "Allenby?"

"Kilkenny is with him."

I nodded. "A life for a life. Your promise."

He smiled. "Still my impatient youngling." His tone was playful, but his flaming blue eyes met mine, and in them I saw fathomless patience and knowledge, shadowed by a horrible, dark wisdom that he had gained through millennia of existence. He had lived a span no one could truly imagine, and it seemed to me that the years had begun to take their toll on him.

My maker. Sembur.

I gestured toward Bronwyn. "I love her. You were right." She lay still, and although her vampiric blood had closed the wound, she was still horribly injured. Sembur's blood would heal her. I could not think it would fail, and would not allow myself to acknowledge any other possibilities until we had tried it.

He laughed softly. "There is always a reason to keep going. For me it was Kilkenny. For you it is Bronwyn."

I met his eyes with gratitude, and he leaned forward to caress my face with his gentle, iron fingers. "You have re-learnt faith. At last."

It was true. I could finally face my future. It had always seemed a long, black road ahead of me, covered in thin ice, but thanks to Bronwyn, that had changed.

"Help her, please." I was begging him for the second time in my life. The first had been when he gave me the gift of his blood.

"She must drink from you first."

I thought about this. It was true—I had to be the one to heal her. I nodded. "Let's begin."

With trembling hands, I reached for my motionless lover and cradled her to my body, gently tracing the outline of her still cheek. Her face was mercifully undamaged, but there was clotted blood in her hair on the slightly flat side of her head that made me shudder and quail inside. She was a dead weight in my arms, and I really couldn't tell if it was too late for her, since she no longer breathed. Her eyes were closed, her skin pale to the point of translucence, her muscles slack. She was so lifeless, but Sembur had assured me it was not too late—I could still heal her.

"I love you, Bronwyn." Truer words had never been spoken.

I nicked a wrist and held it to her lips.

The most basic vampire reflex sprang into play, and she latched onto the blood I offered her. As Sembur's freshly consumed blood flowed from my body into hers, I welcomed the pain with open arms. I could feel the shattered flesh and bone of her head knit together, sealing her dreadful wounds. She drained me almost to the last drop, and I pulled away from her, whimpering, weak as a kitten. I only barely noticed my crystal tears dripping onto her pale skin, as I leaned down to pull her wrist to my mouth so I could feed from her. My teeth broke her clean skin, and there was a jet of hot blood that went straight back into my throat, a hard slap of life. I felt myself grow stronger again, as she became dead weight in my arms, drained almost to the point of death. Sated, I pulled back slightly, feeling a thin sliver of pain from the nick I had put in my wrist so I could feed her again.

As she sucked in my blood in great drafts, her muscles firmed and she gained control over them, although she was still unconscious. The blessed relief I felt as I watched torn flesh become whole again almost stopped me from being able to pull my wrist away from her mouth before she drained me to the last drop.

Sembur left us to feed, to replace the blood I had taken from him, and to give us some privacy. Alone, with only the still crackling, demonic flame to keep us company, I held my wounded lover until she stirred. Her eyes fluttered open, and once again full of blessed life, her gaze held mine and swallowed me whole. I was so wrapped up in her gentle regard that I almost didn't notice that her eyes burned with bright, green flames.

"My angel."

Those whispered words brought more tears to my eyes. "Bronwyn."

She shifted in my arms so she was more comfortable. "I'm okay. What happened?"

"It's a long story. Aristotle happened. Then Sembur happened."

Despite her weakness, Bronwyn stiffened in my arms. "Sembur is here? How did he find us?"

"I asked him for help, and he came, but he's not here at the moment. He went to feed."

"I want to meet him."

"You will." I paused, trying to frame what I had to say next. "Bronwyn, I'm sorry. For everything. I never meant for any of this to happen to you."

Bronwyn smiled. "We're both still alive, aren't we? If you really wanted to die we'd both be dead by now. I knew you were going to weasel your way out of trouble somehow, I just had to trust you." She ran a finger down my cheek. "I love you and I forgive you. I am with you by my choice and my choice alone, so forget the guilt trip."

I kissed her. She held me tight, tracing the muscles of my back under my torn shirt.

"Bronwyn."

My lover yelped in surprise at the soft male voice.

I looked up at the smiling face of my mentor and grinned. "Sembur. Still enjoy shocking the hell out of people?"

Sembur shrugged and looked apologetic as Bronwyn gnashed her teeth in frustration. It was quite clear she thought she'd struck another bloody Crowley.

I exchanged an amused look with him as Bronwyn heaved a deep sigh.

Sembur studied the stars and then looked closely at me. I nodded. I could feel the pull of rapidly approaching dawn.

"We'd better get out of here," I said, remembering the carnage that was once Bronwyn's and my home.

"Our place is trashed." Bronwyn looked at me and sighed. She struggled to sit up, closing her eyes against the dizziness that threatened to steal her balance.

"I know." I gave her a crooked grin. "When was the last time you went camping?"

She frowned. "You mean, sleep outside? We can do that? I thought we had to sleep on the ground we were buried in."

"Well, yeah, you have to sleep underground so you don't get a sunburn. Not all vampires have to sleep in the earth they're buried in. You don't—you didn't get buried, remember? Besides, could you imagine lugging around a whacking great coffin stuffed with dirt for the rest of your unnatural existence?"

Relief glowed in Bronwyn's eyes. She nodded. "Yes, I did notice I never ended up in a pine box. I was kinda wondering about that." She paused. "But I was also kind of curious about what you would've picked out for me."

I gave her a calculated look. "How about something bright red? With wheels and a windscreen painted on to it? You could race the hearse to the cemetery."

Bronwyn winced. "I don't think so. Bright red? Because you think red ones go faster? What do I look like, a blonde?" She leaned forward, fiery eyes twinkling. "Everybody knows silver cars go faster than red ones."

I chuckled. "Is that right?"

Bronwyn looked thoughtful. "Absolutely!" She gave me a sharp glance. "Don't go there. We are *not* trying it."

I grinned and opened my mouth to respond, but Sembur's strong hands on each of our shoulders stopped me. "You may stay with me, if you like."

Bronwyn looked pathetically grateful. "You have place for us to sleep?"

"Yes, of course. I have a spare pair of shovels—large ones—so you can dig a shallow grave in my vegetable patch." He leaned toward me. "Please watch out for the carrots, and try not to kill the tomatoes, I only just planted them."

I smiled gratefully. "Well, looks like that's settled, then." I nodded in satisfaction. "We happily accept your offer."

Bronwyn's mouth was a perfect O of horror. She looked at me as though I'd lost my mind, and shot Sembur a respectful look, the type that was reserved for childless uncles with lots of money and no marbles.

I managed to keep a straight face for a few more seconds until Sembur's snicker made me laugh outright.

Bronwyn realized she'd been had and collapsed back on the ground, sighing, as Sembur and I laughed.

"Come," said Sembur. "I think it's time to go to ground."

I nodded. "Sounds good to me." I held out my hand for Bronwyn. She took it and levered herself up off the floor.

"How are we going to get back to your place?" she asked, tangling her hand with mine as Sembur walked ahead of us, leading us to the sacristy and out of the church.

I squinted against the lightening sky. "We had better move."

Sembur glanced at me and nodded. He gestured toward my car, parked before us, I noted with some amazement. "I think Allenby liked your car."

I wrinkled my nose in disgust. "Do you mean he drove it?"

Sembur shrugged. "At least he did not destroy it."

"Where's your current hideout?" I asked.

"I'll lead you to it," he said, slowly dissolving into mist form and surrounding the sports car.

We got in and a ball of mist—mercifully not clouding the windscreen—surrounded us with a distinctly supernatural air. It did not disperse as we drove, a silent Bronwyn watching it with great interest.

I was geographically confused and trusted my mentor to lead us to his home. After fifteen minutes of high speed driving, we reached Sembur's home. The wrought iron gates that marked the edge of his estate were wide open, and as we pulled up in front of the house we caught a quick glimpse of Kilkenny, an almost comatose Allenby slung over her shoulder disappearing into the house.

Bronwyn and I ran through the open front door into his deserted house and looked at the unused furniture and dust circling the air. He took me into the quiet kitchen, full of unused appliances and opened what should have been the refrigerator door. It was actually the door that opened onto the landing at the top of the stairs that led to his basement hideaway.

"Whoa," Bronwyn said, taking my hand as we found ourselves in a dimly lit foyer at the bottom of the stairs.

"Cool, huh?" I said.

Sembur strode across the foyer toward a set of stairs leading to another lower level. "Guest room is first door on the right downstairs. Library is on this level at the end of the hallway before you. Come to us there once you have rested."

I nodded. "All right." I paused, studying his handsome, impassive features. "Thank you, Sembur."

His gave me a broad grin, revealing his sharp, white fangs. "You're welcome, fledgling."

"Isn't Sembur going to ground as well?" Bronwyn asked as she watched him walk way.

"No," I said. "He doesn't need to. He stopped having to go to sleep at dawn about nine hundred years ago, so he said. Unfortunately he hasn't met anyone the same age as him to ask."

I felt my limbs grow heavy thanks to the brilliant dawn that burned through the above ground levels. Bronwyn took my hand, and we went downstairs, barely making it to the bed before sleep claimed us.

ℴℴ

We woke in each other's arms the next evening, both of us hungry, but I didn't want to take us out to hunt. We had to talk to Sembur first. Bronwyn looked more focused than she had the previous evening, and her eyes were recapturing their old sparkle as she gazed at me. I stole a kiss from her, and then led her up darkened stairs and hallway toward the library. I knocked on the closed doors and then opened them.

Sembur and Kilkenny were waiting for us, and both smiled when they saw us.

"There, this is much better than that nasty crypt, isn't it?" Sembur asked.

"It certainly is," I replied.

Bronwyn and I sat close on an expensive, brown leather lounge, fingers tangled together. Sembur and Kilkenny sat opposite us, on the twin of our sofa, equally close. Bronwyn could not take her eyes off Kilkenny. I had told her the woman was beautiful, but Bronwyn clearly had not been prepared for the shock of seeing a living, supposedly dead vampire as utterly stunning as Sembur's lover. The fact that both Sembur and Kilkenny looked like statues was almost a side issue. Their eyes burned so fiercely that they almost glowed, and the white skin was arresting. They were specimens of physically perfect human beauty, combined with a mysterious, supernatural quality that made them magnetic, completely irresistible.

Bronwyn stiffened in shock when she saw the almost catatonic Allenby, seated in a large leather chair opposite us. A faint scar marred the bridge of his nose where skin and bone had shattered. His eyes had changed, and I didn't know if it was for the better. They had always been dark and vicious, with a ratty gleam of intelligence that had set my teeth on edge, but now they were distant, almost unfocused, gazing into eternity with an unfathomable, hollow stare. It was as though all the self-awareness had disappeared in a spray of blood. Kilkenny had healed him, but it seemed something inside him had been irreversibly damaged.

Sembur saw my attention was focused on Allenby. He signaled me and shook his head. I knew that he would not tell us what had happened to the ex-biker.

"Is Allenby going to be all right?" I asked.

"I don't know," he said.

I nodded and turned to Bronwyn. "I know I have to try and explain all of this to you."

She nodded. "That's an understatement. But since I know how elliptical you can all be, I want to ask the questions. Maybe someone will tell me the truth—all of it."

I had to grin. Kilkenny and Sembur were very old, and they would tell us youngsters what they wanted when they wanted to. "Be my guest."

"Crowley told me Kilkenny was dead." She looked apologetically at the red head. "No offense, but how come you're still alive? What really happened?"

Kilkenny smiled. "I rather like being alive."

Sembur smiled. "I am familiar with what Crowley shared with you."

He and his lover exchanged a quick glance.

Kilkenny nodded. "I was captured by Aristotle, and kept drained almost to the point of death by him for a century. Then your friend Crowley came along. We agreed to hate one another for appearance sake, and then Sembur came to my rescue. We burned the corpse of one of his victims." Her voice was as beautiful as her face—deep, melodic, and somehow hypnotic.

Sembur squeezed her hand. "I had searched for Kilkenny for the entire century. I could not find her. My young apprentice, Crowley, found her, and told me she was alive, but would not tell me where she was. That information came at a price. I could rescue Kilkenny, but only if I agreed to kill Crowley. After all the trouble I had taken to bring her over to our side, I was not about to let that happen. We fought long and hard; I did agree, eventually, to the plan of placing the guilt of the supposed murder of Kilkenny on Crowley's shoulders, so Aristotle would hunt her and kill her."

"But then I came along." Bronwyn's voice was a whisper.

Kilkenny nodded and smiled. "Then you came along. We watched you both and stepped in when the time was right."

"It was you who warned Crowley at the fountain. Sembur, why couldn't you find Kilkenny by yourself?"

"Yes." Kilkenny smiled, ignoring Bronwyn's question.

I could see Bronwyn heave a deep, mental sigh, knowing the question would be answered when they felt like it.

I furrowed my brow and stared at Bronwyn. "How did you know what happened at the fountain?"

Bronwyn gave me that exasperated, affectionate look of hers. "I keep telling you, I'm not stupid. It didn't take a degree in rocket science to figure out that something was up. I just didn't know what it was."

I kissed her. "I'm sorry for everything. I never meant for you to get hurt by all this."

"Crowley." She sighed. "You kept warning me off, you still keep warning me off, but you still don't get it. I love you. I always have and I always will. The fact that I'm a vampire now just makes you all the more attractive because I get to spend the rest of eternity with you and never grow old. I'll never be on my deathbed, dying of old age while you bring a young lover to meet me. I'm the jealous type and would never have taken kindly to that."

I was once more amazed by her love for me, and how lucky I was that she was so persistent. I loved her all the more for it. "I love you too, and I know you're a very smart girl. I'm sorry I didn't tell you about the warning, but I just couldn't tell you about it. Sembur, Kilkenny, and I have more you need to know. Ask your next question."

Bronwyn smiled and nodded. Then she gave me an odd look, almost as though something was on the tip of her tongue, but she could not quite say it yet. She shook her head in frustration and turned to Sembur. "Why did you make Crowley? If you loved Kilkenny as much then as you clearly do now, how could you do that?"

Sembur was silent for a moment. Kilkenny gave his hand a small squeeze, and he looked at her, clearly deciding what to say.

"I stopped a man from beating his wife," he said in a soft, almost distant voice. "I saw a creature that was just like me. When I made Crowley, she was dying."

I closed my eyes in pain at the sudden memory of my human life and my death.

Bronwyn's eyebrows shot skyward, and she looked at me, horrified. "David beat you? Who turned that fucking creep into a vampire?"

Sembur smiled ruefully. "Don't look at me. I certainly didn't do it. I think it was Aristotle, because he knew about David's small ability."

I gave a sad smile, lost in memory of an ugly time. My marriage had been one of the most stupid mistakes I had made. Nobody had known what would happen to me, and I had been too afraid to tell anybody but Rose. "He beat me, but that wasn't what killed me. I was dying from a loss of blood."

A piece of the puzzle slipped into place behind the green eyes. She was unconsciously asking the questions they wanted her to ask. "Sembur, what do you mean, 'just like me'? Crowley, what were you dying of?"

I met and held her gaze, and her fingers caressed the back of my hand, distress apparent in the almost jerky movement. "I used to like to sing. David was jealous and claimed I did it to attract other men because he wasn't good enough. So one night he tried to strangle me, and then stabbed me in the throat. I don't know what happened because I wasn't conscious at the time. I found out later my vocal cords were gone by the time he finished with me. The blood of the vampire heals torn flesh, but it cannot replace what is missing in one who is about to be made."

Bronwyn stared at me, stunned. "You're mute?"

I nodded, and this time did not bother to move my lips when I spoke to her. "Yes. As is Sembur, but his condition springs from being born without vocal cords. You already know that on some level. Didn't you ever wonder how you were able to hear me talk to you while I was in the lion's den in the zoo? The glass is very thick to stop the cats from playing with the people. Humans can only hear certain frequencies and you didn't hear me shout at any of them. I talked to the wolves, but they sure as hell don't understand English, so I had to have done it some way other than using sounds." Sembur had taught me that it was easier to project thoughts if I moved my lips to frame words. Moving my lips when pretending to speak was something I'd never forgotten to do. Ever.

Judging by the utterly gobsmacked look on Bronwyn's face, Sembur had taught me well.

She turned to me, her gaze inward. "How is it that I can hear you? Can you read my mind?"

"Sembur's blood. No I can't."

Sembur smiled, and Kilkenny cleared her throat.

"David was made because he had a dampening effect on my ability to reach Sembur," she said. "It took almost ninety years for Sembur's fledgling—Crowley—to stumble on my whereabouts. Aristotle hated David with a passion, but that ability was why David was allowed to live." Sembur and Kilkenny nodded to one another, squeezing each other's hand. "That brings us to the matter of the gift you wanted us to give you."

I nodded.

Bronwyn's brow furrowed. "What do you mean, ancient blood? What gift do you have to give?"

I smiled at her, willing her to understand. "Blood, Bronwyn. It's the gift of ancient blood."

"I don't get it."

"I have the ability to speak to other people with my mind because of Sembur's blood. It's the gift it carries. I made a bargain with Sembur when we decided to rescue Kilkenny—I agreed to wait to see if he was right about eternity, and not intentionally confront Aristotle, if he would give me the gift of his blood when I asked for it. He asked me to have faith in the future and my eternal life, and I never really did until you and I came together." I smiled at her confusion. I couldn't tell her more because it was too difficult to explain. I had to show her. "If you want that gift, tell us. I ask only that you trust me one more time. Take your time and think it through."

I could see Bronwyn had reached her capacity for one evening. She nodded and arose, but not before kissing me. She wandered out of the room, seemingly headed nowhere, to think and put all the pieces together, to complete the puzzle.

I curled up on the sofa, deep in thought. I was dimly aware that Sembur and Kilkenny arose and went to Allenby. Sembur took one hand, while Kilkenny took the other. They tugged a sluggish him to his feet. He looked as though he didn't want to control his body anymore. Kilkenny led him from the room. He moved robotically, on autopilot, the quality of his now almost horrified gaze not changing. I felt pity for him; he had not been prepared for Kilkenny's blood, and I wondered why they had not asked me to heal him as well, since my blood would not have had the same effect on him. Sembur and Kilkenny moved in ways I often could not fathom.

I watched the empty doorway, listening to the crackling fire, feeling its warmth. I thought about what I'd just offered to Bronwyn. Could we do it? Would we survive Sembur's gift? Would we still love one another?

I mentally slapped myself upside the head at that thought. Bronwyn had become one of us and still loved me as much as I loved her. Even more amazing, she had continued to love me through what had to have been the worst vampire birth in all history. She had almost been killed for real before she had discovered the true pleasures of the night.

I sat there for the entire night, thinking about my long life. I had reached the end of what should have been my mortal years, and had spent the majority of my adult life as a vampire. I had tasted freedom and independence and found that I'd loved them both. It was wonderful to be able to make one's way through the world and not be bound by human standards of behavior and morality. I had gotten myself into trouble and back out again. Yet I had been drifting, searching for an end to the first gift Sembur had given me. Even though I had known that theoretically my vampire's blood should have given me eternal life, realistically I knew my life would come to an end at Aristotle's hands, if I so chose. I unconsciously had been attracted to the idea that I would have the normal span of a human life, but not be subject to slow death by aging. Bronwyn had changed all that for me. She embraced life and she had taken me right along with it.

I loved her for it.

I loved her compassion, her patience, and her fiery spirit. She was a young girl who had given her angel more pleasure and unconditional love than anyone else ever had. What had she gotten in return? She had been almost killed by vampires I couldn't stand because of my selfish stupidity. I knew I had to give her something back. Even though she had come over to our side willingly—the flames in her eyes told me that—she had sacrificed some fundamental gifts humanity enjoyed. She needed to know what could replace them. She deserved to know the gifts that vampires grew through age to enjoy.

I was glad that she had joined me willingly in the night world. I hated the idea of not having her in my life. I didn't want to mourn her for eternity, while others came and went in my life. We never had to grow old together, and we would have an eternity to enjoy our youth and each other. I, for one, couldn't do that as just friends—I wanted more. Mortal death had taken a lot from us, and I wanted some of it back. I wanted a true vampire relationship with her.

I stared into the flames. As my nervousness increased, my mind drifted, and I found it harder and harder to focus on any one thing. I got restless and compensated by roaming through the house. I avoided Bronwyn, because I wanted to give her the distance from me that she really needed to think things through. If she needed to talk, Sembur or Kilkenny drifted close by, ready to offer a steady hand or word of advice. Finally, I felt the pull of the morning, and I knew I had to rest for the day. For once I was glad of the oblivion that sleep would bring. I would not spend every moment until Bronwyn made her decision tying myself into insecure knots. When I went to bed, I went alone. I fell asleep before Bronwyn joined me, and I knew that she must have taken her rest elsewhere.

Early the following night, I sat out on the rear stairs of Sembur's house, just watching the stars drift by, taking my solace from the night. The breeze stirred the tops of the trees bordering the rear path, harsh moonlight making them cast jagged shadows on the concrete. Off to one side I could hear an animal crashing through Sembur's beloved vegetable garden. Much to my surprise, he had not been lying. He had planted tomatoes, and was expecting them to bear fruit any day now. I wondered why he did it. He could not, after all, enjoy the fruits of his labors.

I had not yet seen Bronwyn, and I wondered what she had done with herself during the day. I wondered if she had vanished last night, after we had told her a little of what we knew. I didn't think she would react like that, but who knew when it was the last straw?

A presence stirred behind me, and I knew Sembur was watching me. "Sembur."

He sat on the step beside me. We watched the night for a little while, and he sighed when he heard the animal in the distance. He shook his head ruefully and then turned to me. "It's time. She's waiting."

With those four words, my spirits soared. He got to his feet, and then grinned and held out his hand to help me up. I took it and allowed him to pull me to my feet.

We went down the darkened stone hallway to the library. Sembur opened the door for me and gestured for me to go in. I did so, and if I had a heart it would have been beating with anticipation. Bronwyn sat on our sofa, arms crossed, legs stretched out in front of her, Kilkenny by her side, caressing her arm.

When Bronwyn saw me, she rose to her feet and threw herself in my arms. "My angel."

Sembur smiled. "Are you both ready?"

I nodded. "I certainly am."

"So am I," Bronwyn said, giving my hand a quick squeeze.

"Let's begin." Sembur seated himself on his overstuffed leather chair, Kilkenny by his side to assist him.

Their fiery eyes shone in the darkness, shadows shifting and changing on their faces in the crackling firelight. He nicked his wrists, and we both knelt to catch his blood. The explosion of sensation that the first drop produced made me reel, and I clutched him to hold off the dizziness that threatened to knock me over. As I took each draft, the sensation worsened, but so did the sensation of raw strength and heady power.

I had feasted of Sembur's blood before, so I knew what was going to happen when I consumed his blood. I had had a refresher just before I had healed Bronwyn. Feasting nonstop on Sembur and Kilkenny as we were both doing was something that I had never done before, so I was not prepared for the explosion of sensory input. The dim lighting seemed to brighten to the point of being painful, each sound deafening. My ears became a hundred fold more sensitive, and I could hear every whisper the night produced. I was ultra aware of Bronwyn beside me, the sounds of her feasting, and the soft moans from our hosts as the blood left them.

Bronwyn was much more sluggish, reeling when the first drops of blood hit her lips, almost falling over from the power of the blood. I tried to help her as best I was able, but the dizziness that the increases brought sent me reeling. Eventually Sembur and Kilkenny caught us, and we ended up cradled in their arms, lost in our mutual feasting.

I cannot tell you how many times we all drained each other of the precious blood. It was well into the wee morning hours, not far from dawn, when we were all forced to go out in search of food.

I got behind the wheel of Sembur's car, Bronwyn beside me and Sembur and Kilkenny behind. Bronwyn looked amused that we were taking such an antique form of transport to dinner. The trip was silent, and by unspoken consent I pulled up in a shadowed, residential area. There was garbage in the streets and cars haphazardly parked along the sides of the roads. I could hear honking horns from the cars on the main street close to us, and the sounds of drunken laughter from people leaving the pub on the corner.

Sembur and Kilkenny both focused in the direction of our prey, faces still and guarded, eyes flaming.

I glanced at Bronwyn, who was frowning at them.

"They're calling the humans," I whispered.

"Oh."

After a moment or so, we watched a party of four leave the pub and look uncertainly in our direction. They split off into two couples, two of them walking toward us and the other two heading in the opposite direction.

Bronwyn and I exchanged a grin.

The four of us broke into a silent and deadly run toward them, so swiftly they could not see us coming.

Sembur and I grabbed the male half of the couples, and neither one gave us much more than a puzzled, unfocused stare as our fangs sank into their necks.

As the hot blood jetted down my throat, I thought I heard a strangled squeak from Bronwyn's prey, but I had to concentrate on not killing my victim.

I was hungry. Starved.

I felt my young man go limp in my arms, and I put him on the sidewalk in the shadows. I nicked my wrist with my fangs and spilled blood on the wound, watching the skin close.

I could still hear the sound of a light scuffle, courtesy of Bronwyn's victim, and I turned around to see what was happening.

Bronwyn's victim was struggling and trying to punch her with one hand, the other flailing what looked like a butter knife. She was so drunk she could barely stand.

Bronwyn watched her, arms crossed, head tilted. I felt what could only be described as a kind of mental slap from Bronwyn. The drunk girl's eyes widened, and her body went rigid. She stayed that way for a second or so, and then fell forward into Bronwyn's waiting arms. Kilkenny joined Sembur and I and watched Bronwyn take her victim.

"That's interesting," I said, glancing at them both. "I didn't think it would happen so quickly."

"It's because of your blood," Kilkenny said. "It's stronger than it should be for someone of your age."

I nodded. "True. I wonder if I can get her to remember how she did that."

"Probably not," Sembur said. "I think she's going to have to practice that skill. It's not an easy one to master, and it's difficult to explain."

Kilkenny and I nodded as we watched Bronwyn drip blood onto the girl's bite marks, making them disappear.

"Are you all right?" Kilkenny asked, studying me closely.

"I'm not sure," I said. "I needed the human blood—although I really wasn't all that hungry—and now it's not sitting well with me. I feel like I've over eaten." I grimaced. "I'd forgotten what that felt like."

Bronwyn staggered toward us, looking as though she wanted to retch. I understood how she felt.

Sembur studied us and exchanged a glance with Kilkenny.

"I think it's time to get you both to bed."

I nodded, watching the world waver and feeling my stomach contract uneasily.

"I think I'm going to—" I said, clapping a hand over my mouth.

"No, you're not," Sembur said. "That's one thing that's not going to blend in easily on a city street." He scooped me up into his arms, and Kilkenny followed suit with Bronwyn.

I closed my arms and concentrated on keeping my food down.

I swore to myself again I would *never* feast on another drunk human.

Sembur and Kilkenny put us into the back seat of the car and took us home. He drove considerably faster than I did, for which I was grateful. My eyes were watering against the painful predawn light teasing the edges of the sky.

By the time we got back to Sembur's house, we were both able to stand and walk by ourselves. I didn't feel quite as sick, and Bronwyn had lost her pallor, an almost rosy glow returning to her cheeks.

Bronwyn and I couldn't do much more than stagger back to our comfortable bed, stomachs ill at ease with the human blood we had consumed. I lay on the satin sheets, staring queasily at the spinning room, head pounding with the sights and sounds of the amazingly noisy night.

Bronwyn lay by my side, probably as thankful as I that we didn't breathe. Neither one of us needed the cacophony that would have produced. Poor Bronwyn was much worse off than I was. She looked paler than death, and almost as though she were resisting the temptation to run to the nearest corner so she could be quickly and tidily sick.

I felt the pull of dawn come over me and tried to resist it as much as I could. Much to my surprise, it worked. I knew I could walk around in darkness during the day, but I didn't think that was a good idea. The blood was working miracles to my poor body, but I felt as sick as one could get while not being alive. It felt too much, too soon, so I made myself pass out.

The next evening, when I woke up, I kept my eyes closed, prepared for the same rotten hangover I'd had at dawn.

"Crowley?" Bronwyn asked hesitantly. "Are you all right?"

My body felt rested and pain free, so I waited for a moment to see if it began hurling abuse at me. I leaned up on an elbow, feeling her body close to mine, bracing myself for vicious stomach contractions.

I cautiously opened an eye and blinked uncertainly against the savage light that flooded my eyes. I groaned.

"It's all right," Bronwyn whispered, pulling me into her arms. "It'll pass."

"Uh, huh." I kissed her chest and smiled at the sensation of her skin against mine. "I think I'm fine."

"You know," she said, pulling away from me and sitting up, "I feel terrific."

I grinned, taking in her inhuman beauty. "So do I, actually."

She smiled happily at me, and bounced out of bed.

I tried hard to help her dress, but we were both hampered by the kisses we exchanged. I'm not sure how, but we managed to pull on our clothes, leave the guest room, and head toward the library where Sembur and Kilkenny waited for us.

When we entered, they exchanged a fond glance and smiled at us.

"Are you ready to begin again?" Sembur asked.

"Yes, we are," Bronwyn said.

Sembur sighed and leaned back in his comfortable chair. "Come." He held out his wrist, and Bronwyn went to him. She knelt before him, eyeing his wrist with an intense gaze. I settled myself before Kilkenny, grateful that I could not blush anymore. Sembur's lover was so beautiful that she always threw me off balance, and I felt awkward about taking the blood gift from her. I gazed at the blood pulsing through the veins that ran under the alabaster skin of her wrist.

I began to drool. The hunger for blood was intense. I was so focused on the hot blood that I forgot myself and plunged my fangs into her wrist, drawing in a great draft of blood that left me reeling, and Kilkenny hissing in pain.

"Take, young one," she said.

I could not stop even if I had been of a mind to. No more than an animal, I pulled in her blood, feeling it jet down my throat.

I was dimly aware of Bronwyn moaning close by, almost sickened from the power that I knew from personal experience was flooding into her from Sembur.

He pulled away from her, as Kilkenny pulled away from me. Both pushed us back, and then took us into iron arms and held us close as their fangs took the precious blood that had been given to us.

Drained almost to the last drop, we again feasted from them.

We did this until dawn, when Sembur stopped.

"It is time for us to feed," he said.

I shook my head. "I'm not going out tonight. I don't need to."

Sembur nodded and held out his hand for Kilkenny. "We will go. We will see you again in the evening."

Kilkenny took his hand and smiled gently at us as they left the library.

I crawled over to Bronwyn. "Are you all right?"

She gazed at me in wonder. "I feel terrific. It's almost like there's something just beyond my reach. Like a whispering around me."

"That's Sembur's blood working in you," I said, pulling her into my arms. "It'll get loud enough for you to want to tune it out in another couple of nights."

"What's happening to me?" she asked, her arms tightening around me.

I smoothed the hair back from her forehead. "Sembur's blood is changing you. You'll be as strong as me in a couple of nights."

"I feel as weak as a kitten right now."

I stood, bringing her with me, and cradled her against my chest. I walked from the library, kissing her forehead. "I'll take care of you. The weakness will pass."

She nodded against me, and I pushed open the door to our room. I put her on the bed and collapsed beside her.

It was like I was coming out of a drunken stupor, and I closed my eyes to stop the room from spinning around me. Bronwyn was right about the whispering, I thought as I drifted away into sleep.

The feast lasted for several nights, as Brownyn adjusted to what the ancient blood was doing to her. I was much quicker, and all that was left in its wake was exultation and drunk enjoyment of my heightened vampiric powers.

It took another couple of nights of feeding from Sembur and Kilkenny for Bronwyn to reach the same level as me and to truly feel comfortable with her new blood. I awoke that fourth evening, energetic and eager to hunt. Bronwyn rolled over and smiled at me, her burning green eyes gentled with love.

"You feel like hunting?" I asked, caressing her with my mind.

"I feel like more than that," she said, kissing me.

"I heard that," Sembur's amused mental voice said, followed by Kilkenny's soft, mental laughter.

I stared at Bronwyn in amazement. "Whoa."

"What happened?" she asked, frowning and using her voice.

"You're telepathic," I said, unable to control my grin. "I think you just shared a little too much with Sembur and Kilkenny."

"Fuck," she mumbled. "How the fuck did that happen?"

I nibbled my lip to keep from laughing. "It's Sembur's blood. My suggestion is to keep using your voice to form thoughts for the moment."

Sembur and Kilkenny's laughter increased.

Bronwyn frowned and shot daggers at the door.

"Young one," Kilkenny said. "That wasn't nice."

I gave her a curious look. "What did you just say to them?"

"You didn't hear that?" she asked.

"No," I said, "and judging by the silence I'm sure it's a good thing."

Bronwyn gave me a rueful grin and kissed me. "I'm never gonna get the hang of this, am I?"

"I'll help you," I said. "But in the meantime I suggest you keep your mental mouth shut."

"Agreed," Sembur said smoothly.

"Sembur, do you mind?" I asked.

"Stop broadcasting," he said archly. "You're echoing throughout the neighborhood." He laughed, and I sighed.

"Focus just on me, lover," I said, capturing Bronwyn's gaze. "Just on me."

She gazed deep into my eyes. "I think I could get used to this," she murmured.

"Did you get that?" I asked Sembur and Kilkenny.

"No," Kilkenny said. "Better. Thank you."

Bronwyn sighed in relief. "Do you want to get out of here for a little while?"

"Sure," I said. "You want to practice your mind control skills?"

She glared at me.

"Easy," I said, stroking her cheek with the back of my hand. "I didn't mean to offend you."

"I know," she replied, leaning into my hand. "Okay, let's go."

න

I stopped my car in the darkness of the inner city under a broken streetlight. We were in an abandoned area, the streetlights providing the only illumination around us. It was an industrial section, and my keen eyes pierced the darkness, finally spotting what I had been looking for. I smiled and got out of the car, Bronwyn following close behind me, gazing quizzically at me.

"There," I said, pointing to a "For Lease" sign outside one of the vast brick structures that bordered the potholed road. "You'll find homeless people in there sleeping."

Bronwyn stood close beside me, tilting her head and staring doubtfully at it. "All right."

I watched the shadowed planes of her face and her burning eyes.

"Call to them." I leaned back against the car. "Feel them. Let them know you want them to come to you."

"How?"

I pushed my will toward her, ensnaring her, caressing her. Her eyes were slightly glassy as she sank into my arms, sighing.

I stroked her hair. "Like that," I whispered.

The spell was broken, and her arms tightened around me. "Like that, huh?"

I nodded.

She pulled out of my embrace and pushed her will toward the building.

"Come out!" she screamed with her mind and I winced, holding the sides of my head.

"Right idea, wrong volume," I said, shaking my head to still the ringing.

"Effective, though," she said, nodding toward the building. Four people spilled out of a wrecked door, blinking owlishly in the darkness. They could not see us.

Her eyes lit up, and she grabbed my hand. We ran toward them, blurs in the darkness, and took them. We drained them to the point of death. Bronwyn nicked her wrist, dribbled her precious blood over the marks, and watched them disappear in seconds.

I stood, reveling in the power of the night, drunk on the heady feel of blood that rushed through my system. Bronwyn stood with me, and I felt her gentle presence reaching out for me.

"It's time to go out on our own again," she said, squeezing my hand and drawing the scents of full night in the city into her lungs.

I nodded. "Love to. I think it's time to go back and say goodbye to Sembur."

We walked back to the car, drowning in the sweet sensations of living, breathing mortals whispering with their minds in the distance.

CHAPTER FOURTEEN

I leant against my car next to Sembur. Bronwyn was talking to Kilkenny close by.

"Thank you, for all you've done for us," I said.

Sembar nodded. "Where will you go?"

"I have another house. It's on the beach. We won't be able to stay there for long, the hunting's lousy." I grinned.

He returned my grin, and we were comfortably silent for a moment.

"What are you going to do with Allenby?" I asked. "The changes that Kilkenny's blood made to him are the same as what it's done to us."

"Not quite," Sembur said, his eyes shadowing. "The blood seems to act differently with different vampires. You, for example, have stronger control over broadcasting than Bronwyn seems to. Allenby has been catatonic since Kilkenny gave him her blood. I think he is overwhelmed by the voices he is hearing, but I cannot sense anything from him."

"Is he going to be all right?" I asked. I still didn't like him, and if Sembur was right, I found it fitting that he should be sentenced to listen to others.

Sembur shook his head and sighed. "Only time will tell." He straightened and glanced at Kilkenny. Bronwyn approached us, smiling. I gazed deep into Sembur's eyes, the color so reminiscent of my own, and smiled. "Thank you, my maker, for all you have done for us."

"Until we meet again, fledgling." He pulled me into his arms, and kissed me gently. "If ever you should need me again, please call for me. I will come."

"Same offer goes to you, my maker," I replied. I felt an abrupt bolt of sadness and forced back tears. I didn't want to spend forever around him, but I also hated leaving him.

Kilkenny followed Bronwyn, and I took my leave of her, accepting her gentle hug.

I looked in the rear view mirror as we drove away, and saw Sembur and Kilkenny standing close together, watching us disappear. The tears I struggled to hold back snuck out of my eyes.

Bronwyn took my hand and stroked it. "Where are we going?" she asked as I took us out onto the open road, headed for the coast.

"I have another house. We'll just have to use it until our normal one is fixed."

"Yeah." She sighed. "I suppose traveling for us is out of the question, isn't it?"

"Not necessarily," I said. "It's just going to be interesting, that's all. You may find us traveling by sea."

"You mean we're going to feast on rats in the hold?"

I burst out laughing. "Only if we get to leave one sailor tied to the helm of the ship as she hits ground."

She laughed. "So where is this house of yours?"

"It's on the coast, in a nice little resort town. It's sitting on the edge of a cliff."

"What do you do to entertain yourself?" she asked doubtfully.

"Well, for starters you can build some pretty cool sandcastles on my private beach and swim by moonlight. You can look out of the bay windows at the sea through my telescope. We can drive into town and have a bite to eat."

"That sounds . . . um . . . terribly interesting."

I aimed a mock severe look at her. "You haven't even seen it yet. Would it make it more interesting for you if I told you that it was reputed to be haunted?"

"Yes, thanks, my beloved angel. Sure. Whatever."

I laughed. "Don't believe me?"

"Of course I believe you," she said.

"Just wait until you see the house, all right?"

I turned onto a country road and flicked off the headlights. I didn't need them to see, and neither did Bronwyn. I amused myself by looking out for kangaroos and other assorted wildlife. I saw a couple bounding by the side of the road and pointed them out to Bronwyn.

"Sure," she said. "Tell me, is roo blood as nasty as roo meat?"

"I don't know. Why don't you try biting one and tell me?"

She slapped my arm. "Brat."

"Hey, you suggested it."

"Did not!"

"Did too!"

I slowed the car and drove up a sandy driveway, and the house came into view.

"Whoa," Bronwyn said, straightening as her wide eyes took in the house. "This is spectacular."

I nodded. "I know."

It was a massive three story house, with floor to ceiling bay windows on the ground and second floors overlooking the ocean. The full moon glinted off the windows. Bronwyn's wide eyes took in the open, grassy space that led to a narrow path down the cliffs and the silver streamers of reflected moonlight off the calm ocean before us.

I pulled into the garage, and Bronwyn got out of the car, still gawking at the scenery.

Bronwyn took a step toward the house, and I stopped her with a hand on her arm. "I can't let you do that."

She gave me an odd look. "What do you mean?"

I grinned. "I mean, it's your wedding night. I can't just let you walk through the front door, can I?"

Her fiery green eyes became brighter. "What do you mean it's my wedding night? Wasn't that quite a long time ago?"

"You'll see. Just let me do my thing, will ya?"

She slipped her arms around my neck as I scooped her up off her feet. I tested her weight, and she giggled. I had the strength of ten men, more now that Sembur's blood had enhanced my vampire's body. I smiled at her, and she opened her mouth to speak, but then stopped and looked abashed.

I raised an eyebrow. "What's on your mind?"

"This is going to sound really stupid."

"Go on. Nothing can sound more stupid than telling someone you're a blood-sucking corpse."

She rolled her eyes. "My angel speaks again. Be serious, will you?"

I grinned. "Just for you, Bronnie."

She cleared her throat. "I just never thought this was going to happen to me."

"What do you mean?"

"I mean getting carried over a threshold while conscious and actually able to understand what was happening to me."

I was glad death had robbed me of the ability to blush. "Err . . . well . . . I'm sorry that I dragged you along with my miserable life. You really didn't deserve that."

She gave me a serious look and shook her head. "No, that's not what I meant. Stop apologizing. We've been through this already and it's done, okay?" She sighed. "I meant being carried over a threshold. I died before any of that stuff could kick in for me, you know?"

"I know." I did.

I willed the door to open and carried her over the threshold of our new home.

The house was large and rambling, all of six bedrooms with a comfortable parlor and library downstairs, and a bay window that looked out over the ocean. There was an ancient telescope set on a brass gimbal that I used to watch the ocean waves crash onto the rocks far down below on the beach. The house was as dusty and barren as it had been when I first bought it. I left both floors and the huge, spacious attic for the ghost to furnish and live in. My addition was a basement that was the same size as the ground floor. It was divided into a nice, dark bedroom, a sitting room and library, and a lounge room, complete with an expensive sound system and numerous compact discs. I liked the comfort of my home away from home.

Bronwyn's jaw dropped at the huge foyer and ornate, dusty staircase. Around the ground floor all the doors, badly in need of fresh stain and lacquer, lay sensibly closed in the octagonal space. Jagged streaks of moonlight hit the bare floorboards, breaking through the dusty, stained glass skylight high above us.

"Whoa! This is fantastic." She kissed me and then allowed me to put her onto her feet. "How come you didn't live in here full time?"

"If I'd done that I'd probably gone hungry. The food isn't too good in this town. It will, however, do, until we get our other house fixed." It was true. The population was just a bit too small to support a hungry vampire all year around. My other concern had always been with Aristotle. Being basically lazy at heart, he would never have found me if I'd stayed here all the time. Besides, the house was meant to be haunted, and I thought the ghost might enjoy the solitude.

I took Bronwyn's hand and stepped toward the basement.

"Where are we going?" Bronwyn sounded a bit distracted because of her intense study of the beauty.

"Downstairs."

"But it's not dawn yet." She pulled me to a halt and gave me a look that was part frustration, part wistful disappointment that I hadn't taken her on a tour of the upstairs.

"I have something to show you."

That piqued her interest. She always followed me like a faithful puppy when I told her that I had something for her.

The door to the library opened with a protesting squeak. Our footsteps sounded loud on the dusty wooden floor, echoing around the large, almost empty room. I led her to a bookshelf and pulled forward a copy of *Moby Dick*. One portion of the bookshelf obediently and silently swung outward, revealing a black archway, leading downstairs.

Brownyn crossed her arms and raised an eyebrow at me. She leant back on one leg.

I held up a hand, although she had not spoken, and grinned like a Cheshire cat. "I always wanted one of those."

Bronwyn said nothing, merely waved a hand toward the opening in an "unnecessary ostentation" gesture.

"Oh, c'mon. This is fun. How many times are you going to see this in your life?"

"If I'm lucky, just once. With you." She gestured. "After you."

I chuckled and took her hand. I led the way down the pitch black stairs, not pausing to turn on the lights. I didn't need them and neither did she. We walked down an equally dark corridor to an ornate, oak door at the end of it. I dug into the pocket of my shorts, feeling for almost forgotten keys. Finally, after several balls of fuzz, I pulled them out triumphantly. I slid the key into the tight, new lock and pushed the door open with only a mild squeaking of hinges.

She followed me into the room and tugged me over to the black, satin sheets of the bed. We faced one another, and I smiled at her. I kept eye contact with her as I went to the CD player in the furthest corner of the room. With a gentle touch of a button, the strains of my favorite music enveloped us.

She smiled broadly at me. We had not done this for quite some time, and I knew she missed it as much as I did. She stepped forward and slipped into my arms, and I led her around. She rested her head against my chest, sighing happily. We allowed the music to carry us for a while, and then I broke the spell.

"Do you want to know more about Sembur's gift to us?"

She looked up at me, distracted. "We can enter the houses of our victims by turning into mist, and we can talk to each other without using our mouths. We're closer. Don't get me wrong, it's wonderful, but what could beat that?"

I laughed. "There's a way you can use it that's really obvious, but we haven't tried it because up until now you've still been adjusting to using your mind to speak." I didn't want to mention how dangerous it was. I was well used to it. Bronwyn had had some trouble mastering it, mostly the fine art of not broadcasting to everyone within earshot.

"Okay."

"I think it's best if you lie down for this. I need you to concentrate with no distractions."

I pushed her to the bed. I lay down, taking her with me, then pulled her in close so she was using me as a pillow.

I snuck a quick look at her—curiosity was vivid in her fiery green eyes. "Okay, push your mind toward mine."

"That's easy."

"Shh." I needed silence to be able to do what we were about to do. I relaxed as best I could, and then dug around in every nook and cranny of my brain for everything that was me. No words, just emotion, memory, color, instinct, sounds—basically everything people normally used for thought.

I felt the feather light touch of Bronwyn's mind, circling around the things I brought forward.

I heard her speak in my head and my ears. Both voices were soft and wondering. "Oh my God. Is that you, Crowley?"

"Yes, it is." I dropped the concentration to speak to her normally. It was too much effort to keep both things together. "That's the other facet to Sembur's gift. It's not just words I can broadcast, it's other stuff too." I leant up on one elbow and watched her carefully. "Normally, all you would use the telepathy for is to control your victims and animals. No more than that. Apparently that was a vampire law that Sembur was first taught about when he became one of us. It was a law that he had forgotten about and unknowingly broke when he was testing the limits of his telepathy with Kilkenny."

I paused to allow it to sink in. Bronwyn nodded, frowning.

"All right," I said, making sure I still had her full attention. "Remember, vampire love is all about emotion, since sex can't enter into the equation anymore. I once told you that vampire marriages are forever, and this is why. The law was made for a reason, a very good reason. When Kilkenny and Sembur did what we are about to do, they somehow fused together. She is a part of him and he a part of her and they can't separate."

"I don't quite see what you're saying."

"It means that when Sembur withdrew from Kilkenny's mind, he left a part of himself behind. It's difficult to describe, but it's kind of like an awareness of the other person. If he wants her, all he has to do is call down the link they have together and she comes to him. It works the other way as well."

She looked at me expressionlessly. "Are you asking me if I want to try this with you?"

"Yes."

She rolled over and propped up her head with her hand, so we were eye to eye.

"First of all, there's more here that you aren't telling me, isn't there? How did you get Sembur to help us with Aristotle? I never saw you look for him, or call him, or use any other normal means of communication to get to him. You have a link with him, don't you? Why did it take so long for him to reach us?"

"Yes, we have a link. It happened when he made me into a vampire." I smiled. "I used it to call him when we were at the fountain in Kings Cross. He kept an eye on us after that but he was a long way away and it took time for him to reach us. After all, he can't just get on a plane and fly to the other side of the world."

Bronwyn stared at me, taken slightly aback. "Okay. That was easier than I thought it would be."

"What's the point in lying? If you agree to do this, it's not going to work on you anymore, is it?"

She nodded, silent for a moment. "What do you mean, if? Why wouldn't I agree to do this with you?"

"I don't know. I thought it might be too much for you."

"Too much for me? How? After all the shit we've been through, this is a real walk in the park."

I got a little angry. "This is something huge and irreversible. You are going to be with me for potentially thousands of years. It's not a small, trifling thing. We both have to be sure we don't want to do this because we're afraid of being alone. I want to do this because I love you and I want more out of a relationship with you, in the way that vampires do it."

Bronwyn smiled. "That's not my fear. I'm not like you that way. I'm not afraid of the future and never have been. Things always work out for the best, and it doesn't really matter if it's something you think is horrible at the time. I want to do this for exactly the same reason you do."

I reined in my anger. The criticism, at heart, was true—but only in the past. I'd always clung to the past, but I wasn't prepared to do that anymore. It was time for me to live. It was as though I'd been given a second chance with Bronwyn.

"You see the world through the eyes of youth." I held up a hand to silence her. "As life goes on, it becomes more difficult to live because you do get stuck in ruts, be it ways of life or ways of thinking. You are, however, right—life is a dynamic thing. You have to change as time changes. But we're getting off the subject. Do you want to do this with me?"

"I thought I already said yes." She kissed me. "Now, how do we do this?"

I leaned forward for my own kiss. I adored her. "Well, once I start, you're going to work it out. I'll be open enough for you to see how I did it, and you can copy it. I can't really describe it in words."

She pushed me back down and settled into my arms. "That's a much nicer position, isn't it?" She kissed the angle of my jaw, as I had once done, so long ago it seemed, on the night of her graduation ball. "I'm ready if you are."

I sank into the concentration that I needed to open myself to her. After a moment, I dropped the barriers to my mind a notch, and she moaned softly as she took in what I was giving her. I felt her gentle touch, softly sorting through the torrent that I tried to slow down a little for her to assimilate. I felt a sliver of triumph I knew didn't come from me as she found my memory of what I had done to open myself up to her. Slowly, she opened up to me, and I gasped at the flood of raw feeling that poured into me from her.

I watched over her as she sat by the side of the road, terrified, as an angel approached her. I was with her when Robbie McMahon stole his first kiss from her, and then took her virginity. We won an English prize when she was little, came top of the class in math a year later. She longed to meet her angel just one more time to tell her about her life and what was happening to her. She had tried to find love, but had never known it. All the emotion she had felt for other people had been empty and hollow, robbed of the passion she had for her angel.

I was with her when one day she had been sick as a dog from drink, and her angel had found her and cradled her once again in strong arms.

The final night she had spent with her parents held a special flavor for her. She loved her parents dearly, of that there was no doubt. Her father was a man who smiled with his eyes and told wonderful jokes. He hugged her with the scent of tobacco and aftershave hovering around him. His hand steadied her as she rode her bicycle for the first time, and he helped her into a tree, with her worried mother standing behind them, and laughed as she giggled while trying to grab a branch. Her mother made wonderful birthday cakes, fantastic pizza, and brilliant costumes for school plays. They could not really talk much, because her mother was worried about Bronwyn's love for her angel.

It continued on, a torrent of power, love, and memory. I held her and loved her through everything in her life, my strength and passion reassuring her, as my words never could.

At the same time, I felt her gentle touch on my mind, sorting through the things I was feeding her.

She held me when I fell out of a tree as a child and broke my leg; she was with me on my wedding day, and held me the first time David beat me to within an inch of my life. She saw Rose as she had been as a young woman, saw some of what we shared, and was with me on the night of my human death. She struggled with me as I became an immortal, stood with me and loved me as I fought Rose's family. She was there when I found a little girl by the side of the road, a memory of the loving woman she was to become. She felt my every moment of torture around her, loving her but unable to bring myself to admit it. I could feel Bronwyn's loving strength inside me, and most importantly, the emotion she felt for me. I was humbled by the depth and strength of it. Now I finally believed it. She did not have a crush on me, she truly loved me for everything I was.

We continued on for a time that could not be measured by either of us, we explored one another, learning more and more about each other, gradually fusing together. We finally slowed down, feeling the approach of dawn, knowing that we needed to sleep. The sharing left us both drained and in desperate need of rest. After we withdrew each side of the flow, we snuggled together, satisfied. Just before sleep claimed us, Bronwyn kissed me with a passion that had always before been restrained. We had no more secrets from each other, even if we had wanted to keep them.

This was the true gift that Sembur and Kilkenny shared, that ran through their veins, and that I had been blessed enough to give to Bronwyn. In a corner of my mind, I could feel a bubble of emotion and love that I knew didn't belong to me. It was Bronwyn, and I stroked it gently with my mind, returning the love that was given to me. I could not imagine how we had stayed together before we had done this. Trust was all well and good with humanity, but it wasn't something that worked for vampires, because vampires were always more primal, surviving on raw instinct. Life was a commodity that was cheap to a vampire.

Now I finally understood the depth of the Sembur's rage at Aristotle for taking Kilkenny away from him. Sembur and Kilkenny had shared the ability to create the bond with us, unwilling to force us to wait the millennia it would have taken for it to appear naturally.

The next evening, I awoke, my arms tightening around her. Her muscles tensed, and I gazed at her beautiful face. She avoided my eyes, squeezing my arm and sliding out of my grasp. She pulled her clothes on, keeping her stiff back to me.

I walked out of the room, and she lingered for a moment or so behind me.

I had to feed. I was starving.

I was acutely aware of Bronwyn behind me, jogging to my side as I walked out of the back door.

I looked at the moonlight turning the ocean into a solid blanket of silver. I drew in a deep breath of brine air, closing my eyes and feeling Bronwyn in the center of my mind, feeling her quiet and almost timid affection.

I turned to her, and she slid into my arms and held me tight, head against my chest. I stroked her hair and disentangled myself. She slid her hand into mine, and we walked down the rocky path onto the beach, bathed in silvery moonlight.

I saw two figures on the white sand before us, and Bronwyn pulled me to a halt.

"I'm hungry," she whispered.

I smiled, running my tongue along my sharp fangs. "So am I."

"After you," she said.

"Together." I pulled her forward at a dead run, and we leapt onto the two figures.

This time I got the boy, and my fangs were in his neck before he had a chance to make a sound. His warm blood filled my mouth and I drank deeply of him, draining him almost to the point of death. I felt Bronwyn flare in my mind as our connection became as bright as the sun from the raw power of it.

I picked up the boy's unconscious body, motioning for Bronwyn to follow suit.

I led her down the beach to a sandy clearing on the opposite side of the path we had taken. As I suspected, he had left his ancient car unlocked—and I think his rust bucket was lucky to have had doors anyway—so I put him behind the wheel. Bronwyn put the girl in the passenger seat, carefully avoiding my gaze.

I straightened and crossed my arms. "You're going to have to look at me some time, lover."

Bronwyn fidgeted and then looked at me, her heart in her eyes. "I'm sorry. I just . . . I can't . . ."

The vulnerability in her naked gaze twisted my heart. "I love you, BronwynHunter," I said, taking a step toward her. "More than anyone or anything in the world."

She threw herself into my arms, and I felt her tears against my chest. I held her, letting her cry herself out.

"I'm sorry," she finally managed to say. "Last night . . . I've just never done that before. I'm almost embarrassed . . ."

"I don't know why," I said. "If you're worried about what I think, don't worry, just feel me."

She nodded and let it go as we walked hand in hand back to the green grass of the rear of our house. She snuck glances at me as she sat close to me.

It was the same for me as it had always been. I could feel her undiminished love for me, and it gave me confidence in us.

"Do you know what you want to do this evening?" I asked.

Bronwyn was lying on her back, arms pillowing her head, as she gazed at the stars. "Did you have any plans?"

"Well, I do have an idea, if you're interested."

"You know I am, so just spit it out, will you? By the way, you know I love *you* more than ever, don't you?" She looked as though she thought she was blushing. I'd forgotten to tell her that it was impossible for her to do that anymore, and amazed she hadn't noticed it herself.

"Are you accusing me of procrastinating? I know. You know I love you more than ever, don't you?"

"No, I'm accusing you of being mysterious. Thank God for that. I was afraid you were going to think I was a total child."

"Really? Me? If you had looked closer, you would have known how I felt. It's okay for you to do that."

Bronwyn gave me one of her patented exasperated stares. "Yes, really. Like I said before, just spit it out. You're one of the most amazing people I've ever met."

"So are you," I said. "I want to go and visit your parents, because you really need to talk to them again."

Bronwyn sat up and stared at me. "What do you mean you want to visit my parents?" she asked in a controlled voice.

I sat in front of her, and she shifted position so our cross-legged knees touched. I took her hands into mine. "I know how much you love your parents. I've seen it. I know you miss them and you want to know how they're doing. So I want to take you to find out."

Her fiery green eyes almost glowed in the pale moonlight. The muscles in her jaw worked as she tried to argue with me. Finally, her shoulders sagged a little, and she studied the grass, troubled. "I guess so."

I cradled her face in gentle hands, so we were eye to eye, and I smiled. "Your parents will forgive you. You just have to ask them. They really do love you, you know."

"How can you be so sure? They told me never to come back. I really burnt my bridges with them."

"Trust me, it's a good idea." I wasn't sure if she had seen my memory of my father's death bed. My parents had exchanged harsh words when I had announced that I was going to marry David regardless of what they thought. Then David's true colors had come out, and I had not known how to go back to them. I had always been Daddy's girl, and my apology to him had come too late. It had taken me quite a while to come to terms with it all, and the regrets I had fueled my disquiet with eternity.

"I really don't know about this. When did you want to do it?"

"No time like the present."

She looked absolutely horrified. Before she could come up with a million excuses, I held up my hand. "Take it easy. Just trust me. One more time. Can you do that?"

Her jaw worked as she thought about it. Finally, she turned to me, fiery eyes glinting. "Okay, I'll trust you. But don't you leave me."

"I can do that." I kissed her. "It won't take us more than a couple of hours to get there." I levered myself to my feet and brushed off the seat of my shorts. I held out my hand to help her to her feet.

She looked lost in thought as I led her toward the garage. She was distressed, but not to the point of cold feet.

We screamed down the driveway at breakneck speed, me negotiating the corners with practiced ease.

I left the top of my sports car down, and the wind streamed through our hair. We saw a shooting star and a satellite, and more than one kangaroo bounding through the pitch black bush that bordered the road. The lights from small towns came and went, with no signs of the police, as we approached the city. Bronwyn was silent throughout the trip, deep in thought.

When we finally hit the city and started encountering some light traffic, I turned to her to try and get her to untwist some of the knots she had put together inside herself.

"You know what the most important thing is, don't you?"

"Hmm?"

"Don't forget to breathe. You don't want to have to explain that you lived fast, died young, and are a good looking corpse."

She stared at me expressionlessly.

"Bit too stressed for humor?"

"Yes, I am."

"Relax. These people love you. You have a home with them. I love you. You have a home with me. If it doesn't work, at least you tried. I know perfectly well you want to see them and talk to them."

"You're not helping."

"I know I'm not. We're there."

She looked as though she wanted to hurl herself through the windscreen to escape. I took her hand. If she had been human, she would have been sweating. I gave her hand a comforting squeeze as the porch light came on.

Bronwyn undid her seat belt and half climbed out of the seat.

The front door of the house opened, and her father emerged.

She got out of the car and stood uncertainly by the passenger side door. "Daddy?"

He shielded his eyes against the glare of the porch light. "Bronwyn?" He smiled and gestured toward the figure that stood behind him in the doorway.

"Dad!" Bronwyn jogged up the footpath and leapt over the front gate.

He held out his arms for her, and she launched herself into them, hugging him with energy that I'm sure left him breathless. Her mother stood uncertainly behind them. I smiled when Bronwyn and her father both extended their arms and drew Mrs. Hunter into their embrace. They stood like that for some immeasurable period of time, simply taking comfort in each other's presence.

Finally, Bronwyn pulled back from their embrace and spoke for moment. She looked down at the concrete of the porch floor, arms crossed, clearly uncomfortable. She gestured toward the car, and then looked up at them. They frowned. She turned toward me in mute appeal, so I got out of the car.

Things looked like they were not going well, but I had half expected that. Bronwyn had not come crawling back to them, as they had obviously thought she would, she had lived without them for more than a year. Even though she looked repentant, they clearly didn't fully trust her and they would all have to work to repair the relationship between them. I wondered what they had said on the last night she had gone out looking for me. I hadn't found that part out from my exploration of Bronwyn, only that she needed to go to them.

Bronwyn signaled for me to come over, so I closed the car door and walked up the path to the front gate. Unlike Bronwyn, I didn't leap over it, I undid the latch, let myself through, and closed it behind me. I walked up to them and could feel their eyes resting on me, not with hostility, but full of curiosity, uncomfortable.

The silence stretched out as I came to stand beside Bronwyn, touching her back with a gentle hand. I could sense the turmoil coming off her in waves.

"Hello. I'm Carlisle Crowley." I held out my hand out to Bronwyn's father, not really expecting him to take it.

Much to my surprise, he shook it with a firm grip. "James

Hunter. This is my wife Eloise." Bronwyn's mother also came forward to shake my hand, her grip nowhere near as firm as her husband's.

"Pleased to meet you."

I studied them in the awkward silence. They had aged gracefully in the thirteen years since I had first met them. Bronwyn's father was now a handsome, distinguished man, mercifully free of middle-aged weight gain. He obviously kept himself physically active. Bronwyn's mother had not been so fortunate. She had thickened a little around the waist. Their eyes remained trained on me, not exactly hostile, but not exactly friendly either.

James Hunter brow creased, spark of recognition flaring in his eyes. "Do I know you from somewhere?"

I opened my mouth, but was cut off by Bronwyn's quick response.

"You should know her. She brought me home when I was five years old. Remember that time when I went exploring, and you got so worried you were about to call the police?"

I could see the wheels turning behind their eyes as they studied me.

"I remember that night," Eloise said. "It always seemed like a bad dream."

Bronwyn looked at her as though she'd lost her mind. "It was real and she's real. My one and only angel." She glanced at me, and she would have smiled had she not been so tense.

"I've been real as long as I've been alive." I smiled, careful to conceal my fangs.

"So I see. So this," Eloise Hunter waved her hand at me, "is the reason for your bad behavior."

Bronwyn and I exchanged a glance.

"Well, yes," Bronwyn said.

I sent gentle reassurance to her, trying to cut through the whirl-pool of negative emotion spilling out of her. Their anger didn't faze me. My parents had been furious on occasion, but they had loved me, and we had made it through all kinds of disagreements. Bronwyn straightened, so our bodies lightly touched, her chin firmed, but her arms remained crossed. She looked her mother in the eye.

Eloise Hunter returned her stare with something that was now openly hostile. "And this is supposed to excuse everything."

"No, Mum, it's not." Bronwyn sighed. "Enough of this. You're really fucking pissing me off. Do you want to sit down and talk like rational people or do you want to scream at me some more? I'm not a child anymore."

Eloise's face darkened with anger, and she drew in breath to say something that undoubtedly wouldn't be nice. James Hunter laid a restraining hand on her arm. He was much calmer than she was, so his mind was more open to whatever Bronwyn had to say to them. He also cast a glance at Bronwyn, nowhere near as angry as her mother, thanks to the reassurance and support I was giving to her. James seemed to be the peacekeeper between the two of them.

He cleared his throat. "Why don't we go inside and have a cup of tea and try to talk this through?"

Bronwyn and her mother glared at each other.

Her parents stared each other down in a real battle of wills, which James eventually won. Eloise dropped her eyes from his, settling for glaring at the welcome mat in front of the door.

"Sure, why not?" Bronwyn said.

"Good," her father said, holding open the ornate screen door so that they could all go inside.

I gave Bronwyn a brief, encouraging smile. "I'll wait for you out here."

"Oh, no you don't," she said. "You're a major part of this, so you can go right on in there with me."

I shook my head. "I don't think so. This falls into private business between you and your parents."

The smooth, deep voice of James cut in, a little awkwardly. He looked at me with shrewd eyes. "Are you together with her?"

"Yes, I guess I am," I said, looking him straight in the eye, brief smile flickering about my lips.

"Well," he responded, "you should be taking better care of her. She looks like hell, and so do you, if you don't mind my saying so."

It was the pale skin and flaming eyes that did it. I exchanged a long suffering look with Bronwyn, and we both sighed.

"After you, Dad." She gestured toward the front door and then leaned forward to hold it so that he could walk through ahead of us.

I looked out into the clean, night air, giving one last glance to the freedom I, and now Bronwyn, enjoyed. The stars were bright in the clear sky, and a gentle breeze blew, teasing the leaves on the branches of the huge trees across the road. It felt strange to be part of a normal, run of the mill problem, not involving blood, garlic, or wooden stakes. Although I knew I was about to be yelled at by people who mistook me for a child even though I was old enough to be their parent, I suddenly felt great.

I had my beloved Bronwyn by my side, a beautiful home, a dark night, and a clear eternity.

"Are you coming?" Bronwyn looked at me from the front door, smiling because she had picked up on my sudden feeling of liberation.

I leaned forward, gave her a quick kiss, and stroked her face, feeling her smooth, pale skin. "I love you. Of course I'm right behind you."

She returned my smile and gave me a hug. "I love you too, my beautiful angel. Let's get this over with so we can go and enjoy what's left of the night."

"I couldn't agree more."

James Hunter watched us, frowning, but we didn't care.

We had been through life, death, and Sembur's tomato patch. What more was there to fear?

ABOUT THE AUTHOR

Jordan Falconer was born in Sydney, Australia, and from a very young age had an interest in ghoulies, ghosties and long legged beasties and all things that go bump in the night. After surviving Catholic school (twice!) she graduated from Sydney University with an honors degree in Psychology. She currently resides in Canada with her other half and three small, demanding dogs.

Visit the vampire Carlisle Crowley's My Space page at: http://www.myspace.com/carlislecrowley

www.ingramcontent.com/pod-product-compliance
Lightning Source LLC
Chambersburg PA
CBHW020421180626
46812CB00003B/1080